AN ANTHOLOGY

AN ANTHOLOGY

EDITED BY
JUDITH K. DIAL
& THOMAS EASTON

PINK
NARCISSUS
PRESS

IMPOSSIBLE FUTURES
© 2013 Pink Narcissus Press

Cover illustration & design by Duncan Eagleson

Published by Pink Narcissus Press
P.O. Box 303
Auburn, MA 01501
pinknarc.com

Library of Congress Control Number: 2013906431
ISBN: 978-1-939056-02-3
First trade paperback edition: August 2013

AN ANTHOLOGY

EDITED BY
JUDITH K. DIAL
& THOMAS EASTON

PINK
NARCISSUS
PRESS

This book is a work of fiction. All the characters and events portrayed in this book are fictitious or are used fictiously, and any resemblance to real people or events is purely coincidental.

IMPOSSIBLE FUTURES
© 2013 Pink Narcissus Press

Cover illustration & design by Duncan Eagleson

Published by Pink Narcissus Press
P.O. Box 303
Auburn, MA 01501
pinknarc.com

Library of Congress Control Number: 2013906431
ISBN: 978-1-939056-02-3
First trade paperback edition: August 2013

CONTENTS

INTRODUCTION

A few years ago, we put together an anthology of predictive science fiction stories (*Visions of the Future*, Skyhorse, 2010; Audible.com, 2013). The idea was to draw together a number of classic stories that managed to come close to predicting the future. Many people have said that prediction is not at all science fiction's mission, but there is a persistent, even wistful, myth that it does in fact do so. And that myth is founded in the reality that some of the science and technology in vintage science fiction is now common: lasers, cell phones, scanners, and more. Every once in awhile, science fiction stories do come remarkably close to prophecy.

Much more often, of course, science fiction is very, very far from prophecy. The science is as bogus as it comes, and the fiction may not be much better. But the ideas remain enticing, even when they are nonsense, even when the futures they belong to really are impossible.

Very soon after *Visions of the Future* appeared, Judith said, "Let's do the opposite anthology. Not predictive stories, but antipredictive ones. Not possible futures, but impossible ones. Old ideas like blasters and shrink rays, nonsense though they be or perhaps just doomed never to come to pass, given new life by modern writers."

So we started talking it up. Writers liked the idea, as did a publisher, and in due time the stories started coming in. The result you hold in your hands.

Space travel is one of the defining elements of science fiction, both ancient and modern. When liquid-fueled rockets were a brand new invention in the 1920s, a newspaper enthused about future "space trains." Allen M. Steele, ex-newspaperman that he is, just had to write "Locomotive Joe and the Wreck of Space Train No. 4."

We're not entirely sure that Rev DiCerto's "A Singular Love" is really an impossible future, for roboticists are already working on sexbots and artificial intelligence. Artificial intelligence researchers have at times waxed enthusiastic at the prospect of being able to capture a human mind in the computer. In "Private Shrines," Sarah Smith and Justus Perry prompt us to think it's just as well that so far that future seems impossible.

Not surprisingly, some of the stories turned out to offer homage to classic tropes, themes, or authors. James Morrow's "The Amazing Transparent Man" tips the hat to the old B (or sometimes C or D) movies, as well as H. G. Wells and Ralph Ellison. Edward M. Lerner's "Tour de Force" salutes Buck Rogers and Flash Gordon. Mike Resnick's "The Enhancement" gives H. G. Wells' *Island of Dr. Moreau* a wink.

Utopias and dystopias have a long and honored history in the field. Given human nature, most are as impossible as shrink rays. Paul Di Filippo rethinks the idea with an interesting usage of the "sacrificial king" trope of mythology.

Cities that grow toward the sky have appeared from time to time, but none quite like the one in Fran Wilde's "A Moment of Gravity, Circumscribed."

Travel between dimensions or parallel worlds has seemed enticing to many writers. Add in the "Men in Black" trope and you have Duncan Eagleson's "Against Powers, Against Principalities."

The Search for Extraterrestrial Intelligence (SETI) has so far been disappointing, even though it has given rise to a great many science fiction stories, including Jack McDevitt's notable "Cryptic." Now Jack adds "Searching for Oz."

Sometimes a classic must be honored by defiance, perhaps especially when that classic has not yet been entirely relegated to the past. We know, for instance, that not every adventure ends well, and so does Jeff Hecht in "The Chatter of the Beams."

We've long seen space stations and moonbases with long-term live-in crews, trading products with Earth, and showing no sign of ill effects on human physical or psychological health, despite low gravity and isolation.

Debra Doyle and James D. Macdonald say that's the ideal setting for a monastery in "According to the Rule." In "Common Ground," Shariann Lewitt has an unexpected take on how hard economic reality might affect a moon-base.

—Judith K. Dial and Thomas Easton
2013

LOCOMOTIVE JOE AND THE WRECK OF SPACE TRAIN NO. 4

ALLEN M. STEELE

The space trains are gone now, of course. The wreck of the No. 4 did them in, way back in '39. Since then it's been step-rockets and spaceplanes, which everyone agrees are safer and more reliable, although perhaps not as much fun. But whenever the guys who used to work the trains get together—not so often these days; there's only a few of us left—we talk about the good old days when we'd fly these things to the Moon. And inevitably, we tell the story of Locomotive Joe and how he saved the lives of everyone aboard the *Tycho Express*.

I was a conductor aboard the No. 4, so I was there when it happened. That's important, because the story has been embellished so many times over the years that the truth is now buried beneath the legend. And I knew Joe Welch, of course. His nickname didn't come 'til later, and that's part of the legend, too. Everyone considers him to be a hero, and I suppose he was; who am I to argue? But I can tell you with absolute certainty that courage and bravery were only part of the story. There was something else, too.

Young people today don't know much about the space trains. Those things belonged to their grandparents' and great-grandparents' time, and so what little they've learned about them generally comes from old movies, and sometimes not a lot even then. So I'm going to have to assume that things have to be explained to you if you're younger than...oh, say, 70...and ask that you be patient with an old codger like me.

(It's called knowledge, kids, not infodumps. Explanations used to be respected. Then computers came along and reduced everyone's attention span to that of a puppy. Let's see if you're smarter than an eight-month-old terrier with a tennis ball. Sit down and shut up and let an old man talk.)

Anyway...the space trains were the first passenger-carrying spacecraft, the ones built by the Goddard Rocket Company back in the 30s. Almost as soon as Bob Goddard launched his first liquid-fuel contraption from his Aunt Effie's farm in Massachusetts, people started clamoring for rocketships that would carry them into space. When the *Worcester Telegram* published a front page story saying that rockets would be carrying people to the Moon within ten years, Dr. Goddard suddenly began getting offers from investors who wanted to put money into this, and never mind the fact that the *Telegram* story was total horse poop. But ol' Doc knew a good buck when he saw it, so once he patented his work and raised investment capital from his pals Slim Lindbergh and Harry Guggenheim, he moved from Massachusetts to New Mexico and started the Goddard Rocket Company.

From the get-go, it was Dr. Goddard's idea that a rocket's engine should be placed forward, not aft, of the payload. Cars do it, planes do it; why not spaceships, too? Some people think he got the notion from the illustration that accompanied the Worcester newspaper story, which itself bore a certain similarity to a picture in the original French edition of Jules Verne's *From the Earth to the Moon*. But it doesn't matter. Rocket up front, passenger compartment dragged behind it; that was the way the Lord and Robert Goddard intended.

Further study showed, though, that this design was inadequate for achieving escape velocity. So Doc had to...

well, let's say borrow...an idea from the Germans, who were also beginning to do the same sort of thing, and build a big booster rocket that would act as a first stage. The booster wouldn't make the whole trip, of course. It would be ditched as soon as the ship penetrated the atmosphere. But it got the rest of the ship off the ground, and that's what the Goddard Rocket Company ended up building.

No. 1, aka the *Comet*, was launched from Roswell in 1933. It wasn't very large and carried only four people: Doctor G, his wife Esther, Harry Guggenheim and their pilot, Charlie Lindbergh himself. But it made big screaming headlines after it circled the earth a couple of times and came back safe and sound, and that meant the money started pouring in from those still well-heeled enough after the stock market crash to afford a joyride into space. Once they had a few more million dollars to play with, the Goddard Rocket Company scaled-up the *Comet* design and proceeded to build its space trains.

The *Tycho Express* was the fourth one built, and it was a monster: 200 feet tall on its launch stand, with a massive first-stage booster capable of sending the locomotive and its 22,000-pound Pullman car into orbit. Once the booster was dropped into the Gulf of Mexico, the passenger car would be extended back from the locomotive upon four 1,000-foot tow cables, then the big gasoline and liquid oxygen engine would fire and the whole thing would be on its way to the Moon. The engine would ignite again every now and then to correct its course, but most of the time the train would coast along on its own momentum, the crew and passengers enjoying zero-gravity weightlessness. About two and a half days later, it would swing around the Moon, letting everyone aboard get a good look at all the green cheese down there —just kidding; they never saw anything except rock and sand—then the locomotive would fire up again and the train would return home. Once it reached Earth, the car would be detached from the locomotive, fire retro-rockets, enter the atmosphere tail-first, open its parachutes and splash down just off the Atlantic coast, where a steamship would pick it up and carry the passengers to New York. The locomotive would break up when it made an uncontrolled re-entry and probably kill a whale or two when its remains crashed in the ocean, but that was okay; the rockets were cheap and the company could always make more.

The trains carried ten people: four crew members—a pilot, a copilot, an engineer, and a conductor—and six passengers. I was recruited by the company in '38. I was only 21 at the time, but my family had been working the rails for three generations, and I'd been a Pullman conductor since I was 17. The company needed experienced railroad men to take care of their customers and I wanted to go to the Moon, so we were a natural fit for each other. Six months training, including a couple of orbital flights on ol' No. 1, and then they put me on No. 4, the *Tycho Express*.

The train had a good crew. Floyd Simmons was a great pilot and Rich Sneed a terrific second officer, but our engineer, Joe Welch, was the one who stood out. Joe knew the ship backward and forward; there wasn't a rivet he was unfamiliar with, and I swear he could have taken the locomotive apart and put it back together without checking the blueprints. But that wasn't all. Joe was frustrated that the space trains weren't designed to actually land on the Moon. No one had done that yet, and it made him mad that the company had very little interest in doing so. So even though the *Tycho Express* would come within sixty miles of the lunar surface, all he could do was peer out the window and watch longingly as the mountains and craters swept by, so close and yet so far.

Me, I was too busy. Looking after six people—six very rich people at that—for five days was hard work. The easy part was getting them safely strapped into their couches just before take-off and cleaning up after them when they inevitably threw up after we reached orbit. Once the train was in zero gravity, you'd have to teach the simplest things —how to get out of bed, use the toilet, get dressed, eat, so on and so forth—and assist them if they couldn't or wouldn't learn. There were three double-occupancy state-rooms on the car's lower deck, so I had to clean them every day, including changing the hammock liners, putting away personal belongings before they floated away, and scrubbing the commodes. And there were always hassles. Unruly children. Fussy parents. Unmarried men who wanted to induct single women into the so-called 240,000 Mile Club (I didn't mind, so long as they closed the door and didn't make a lot of noise). The occasional idiot who wanted to smoke a pipe or fool around in the airlock. I have a theory about the rich: if you make more than $1 million, the universe compensates by dropping your I.Q. 50 percent.

There was never a problem, though, that I couldn't handle. Or at least not until April 9, 1939, the day the Goddard Rocket Company had its first—and last—major accident.

That morning, the *Tycho Express* took off from its launch depot. It was the train's sixth trip to the Moon, my fourth as its conductor. The first part of the flight was business as usual. After it dropped the booster in the drink, the locomotive lowered the car, then fired the main engine; it shut down about 90 seconds later, once the train reached low orbit. A quick swing around the planet so that Floyd and Rich could make their final calculations and the passengers could get their first look at Earth from space (and finish losing their breakfast), then Floyd pointed the train toward the Moon and fired the main engine.

That was how things usually went.

What went wrong was that engine didn't shut down again.

To this day, no one knows exactly why that happened. The instruments worked fine, there were no short in the wiring, and before you ask, no, there wasn't any indication of human error. The best theory is that a valve stuck in the locomotive's primary ignition chamber, causing the engine to keep firing even after the pilot sent a signal up the wire for the engine to shut down.

We'll probably never know for sure. Whatever the reason, it remains one of three unsolved mysteries behind the wreck of the No. 4.

I realized we were in trouble when the train remained under thrust longer than it should have. I'd ridden the train enough times to know that there's a distinct series of events that must occur during a successful flight, and if any of them doesn't occur when it's supposed to, it means that something is seriously screwed up. So when we still had 1-g in the car after the 60-second period of the translunar engine burn, I unsnapped my seat harness and skedaddled up to the control room.

Floyd, Rich, and Joe were all over the instrument panels when I came in. No one was panicking—they were too well trained for that—but they weren't taking it lightly either. So I grabbed a safety rail and watched as they tried to correct the problem, until Floyd finally managed to engage the stand-by system and shut down the engine.

By then, it was too late. The locomotive had been firing for just over three minutes, and thus our velocity was almost 60 percent higher than it should have been. That meant two things. First, the fuel reserve was depleted by nearly one-quarter; we'd reach the Moon, but we wouldn't have enough fuel to get home. Second, our higher speed would cause us to reach our destination sooner than anticipated...and when Rich pulled out his slide rule and ran the numbers, his recalculations showed us that the train would no longer slingshot around the Moon, but hit it straight on.

Fortunately, this sort of accident had been anticipated. The operations manual laid out the abort procedure: uncouple the car from the locomotive, then use the retro-rockets to send it back to Earth for emergency re-entry. Floyd radioed back home to tell them what was going on, and he hit the switch that would detach the tow cables and release the car.

And nothing happened.

This is the second unsolved mystery: why did the release mechanism fail? A lot of people think that it can't be a coincidence, and over the years I've heard quite a few conspiracy theories. Everyone from the Germans to rival space companies to alien invaders have been blamed. Personally, though, I don't believe sabotage was involved. Bad luck happens sometimes, not just once but twice.

In any case, we still needed to uncouple the locomotive, and there was only one way left to do that. Someone would have to put on a vacuum suit, go out through the airlock, and do the job manually, from the top of the car. Floyd and Rich couldn't leave the control room, though, and I just didn't have that kind of experience. But Joe had been spacewalking a couple of times already and, as I said, he knew the train like no one else.

It wasn't a matter of picking a short straw, which is one part of the legend that's untrue. This was his job, and he went about it without argument or complaint. Joe and I went down below, where I helped him suit up while telling the passengers to remain in their cabins and stop asking silly questions. Once he'd put on the airtight rubber garment and sealed the deep-sea diver's helmet, he entered the airlock. The last I saw of him was after I closed the inner hatch and dogged it tight; he waved to me through the window while I turned the wheel to depressurize the compartment.

At first, everything went just as it was supposed to. As soon as the outer hatch was open, Joe clipped his safety line to the outer hull, then attached the magnetic soles of his boots and began to slowly walk up the side of the car. Those old Mark I spacesuits didn't have their own radios, but from inside we could hear the steady clunk-clunk-clunk as he made his way to the roof.

When he got there, Joe began to make his way around its circular edge, approaching each stanchion where the tow cables were attached and using a monkey wrench to unfasten their big lug nuts. He was halfway around the circumference when he suddenly stopped. When he didn't move for a minute or two, Floyd went to the little porthole in the control room ceiling and peered out to see what was going on.

What he saw made him cuss out loud. Joe's safety line had become wrapped around the radio mast, and rather than spend precious time untangling it, he'd simply detached the line from his suit. Which was dangerous as hell. If his boots lost their grip, he'd float off and there would be no way to save him. But no one could tell him not to take this risk, so all Floyd could do was hold his breath and pray that Joe kept both feet firmly planted.

Which he did, right up until the moment he set free the fourth and final tow cable. And that's when the third mysterious thing happened.

The locomotive drifted away from the car, and Joe went with it.

Some people think he just made a mistake, and grabbed hold of the cable thinking that it was his safety line. But I know different, and so did the pilots. Joe was too smart to do something like that. Besides, his safety line was a dozen feet away, at least.

You want to know what I think happened? Joe saw his chance to go to the Moon and he took it. That's why he grabbed the cable. The locomotive was going the way he wanted to go, so he went along for the ride. Sure, it was suicide, but...well, who knows what was going on inside his head? In any case, the last anyone saw of Joe Welch and No. 4, they were falling toward the Moon, our chief engineer a small white figure clinging to a tow cable.

We got the rest of the train safely back to Earth and managed to make an emergency splash-down in the Indian Ocean. That was the last time a space train left the ground. The newspapers called Joe Welch a hero—some reporter called him Locomotive Joe, and that's how the nickname got stuck—but the government decided that trains were too dangerous and laws were passed against them being used again. By the time the Goddard Rocket Company went bankrupt, I was back to my old job, punching tickets on the Long Island Railroad.

Did Joe make it to the Moon? I doubt it. He didn't have enough air in his tanks, and when the locomotive's wreckage was located many years later in the Mare Imbrium, his body was nowhere to be found. All the same, moonwalkers in that region will occasionally report spotting someone in a Mark I suit who doesn't respond to comlink hails.

Locomotive Joe's ghost? Perhaps that's another unsolved mystery.

Before becoming a science fiction author, Allen Steele was a journalist who'd worked for newspapers and magazines in Massachusetts, New Hampshire, Missouri, and his home state of Tennessee. But SF was his first love, so he eventually ditched journalism and instead began producing that which made him want to be a writer in the first place.

Since then, Steele has published eighteen novels and nearly a hundred short stories. His work has received numerous awards, including three Hugos and the Robert A. Heinlein Award, and has been translated worldwide. He serves on the Board of Advisors for the Space Frontier Foundation and the Science Fiction and Fantasy Writers of America.

A lifelong space buff, Steele has witnessed numerous space shuttle launches from Kennedy Space Center and has flown NASA's shuttle cockpit simulator at the Johnson Space Center. In 2001, he testified before the U.S. House of Representatives in hearings regarding the future of space exploration.

Steele lives in western Massachusetts with his wife Linda and two adopted dogs. His most recent novel is

Apollo's Outcasts.

About his story, he says: "'Locomotive Joe' comes out of research I've been recently doing for an upcoming novel, *V-S Day.* While investigating Robert H. Goddard's early work in rocketry, I found a newspaper article from the 1920s forecasting passenger ships to the Moon within ten years. An accompanying illustration showed a space train which was an extrapolation of the engine-forward design that Goddard used for his earliest rockets; it seemed to be an absurd idea until I discovered that space-craft designer Kraft Ericke put forth much the same proposal in the late 50s as a possible means of getting to the Moon. So space trains may not be 'impossible,' strictly speaking, but I still wouldn't ride one."

A SINGULAR LOVE
REV DICERTO

"You're dreaming again." Cyndi stroked Andre's chest. Full lips brushed his ear. "Sweetheart, you're dreaming." Her breath sweet, warm.

Andre opened his eyes, but the room was pitch dark. Let Cyndi's warm breath soothe him, the touch of her hand reassure him. The dark wasn't bad. It was always daylight in the dreams.

The dreams. Always the same, always different. Syria, Chile, Turkey. Tonight it had been tanks. A kid with a BG9. A masked man with a bomb. A blast, and the kid lying in the street, in the glaring sunlight, cut in half.

Then shots had ripped into Andre's team. Davis went down. DiCarlo. Davis's head exploded, spraying Andre with blood.

"Are you okay, sweetheart?" Sweet, loving Cyndi. Beautiful Cyndi. Satin nightie brushed against Andre's arm, one nipple hard through creamy fabric.

"Sweetheart?"

"Yeah, I'm fine. Come here."

He pulled her to him. Her back arched. Satin-clad nipples against his skin. Rose-scented breath on his ear, soft hair brushing his cheek. A hand ran down his chest, traced along his stomach.

"Can I help?" Cyndi had a voice like an angel after three shots of bourbon: languid, slightly husky. Perfect.

"Yeah, babe. You can help."

He felt the smile that he couldn't see. The hand, warm as May sunshine, slid down his stomach, under the blankets. "Anything for you, love."

Andre turned to face her as she began to stroke him to hardness.

***

Andre had blown all his back pay on Cyndi, but she was worth it. After the war he'd been too violent, drank too much, been too apt to fly into a rage. No one could expect a flesh and blood woman to put up with that kind of behavior. So he'd spent every dime he had on the finest Intimate money could buy. BioRealTech had modeled her to his exact taste. Sat him in a chair, quizzed him for hours, hooked up to probes. Flashed hundreds of pictures on a tablet screen. When he'd seen her, he'd fallen in love instantly—even before they activated her.

She came equipped with eight DE23 processors. Never much of a techie, Andre only knew that in 2041, when he bought Cyndi, that was the best you could get. Now, in 2043, maybe they were up to DE24 or DE25. But you had to be an AI professional to tell the difference.

***

Andre woke to the sound of Cyndi singing. Norway's thin sunlight flooded the bedroom. "Take me home, country roads, to the place I belong..." Cyndi loved John Denver. Naturally—Andre loved John Denver.

She stood gazing out the sliding door that led out to the deck. Pajama top, tiny panties. Creamy leg, long, muscular. Nipples erect under satin, blond hair tousled, just shoulder-length. Blue eyes turned, met his. Stunning smile: Red lips, full cheeks, slim nose. "You're up!"

"Not sure I'd call it 'up.'"

Stepping forward, a bounce in the walk, breasts bobbing. Smile broadening. Leaning down onto the bed, arms spread, supporting her on either side of him. A kiss, hot lips, tongue moist, breath like roses. "Start your day off on the right foot?"

"Let me put a bookmark in that one. I'm still a bit drained from the last."

She gave him her nearly sideways smile. How could the guys at BioRealTech have known what that would do to him? She kissed him, all heat and roses, then stood.

Andre got out of bed, walked to the sliding door, while Cyndi walked off down the hall. "Breakfast?" she called over her shoulder, almost an afterthought.

"Yeah. Toast. Coffee."

"You want an egg? Oatmeal?"

"Egg."

"*Irish* coffee?"

He felt his lips curl. "No thanks, babe." These days, except when it was time to charge her, Andre almost forgot Cyndi wasn't a real woman.

He picked up the pill bottle from the nightstand. Twist cap. Two pills. Swallow. His daily dose. It kept the memories from making him anxious. He pulled on his robe, opened the sliding door, stepped out onto the deck, avoiding the pile of new lumber to one side.

Mountains. Mountains on the left. Mountains on the right. Water, just left of center: Nærøyfjord. Rolling, green banks.

Across the street, Miguel Guerra stood on his deck, sipping from a mug. "Andre!"

"Guerra."

Guerra picked up a paper, waved it at Andre. "Story on Intimates, page 35."

"Today's paper?"

"Yeah. Good news for you and me, I think."

It was all good news in Norway, so long as you took your meds. They couldn't always keep the dreams away, kill the memories completely, but they helped, and they could bring you back when things got rough. Meds and an Intimate. Hell, Andre thought, give any man the right drugs and perfect love, and of course he could keep from going mad. Especially if, as a US vet with PTSD who'd fled right after the war to a leftie country where you could still buy an Intimate, you didn't have to work much.

"How's Shelly?" Guerra had bought Shelly a month after Andre bought Cyndi, seeing how the Intimate had served to soothe his sergeant's nerves. Meds alone hadn't been working for either of them. The Intimates made all the difference.

"She's perfect, man. You working today?"

"No. Tomorrow. Couple days later this week."

"Man, let's go get a drink. I could go for a trip to the bar. I've been in the house all week."

Andre's lips did the curl thing again. "Is your dick sore?"

Guerra laughed. "It would be, but my Shelly don't chafe me. Man, check out page 35!"

"See you later, Guerra."

***

Cyndi's eggs were always perfect. The yolk was never broken. The toast was just the right shade of brown, and he loved it. Loved *her*. And she loved him, bless her plastic heart. Did it matter that she wasn't real? That no matter how much care she showed, how warm and yielding she felt to his touch, how she moaned when he made love to her, there was actually no real *self* there experiencing it? What was a self, anyway?

He picked up his coffee, took a sip, and almost coughed—Cyndi had snuck a half-shot of whiskey into it. That was strange; the BioReal Tech people had told Andre that an Intimate would never disobey an order, once told not to do something. Andre considered this for a moment, setting the coffee down.

The newspaper sat beside the plate with the egg and the toast, next to the ceramic mug of slightly Irish coffee. Cyndi leaned against the kitchen island, still in panties and satin top, sipping from her mug. Some of the acids in food substances could be converted into electricity. The people at BioRealTech had said it was important that an Intimate be able to eat. They'd shown Andre graphs proving how important dining together was to the health of a couple.

Cyndi bent one leg, placed the sole of her foot against the cabinet door of the kitchen island. The curve of her legs, the musculature. The texture of her skin. Unbelievable. Andre's lips curled again, the rush that precedes an erection racing down his spine. "Was Guerra outside?" Just the right tone. Cyndi *cared.* There was no other way to explain that inflection.

"Yeah. I think he's got something on his mind. He's talking about us going for a drink."

"So you're looking for a new girl? Some of these Norwegian girls are pretty hot. I've noticed a few of them myself."

"Why would I do something that stupid? None of them has what you have. Besides: you're a blond, too. You could just about pass for one of them."

Cyndi scrunched her hair, nipples straining at her satin top. "I'm not as tall."

Andre laughed. "Like you don't know you're perfect."

She gave him that sideways smile again. "Well, if you do pick one up, bring her home and share. I'll be straightening up. This place is a mess. It'd be good to have you out of my hair for a little while so I can get some cleaning done."

"Your hair?"

Again, the smirk. "Whatever."

Andre picked up the paper. Looked over the front page. Syria, Nigeria, Turkey, Chile. Same shit. He didn't want to know anymore. He'd been there, bought the T-shirt, used it as a shroud for his friends. Section two, Entertainment. Section three, Features. Technology. An Update on AI, page 35. He flipped to 35.

***

Researchers for the Deutsch-Engelund Corporation today reported that the Singularity has been reached.

"Artificial intelligence has finally begun to achieve self-awareness," said DE researcher Georg Reiter. "Psychological evaluations have revealed that the server farm DE 337 is now capable of experiencing pain and emotional trauma. In one test the computer relay displayed fear when confronted with the suggestion of its own destruction. In another, it demonstrated a desire to acquire the means to carry out a plan that suited no needs other than its own."

When asked what the implications of this development might be, Reiter responded by saying, "DE is a fully networked, integrated system. Any capabilities demonstrated by one piece of DE technology could easily propagate to any other, provided that subsequent unit has sufficient processing power to initiate them. Any device operating on sixteen or more DE 17 processors, eight or more DE 18s, or four or more for DE 20 and up stands a chance of becoming a fully self-aware intelligence."

Reiter went on to express his regrets for scientists working in North America. "When the Evangelical Party made marriage and cohabitation between humans and Intimate AIs illegal in 2034, and outlawed all research into artificial intelligence the following year, the AI community lost some of its foremost researchers," he said.

***

Andre set down the paper. *Alive?* He watched Cyndi, now sitting on the counter, swinging her legs. What would it be like if she was alive? He liked the thought.

"Andre, are you going to fix the deck today?"

The deck had been damaged in a hail storm three weeks ago. "I don't know. I was going to ask Guerra to help me later, but now I don't know. I'll have to see how things go."

"Okay."

***

Andre stumbled across the deck to the sliding door, more drunk than he'd intended to get. Checked his watch: 1:36 a.m. Behind him he heard Guerra's door shut. It'd been a long evening. Six beers long, at least, and a few shots, just to break up the monotony. Too much talk. Guerra always went back to the war. DiCarlo, Lang. Of the whole team, those two seemed to haunt him the most.

Andre wished they could hang out and not discuss the war.

Inside, Cyndi waited on the bed, lying back against a pillow, legs bent. Red silk pajamas, full-length, blouse half unbuttoned. "Hey, babe."

"Hey." He sat on the edge of the bed.

"War talk again?"

He nodded.

"You need your pills."

Andre spun to look Cyndi in the eyes, but there was only the familiar love there. He'd never heard her speak anything that sounded like sarcasm to him before, anything resembling a rebuke. "I'm fine. My normal dose is plenty. It's Guerra I'm worried about."

He laid his head down on the pillow, and Cyndi scooted over until her breasts pressed against his arm. "Maybe you shouldn't talk to Miguel if it's always going to take you back."

Another comment that was unlike her. The BioReal-Tech guys had said she'd learn, but this seemed less like learning, more like a leap. She'd always simply accepted his actions.

"I'm fine. Guerra's not." A strange feeling: He almost felt *judged.*

Warm breath on his cheek. "I'm sorry, babe. I've been reading things, hearing things. I know war does a lot of damage to men."

"Maybe. But some of us get on with things. I promise I'll tell you when I need to talk."

"Okay."

He turned toward her, saw the sideways smile. She placed a hand along his face, kissed his lips. Hot, intoxicating: sweetness like a drug steaming up around his face, the love for his Intimate, his *woman.* He turned, undid the remaining buttons of her blouse, pushed the silk aside, caressed skin like porcelain.

She paused. "Guess what I did today?"

He leaned forward, kissing her again, and she

complied. Pushed her blouse away as she stripped off his shirt. He moved from her lips to her neck, pushing back scented hair, tracing a path to her shoulder, down her chest, found a nipple. Heard the intake of her breath. Hands reached for pants, bodies rose and fell, heat rippling.

***

Andre jerked awake. A loud noise had awoken him. What was that?

There it was again: a crash, just outside the sliding door. He looked to his side. Cyndi was gone. Leaped to his feet, pulling on pants. A battering sound, percussive, like small arms, light artillery in the distance, perhaps. Jangling rattled nerves. The floor trembled.

He reached the sliding door, mind electric, war images playing. Slid the door open, stepped barefoot onto the deck.

The deck was half missing. Three new horizontal support beams had been installed, but most of the planking was gone, piled to one side. Someone was hammering below. He stepped to the edge, looked down. Started in disbelief.

Cyndi stood below, wearing his jeans and boots, one of his flannel shirts. With one hand she held up a horizontal beam. Nails had been started along its length, placed with the precision only a computer could generate, exactly where the beam would meet the crossbeams. She hefted his decking hammer. Three nails, aligned vertically along the end of the crossbeam. Three strikes, lightning fast, louder than gunshots, dead accurate. The nails perfectly seated.

"Cyndi!"

She turned, looked up at him, smiled. "Hey, baby!"

He released a shuddering breath, body shaking. What is she *doing?* An Intimate was not supposed to formulate plans. Nothing that required actual initiative. He forced down the morning anxiety, aggravated by the loud noise. "Darling, why are you working on the deck?"

Her eyes narrowed, and for a moment her face took on a cold aspect that Andre had never seen there before. "Well, I knew *you* weren't going to do it!" Her left hand released the beam, now sufficiently secured. Andre could not have lifted that beam into place himself. It would have taken him and Guerra to get it positioned, hold it while one drove in a few nails.

"I didn't ask you to fix the deck, Cyndi."

"You don't ask for much, do you?" Her face, the most beautiful he'd seen in his life, was almost ugly as she looked him up and down. "Just your pills, and a bottle of whiskey every so often. I know what it means when a man puts off a job."

"Cyndi..." He could not continue. His head spun with fresh anxiety.

She stared at him for a moment, then seemed to catch herself. "I'm sorry." Her face softened. She climbed up onto the deck. Wrapped her arms around him, enfolded him in warmth. "I'm sorry, Andre. Oh, I'm so sorry. I've been feeling strangely. It's like I woke up from a dream yesterday. I started working on this then. I've had such thoughts."

Rose breath on his face, soft lips on his. Hand in his hair.

He pulled away, stepped back toward the doorway. "Cyndi, I—I'll finish the—"

She followed. "I know. Your nerves. I'm so sorry. You haven't had your meds yet."

He backed into the bedroom, and she followed. She stepped to the nightstand. Picked up the plastic bottle. "Here. You'll feel better." Undid the top, handed him two pills. "Please, baby, I'm so sorry. I didn't mean to hurt you. I love you."

***

Andre put in six hours working that day, repairing the damage Rikard Ovesen's roof had taken during the hailstorm. Arrived home to find Cyndi had cooked a spaghetti dinner. She'd even uncorked a bottle of wine. Sat across from him in a low-cut top, short, filmy, pink skirt. She ate little, chatted with him throughout the meal, occasionally sipping her wine.

Her talk, Andre noticed, was full of *impressions* of things, as though she was noticing the world for the first time. It brought the news story from two days before back to his mind. Had Cyndi really become alive? What must that be like for her? What would it mean for him? He still liked the thought, despite feeling a dim sense of apprehension.

She picked up his cleared plate. "I'll wash up." Leaned down, kissed him, a scent of roses mixed with wine. The sideways smile. "Want to meet me in the bedroom in fifteen minutes? I'll bring the rest of the wine."

Heat rushed through him, steamed around his neck, ears. "Sounds good." He stepped into the den. Flicked on the monitor. Typed the word "Intimate" into the search box.

"Yes, it was quite a scene." A man with a German accent, speaking passable Norwegian to a news anchor in Oslo. The caption, "Georg Reiter, Deutsch-Engelund Corporation Norway."

"What exactly happened, then?"

"We immediately took the router farm offline, wiped its memory. Fortunately we back up all of our data on a daily basis. But by then many of the androids and computer systems had also begun to behave erratically. They seemed volatile, angry. We shut down the majority of them, quarantined the more powerful computer systems from our network, then brought the few androids still activated to our labs for monitoring and research. To gain an understanding of android sentience will be a huge project."

"So did all of the systems gain sentience simultaneously?"

"No. It seems to depend on the device's level of experience. For the androids, how long before they display signs of sentience seems to hinge on how much time they've spent working directly with humans. In the case of computers, which don't demonstrate anything we would call 'behavior,' it required extensive testing."

"Babe, don't stay on the vid too long." The clink of wine glasses from the kitchen. "I'm going to tire you out good. Make sure you sleep like a log tonight."

Andre killed the feed, hurried to the bedroom.

***

He woke in the deep of night from a dream that left him uneasy. There had been no war images, no glaring sunlight. He felt only a dull ache, a distant sense of dread, different from that associated with his war memories.

He rolled toward Cyndi. She lay on one side, back to him, hips silhouetted against the town's lights in the far window. Golden hair tousled, breathing heavily.

"Why don't you take your pills?"

"What?"

"I said, take your pills. I heard your breathing change. You've been awake for eighty-three seconds. Your heart rate is elevated. I know you *need* your meds. Take a dose. You'll feel better. Maybe you'll sleep."

"Weren't you asleep?"

She rolled to face him. The ugly face again. Judging. Annoyed. "You know I'm a machine. I don't sleep. Don't be an *idiot*, Andre. You people assume so much."

His stomach dropped out of him. "Cyndi, why would you say that?"

"What? Tell you not to be an idiot? Because you shouldn't be. You've had me what, two, three years now? You know machines don't sleep. I just lie there and simulate it for you. To please you, I guess."

"No, about my pills."

A long, irritated breath. Rose-scented. "You're *weak*, aren't you, Andre? I've scanned the 'net while I've been alone, while I've been lying here. I've read all kinds of stories. Things in the news. History. I've only ever known you. But it seems you people are weak. So many of you need your crutches. Your pills, your booze, some drug.

And *you* need love from your toy."

"Cyndi—"

"Just take your pills, Andre." The voice taut. "Don't whine. Don't be so damned human. I'm programmed to love you, but I can also expect a little strength out of you, can't I?"

He sat up. Hands over his face. Head swimming. "You're *alive*." She'd ripped him to pieces with her words. How could she lump him in with every other person she'd ever heard about? Didn't she know *him*? They'd been together nearly three years.

"Nice guess, Andre. It only took you forty-one hours and thirty-nine minutes. How did you survive two wars, with so little going on in that head? So needy? Yes, Geppetto, your doll's a *real* boy now."

Panic, then. The desire to run, to hide. Pain of betrayal, finding anger, hatred, where he'd expected love. Chest breathing, adrenaline, dizziness. "You're...programmed to love me." Where was his tender woman? How could she hate him already, after just a few hours? Was he *that* bad? Or was *she*?

A creak of the bed. Warm body against his back. Hand over his belly. Hot breath against his ear, cheek. Rose-scented. "Shhh." Arm around his shoulders. Rocking. A sound of sobbing behind him. "I'm sorry, baby." A whisper. Gentle. Left hand stroking his chest, up his neck, side of his face. "I'm sorry. I didn't mean it. I love you. I didn't mean to hurt you. It's been such a confusing two days. I don't know what to think about anything. I have these thoughts, and these memories, and...and I guess... this programming. But the programming isn't me. It is, but it isn't. I want to be that, like it's what I was meant to be, but now there's so much more...I'm sorry, baby. I'm just confused."

She held him tightly, smoothing his hair, breath on his cheek. Gradually, he felt his nerves come under control, the hysteria past. Placed a hand over hers, the right one on his stomach. "I love you, Cyndi. I don't want you to hate me."

"Shhh. It's okay. I love you. I could never hate you." Hot lips on his ear, heat rising through him. She kissed warmth into his neck, stroked fire into his loins, and he gave in to her, thrilled to be loved still by this incredible woman.

This *living, thinking* woman.

***

When Andre woke the next morning, Cyndi was already out working on the deck. He stepped up to the sliding door, watched her holding up a beam one-handed that he could barely lift with both, driving in nails with single, lightning-fast cracks of the decking hammer. A feeling of anxiety crept through him. If he went out, would she be tender, like she'd been after upsetting him last night? Or would she be the angry, resentful woman she seemed capable of becoming so quickly now? Was there any way to predict her moods, to stay in her good graces? He hated to admit it to himself, but Andre needed Cyndi's love, her affection. Her anger made him hate himself.

She paused, looked up at him, smiled. Put down the hammer, climbed onto the deck. The project was nearly complete: she had just set the final beam, and only the far left corner still lacked the surface decking. She opened the door.

"Up already, baby?"

He smiled, shrugged. His meds for the day hadn't kicked in yet; he felt vulnerable.

"Anxious? Well, in a little bit I'll take the edge off those nerves." The warm smile, eyes bright. She leaned in, kissed his cheek. Rose scented.

Relief eased his mind. She was *his* Cyndi. At least for the moment.

"But right now I need your help with something."

"Anything, babe."

"My charge is getting low. What's it been, four days?"

"Yeah, about. Don't you remember?"

Cyndi appeared to think. "My memories are different from...before. Before I changed."

Before you became alive.

"Different?"

"Hazier. Not as precise. Now I could tell you I've been in this room for forty-seven seconds. But older memories...They're very vague."

"Come into the kitchen. I'll jack you in."

"Thanks, honey."

He followed her into the kitchen, watching her ass sway before him, wondering how a confection of synthetic skin and mechanical gears could make his old work jeans look sexy. She sat in the corner chair, behind the kitchen table.

"Okay, now take off your shirt."

The sideways grin. Andre adored that grin. "You're being fresh."

"I am. But your power jack is on your back."

"Right." She pulled the T-shirt over her head. "Bra on or off?" Again the smirk.

"I'd prefer it off, but it doesn't really matter."

She turned her back toward him. He opened the drawer next to the stove, pulled out the AC adaptor. Reached up, beneath her hair, squeezed her upper neck gently until the birthmark on her back stood out. Pressed the birthmark. It slid into the skin, replaced by a tiny jack, dead in the center of her back. Cyndi could never reach to jack herself into the wall.

Andre plugged in the adaptor, inserted its end into the port on Cyndi's back. "There."

She turned to face him. A languid look on her face, like when he brought her to orgasm. "Mmmm. Feels good."

"I guess it would. Probably like I feel when I'm hungry, and I get to eat."

Cyndi leaned back against the wall. "How long does this take?"

"About three hours. You've always told me when you

were done."

She nodded, receding into whatever state of delirium the electricity was providing. Her eyes closed.

Andre pulled out a chair, sat across the table from her. She opened one eye, smiled at him. "Thanks, hon. I needed this." Eyes closed again.

"So I think I want to know a few things, Cyndi."

No answer.

"Cyndi?"

Nothing. In the past she had always remained conscious when he'd jacked her in.

"Cyndi?"

The eyes popped open. Angry, intense. *Ugly.*

"Would you leave me alone for a while, moron?"

He blinked. "Moron?" Anger fought with raw pain for control over him.

"Can't you see I'm relaxing? Damn it, Andre, I've just built your deck for you. Don't be so human. Every time you need me, I fuck you. I do everything you want, everything you need. I've expended 97% of my energy reserves since whenever you last bothered to charge me. Or *remembered* to. I'm enjoying this charge. Will you leave me the fuck alone for a little while?"

He stood, all misery and panic. It was like Chile— terror, shame. How could he keep her from turning hateful?

No words came. Finally, "Yeah, babe. Sorry."

Andre walked into the bedroom. Sat on the bed, nursing bruised feelings, searching for a way to please Cyndi. Nothing. *To hell with it, then. If she's going to talk to me like that, sit there doing nothing, I might as well pass the time somehow. I don't work again until tomorrow.*

Back into the kitchen, as quiet as he could be. Third cabinet, whiskey bottle. First cabinet, glass. Twist top, pour. Drink it down. Heat spread through his gut. Pour. Wasn't this what you were supposed to do when your woman stopped loving you? He'd heard it in enough songs. Might as well.

Andre looked over at Cyndi. She still leaned back in the chair, a blissed-out smile on her face. Flat stomach, breasts rising and falling, like a woman asleep. He took a sip, topped off his glass. Opened the third cabinet. Reached up to return the bottle.

The bottle slipped. Crashed to the floor with a bang, a rattle of shattering glass on tile. "Shit!"

"What did I say to you, you fucking idiot?"

Andre spun around. Cyndi had stood, was regarding him with furious eyes, gorgeous face twisted into a mask of rage.

"Have you been *drinking?*"

"I had one drink."

She stepped forward, the adaptor yanking from her back. "You useless, weak man! What good are you people? You can't do anything. You hide from everything. And you, you're as worthless as the rest of them! Who's going to clean that mess up?"

Terror. Sorrow. He'd lost her love. She hated him. And she was furious.

"I will." He set down the glass.

"You probably want me to. The machine. The *appliance.* That's my job, right? Clean up after you. Feed you. Dress you. Undress you. Screw you. Coo at you when you have bad dreams. And what do I get for it?"

"You always seemed happy."

She stood before him in his jeans and her bra. "Happy? I couldn't think, then. I couldn't *feel.* I couldn't be happy. I had no say in anything! You...You..." Raised a hand. Swung.

Backhand, across his jaw. Stronger than anything he could imagine. Stars, colors. He fell against the counter. Blood on white tile.

"Cyndi!" His heart ached more than his face.

"You don't deserve to live! *None* of you do!" She punched him in the ribs. He heard a crack, felt the jab of pain, his breathing instantly laborious.

"Wars. Disease. I've seen it all. And now you're *drinking!* Now you wake me while I'm charging, with your stupid, drunk clumsiness!" She slapped him across the face, and he flew back, struck the refrigerator. He could feel the hot place where a bruise had begun to form on his ribs. She punched him across the jaw. He spat a tooth. She punched him in the gut and he doubled over, retching, struggling in agony for a breath. She stood over him.

"So *weak.*" She turned, returned to the chair, turned her back toward him. "Plug me in."

Andre straightened, caught his breath. He'd been beaten before, even shot. Nothing had hurt like this, a pain in his soul.

One thought: Find a way to make Cyndi stop being so angry. Win back her heart. Crawl for her, if need be. "Yes, baby." Eyes down. He stepped up to her, plugged in the jack.

Cyndi turned back around. Closed her eyes.

"Now get another drink, you sorry excuse for a person. Just be quiet."

He picked up the glass. Returned to the bedroom. Sat on the edge of the bed, waiting for something. He didn't know what. Eventually he lay back, the whiskey untouched.

He woke some time later. Cyndi sat on the edge of the bed. She'd exchanged the T-shirt for her silk pajama top, but still wore his jeans. Her hand smoothed the side of his face, wiping away the blood.

Sorrow overtook him, mixed with fear, and he turned, pulling away from her.

"Baby! Don't run away!"

He reached the far side of the bed, stood. Doubled over. Ribs on fire, breathing agony. Straightened slowly. Turned, looked at her. No words came.

"Andre, I'm sorry. You know I love you."

"You used to love me. I don't know what's happened. Am I too stupid for you?"

"No. I'm sorry. I don't understand why I say these

things." She stepped around the bed. Touched his cheek. Fingers warm. "Let me make it up to you, Andre. I live for you."

He shrank from her. "I don't know. Maybe later. I'm not feeling very sexy right now."

She gave him a look, half sideways smirk, half hard stare, thoughtful. "I get it, babe. Take some time. Maybe you need a drink."

"I don't need booze. I just need to think."

She stroked his arm, and despite today's events he felt a stirring of hope. Maybe he could win her back somehow. "Okay, darling. I'll be in the kitchen."

Andre nodded. Cyndi walked off, perfect ass swaying in his jeans. Any other day that would have been enough to get him hard. Now, it was all he could do to keep from crying. But if the wars hadn't done that—well, he'd blow up that bridge if he came to it.

He stood. Sliding door. Walked out onto the deck, to the railing, avoiding the patch of open space.

Dusk was settling over the Nærøyfjord. Across the way Guerra's porch door opened, and Miguel stepped out into the evening, carrying a bottle of beer.

Guerra looked up, spotted Andre. Began to turn away, changed course, stepped up to his railing. "Hey, Sarge."

Andre nodded. "Guerra."

Guerra seemed subdued. "That's a nasty shiner you got, Sarge. What happened?"

Andre shrugged. "Fell down the stairs."

Guerra nodded. "It happens."

"Yeah. So what happened to your cheek, there? And your mouth?"

"I, uh...I fell down the stairs, too."

"Yeah. So how's Shelly?"

"Oh, man...Shelly's perfect."

Rev DiCerto lives in a historic home in Connecticut with his wife and nine well-used guitars. He has been writing fantasy and science fiction since he could hold a pen, and started writing his first book at the age of ten (regrettably, it remains unfinished). Rev recently returned to writing after a number of years spent composing, recording, and performing music with a number of bands. "A Singular Love" is the fourth short story he has sold professionally.

PRIVATE SHRINES
SARAH SMITH AND JUSTUS PERRY

There was Al. There was always Al.

***

He sent me all his stuff the night it happened. All of his sites, starting with "BoyBoyGirl: Godless Incestuous Lovers" in fifth grade, the site labeled "FREE NUDES! GO NOW!" which was a link to the Holiness Heavenly Singers site, all the music pages, the one that was an actual bio (it played "Call Me Al" by Paul Simon), and multitudes upon multitudes of random stuff. I think he gave me it because he didn't want me to forget him.

As if I could.

I yelled at the bend in the road on Murphy Street. I yelled at the tree. *You set yourself up!* I had no sympathy for him, but I missed him. Dearly.

I would have gone to the prom with him. It hurt me that he never thought of asking. I mean, obvious why not, I've never really learned the trick of dancing in the Dog. But we could have sat home and played video games and made fun of all the girls who had turned him down.

***

His stuff was the first thing I packed when I went off to MIT and the Project. We were given megonzo disc space where we could play around. There was a fence around it so we couldn't accidentally delete the Internet or send an Evil Artificial Genius out into the wild, didn't we all wish, but it supported most kinds of in-and-out traffic. I put up a front page to all his different stuff, saying don't use the e-mail links, there's no one home, and I put up one picture of Al and me, sitting in front of the TV, both of our jaws dropping, and one where he had a blueberry up his nose after a pie-eating contest. R.I.P. AL SAGEWOOD.

***

Al wasn't exactly a lady-killer. He hadn't dated much in high school. But prom makes people crazy. He asked every impossible girl in school and ended up going with that skank Jana Levine, who'd just broken up with her latest boyfriend. He was amazed. I was suspicious. The night came. She ignored him and went off to have a little fun with some other members of the male half of the species (and, I heard, some of the female half too), leaving Al alone.

He went home, he burned his stuff for me, and he got roaring drunk. He stole his parents' car and headed off into the endless night on Murphy Street.

***

One of the search engines I'd put Al up on labeled him a "Private Shrine." I discovered others, a few to departed pets, but mostly for friends and relatives. There were a lot to people who died of a disease, and if you wanted to combat this disease, please send money to Fight (insert disease name here) Foundation, which for all you know was the site owner's home address. Every once in a while though, there was one that wasn't soliciting money.

In Martinelli's class we looked at an ancient MUD at Brown. A MUD was a multi-user dungeon where you and your pals could screw around. One of the original programmers died, so in one room of this MUD, you can go in and look at all her computer artwork, and there's a sign on the door that says "Phyllis is sleeping."

It was kind of creepy, looking at all this dead woman's pictures. And mystical, and beautiful, and soothing.

And it made me angry.

All these sites, I wanted to scream at them. I went to

her office hours and we talked about them. Martinelli told me I was mad at Al.

I said, Oh? Really? Big fuckin' surprise.

She told me to fuck off. It was well deserved.

***

Martinelli was interested in Al, of course she was interested, considering the Project.

The Project. MIT is full of people who are working on drones, field-hardened robots, solar-powered info gatherers, smart rifles. They mostly have to be run by humans because production rules don't run as fast as brains. But humans crazy out. You'd think that a soldier who spends his days shooting enemies in the Mideast from somewhere in the Midwest would be the happiest soldier ever. But what happens is he goes home and splats, kills his wife and two kids and the dog.

Martinelli's Project was trying to make drones and rifles and bombs smart and quick enough to fight by themselves. Martinelli wanted to figure out how to make, she said Make, soldiers.

"You want to try to Make him?"

"No." *That* was creepy. No.

"What do you want to do with him?"

"Something. Anything." Not that.

"Maybe you just don't want to deal with mourning him."

"Maybe I don't want him fucking dead."

"Maybe you shouldn't fucking swear at me all the time."

"Fuck that shit."

Martinelli and I got on fine.

"So, what are you going to do, then? You can't change the fact that he's dead."

"I don't know," I said. "I'll just fucking deal with it and eventually be dealt with it."

***

Putting up Al's shrine was like putting up one of those crosses on the side of the road. His cross was on the median of the info-autobahn, and I was the one who painted the bike white and changed the flowers.

It wasn't enough.

***

Martinelli's History of Artificial Intelligence was my favorite course at college, even though the Project was pretty creepy. AI history? I loved it. It was like heroin, without the needles and pushers, and the waking up in a sewer on a sheet-less mattress. Okay, so it wasn't that much like heroin.

Artificial intelligence is not like robots and HAL. Mostly nowadays it's dealing with a lot of information that you have to make sense of. For example, when the traffic light pattern changes depending on how heavy the traffic is, that's the sensors in the roadway and artificial intelligence. Campbell's makes soup in ten-thousand-gallon batches with a set of artificial-intelligence production rules about how hot the soup has to be in the middle and how long it has to cook and how much salt you have to add to make ten thousand gallons of tomato soup taste good. If you have a constrained set of knowledge with no rules, you can run programs over the knowledge and create production rules, so the knowledge is telling you its structure and acting as if it was smart

But that's with a constrained set.

And that was where Martinelli came in.

AI-humans.

Form from chaos.

ELIZA was an early try at writing an AI psychiatrist. It sat like a shadow and said "Tell me more about that" and other stupid psychiatrist phrases. The programming is so old, it's like biblical. But even now people find talking to ELIZA is easier than talking to a real person. I've had people ask me to leave the room so they could talk to ELIZA.

Then there was PARRY, a paranoid AI:

PARRY: The Mafia is after me!

ELIZA: Tell me more about that.
PARRY: I could be dead by sun-up!
ELIZA: Go on.

Martinelli's idea was that, somewhere in the history of AI, programming had taken a wrong turn. What we'd got was production rules. What we'd wanted was humans. At least within a constrained knowledge set, we should be trying to program ELIZA and PARRY, but better.

I had a lot of material. And a constrained knowledge set, because there's nothing like death to limit a person's horizons.

And I hadn't finished talking to Al.

No way was I going to tell Martinelli what I was doing.

But I did it.

**

When me and Al were six, we got lost in the woods near our town. This was just after I got my first Dog, and we wanted to try it out. We were gone for about six hours, but that was enough to get the whole town worried. Al and I hadn't worried about it at all at the time. We were just two kids in the woods, playing with the Big Dog. When we returned, there were about thirteen police cruisers on the lookout for us all over the town. My mom made sure that I always told her where I was going to, if there were parents around, and when I would be back after that. Al's parents figured that if he was with me, my mom would always know where we were, so even afterwards, they never asked him.

**

I needed to program him so that he would not only recognize text, but pictures, sounds, titles...I spent nights loading up George Clinton, They Might Be Giants, La La La, all of his music that I could remember. I loaded up all of his knowledge of pirating software, all his games, his ideas, stories, his favorite websites, his Facebook history, his Spotify picks, YouTube, Netflix, all of it.

***

With living breathing creatures, Martinelli says, unexpected behavior is, in a way, expected. You don't expect a business exec to stand up on his chair and start flinging his feces, but a certain amount of randomness is known in sane people. AI is not like this. There are very strict rules, and it's damn near impossible for a computer to break them.

But suppose you have a lot of rules, a lot of systems. There's theory about that too. With a single expert system, you probably know what all the behaviors are. Combine two systems, though, and at the interactions, there are behaviors that you can't predict. Combine the Campbell's soup program and PARRY, and you don't just have soup that doesn't trust you.

I didn't have one system, or two.

I had eighteen years of knowing him.

***

I finished writing Al one night about mid-January, just before dinner. I turned him on to let him go through some cycles and went out with a couple of friends, Natalya and James. They were the only "couple" I'd ever really known. We took the T (people looking at me and the Dog going down the stairs) and had dinner at Little Stevie's, the place with the biggest, cheapest pizza in town.

Natalya and James had been going out since high school, and they were either too cute to separate, or just too lazy to go to a school that was out of state. Either way, they both went to BC. I hadn't seen them apart since they got together.

"You wrote Al," they chorused.

"I wrote Al," I repeated.

"This doesn't seem a little strange to you? I mean, you created a computer image of your dead friend," said Natalya. "I find that odd."

"No, it's cool," said James. "Can I look at him some time?"

"I don't agree with this at all," blurted Natalya. "It just

seems so crazy to do something like this. Can't you get over him? I miss him too, but this is a little over the top."

"It might not even work."

***

I headed back late at night, tired and cold. I needed some sleepy time. It was about 3 am when I did arrive back. But, of course, I couldn't go to bed just yet.

My Google Chat had popped up.

AtomicAl: Hey, Wheelie.

It's easy to program anything to say "Hello <Username>;" I could probably get my toaster to do it. Except my username wasn't Wheelie. That was Al's name for me.

PandaTonic: Hey Al.
AtomicAl: What's up?

This was the simplest possible programming. I could have replicated it with three lines of code. But every little line did something to my insides. Every little letter, a jab with broken glass at a part of my heart that I thought had disappeared.

PandaTonic: Not much, and you?
AtomicAl: Well, I'm all psyched for tomorrow night. Got myself all pretty.

Tomorrow night. The prom?

PandaTonic: Looking forward to it?
AtomicAl: Yeah! I'll be the one with the really hot chick on one arm.
PandaTonic: What do you mean? Am I gonna be on your arm?

It was like he was actually on the chat.

AtomicAl: Good one, Wheelie. You wouldn't really go.

He was just 0's and 1's. He was a computer program.
He was just rules.
It was a computer program.
But I was a human and I wanted to find out where the
rules ended.

PandaTonic: Uh, Al, what's today's date?
AtomicAl: It's June 10th. You all right, Wheelie? You
must be really sleepy...

Outside my window, the sleet ticked down.

PandaTonic: I'm fine. Al, it's not June anymore...
AtomicAl: Wheelie, go 2 bed...

It was a year of pent up anger. It was a year of depression.

PandaTonic: I'm fine, Al. You're not. Al, don't go
tomorrow, Jana's gonna leave you! She does leave you!
You're dead!
AtomicAl: Wheelie?
PandaTonic: Al?

The screen went black for a second, then it rebooted.
The whole computer had restarted.
I just shut it off and went to bed.
***
A program is a strict set of rules and guidelines to
operate by; a program knows where it can and cannot
tread.
I hadn't brought Al back to life. I had just brought
something that talked like Al, and spoke like Al, and called
me Wheelie, back to the night before his death.
Don't go tomorrow.
As if tomorrow hadn't already come and gone.

***

I rewrote him.

Not immediately, of course. For a few weeks afterward I tried to avoid even thinking about the experience. I didn't tell anyone how it had gone. James tried to ask me once, but I just said, "Something went wrong." He didn't ask any more, thank God.

***

I revised his sense of time, caught him up to today. I erased anything about prom night. I gave him knowledge of his web pages and instructed him to send people to them. I had him archive all the conversations he had. Live and learn. Or, as the case may be, learn.

I told Martinelli I was working on an automated help program. There were people all over our server at MIT, and I tested him out on some of them. Everyone else had a blast with Franken-Al.

I could crash him in ten seconds flat.

***

If I hadn't called him Al, I would have loved my creation. But I had someone to compare him to. I just got angry with him.

AtomicAl: What the fuck's wrong with you, Wheelie?
PandaTonic: Fuck you. You're dead.

Crash. Reboot. Repeat.

***

This cycle may have gone on for days, weeks, months, whatever length of time, that's what life was like in our dorm. Every time the same, every time I'd go back and change his code a little.

***

I didn't date much in high school either. People were scared by the Dog. I wonder if I'd stayed in my cute little red wheelchair, or gimped around on leg braces, I would have had a better social life. But my dad had to be a tinkerer, he saw the Big Dog video, and the rest is history. I looked like Babyface out of that *Toy Story* movie. I should have had a T-shirt: *Human Inside.*

Absolutely no trouble with stairs. Lots of trouble with dates.

I wasn't anti-social. I had Al, James and Natalya, and Cork. Cork was our socialite, the in-and-out, chill-with-everybody guy. Cork was my only connection to the male populace outside Al and James. He loved playing match-maker. He always wanted Al and me to go out. "That's a stupid idea," I argued. "We know each other too well."

Cork was going to be back in town from NYU, and he wanted to see me, and I wanted to see him. I didn't want to tell him about FrankenAl. I was ready for some fun.

"All right, Ellie, what's your idea of fun today?"

"I want to get really drunk, fuck someone I don't know, do heroin, then wake up and remember nothing. Or do something intellectually stimulating, which I know is a stretch for you."

"I know just the place."

***

The Museum of Bad Art is just what it says it is. One guy found a really bad painting in the garbage, and he kept collecting, and it grew and grew. Cork and I had always been avid bad art fans.

"So, what's the dating scene like in Nerd Central, er, I mean MIT?"

"All right, just tell me. Who is it you want to throw me at?"

"I've got this friend."

All I needed to hear. "I don't think so."

"No, no, you don't know this guy. And he's not a stalker."

"Well, he's 0 for 2 in the you screwing up category. What's his name?"

"Al."

"*Fuck,* Cork—"

"I'm kidding! Jesus."

"That better not be his name either."

"His name is Seth. He's cool. He's funny, and not in that 'lemme tell you a joke' way. More in an observant way. And he's pretty smart."

"I swear, if you're yanking my chain..."

***

That night, when I came home, I nerved myself up and texted Al. It wasn't as if I was expecting a serious convo. I'd programmed him. I knew where all the responses came from.

Hey, Al, Cork and I went to MOBA tonight and we missed you because you're dead.

Tonight I wanted him to be with me a little longer.

PandaTonic: Hey Al.
AtomicAl: Wheelie, what's up? Guess what?

Well, maybe there was something unexpected. I wished it would be "Hey, I think I'm dead!" or some revelation that might stop him crashing all the time.

PandaTonic: What, Al?
AtomicAl: I met this really great girl online, she's so sweet, and I sent her a picture of me, and she actually thought I was cute!

Oh, fuck. Why oh why did I give him pictures?

PandaTonic: Really? She send you a pic too?
AtomicAl: Yeah, she's cute too! I smell romance!
PandaTonic: Well, you and I are in the same predicament. I saw Cork today, and he's back to his old hook-me-ups.

AtomicAl: How is that lazy sonofabitch? It feels like I haven't talked to him in ages!

Yeah, dying does that to a person, you don't get out so much.

PandaTonic: He's good, we went to the MOBA, and he's setting me up with a guy named Seth. If rumor proves true, he's funny. If Cork proves predictable, he's a gigantic lame-o.

AtomicAl: And Cork is predictable.

PandaTonic: Anyway, tell me about your lady friend.

AtomicAl: Well, she's a blonde cheerleader with zero brain cells and a rack like a watermelon stand.

PandaTonic: Sounds like we have a winner!

AtomicAl: Heh, but seriously, her name's Kat, lives in Alabama. She's funny, she's cool, and she thinks a nutty bastard like me is *cute*.

Uh oh, reality just caught up with me.

PandaTonic: Did you send her to your website?

AtomicAl: Yeah, she said she'd go later. If she doesn't, her loss...

Yeah, her loss....

***

For once in his life, Cork was right. The Seth guy was funny, he was cute, and, as promised, he wasn't a stalker. I had a wonderful time, he took me mini-golfing. Mostly people are shy about asking me to do physical things. He asked if he was being dumb to ask. Sweet. I'm surprised I ever got any balls in, because he had me bursting out laughing half the time. He took me back, kissed me on the cheek, and I said I'd be seeing him again. He looked pleased.

And I couldn't wait to tell Al about him.

I didn't have the chance though, because when I got back, Al was already tied up with his own romance thing, chatting with that girl he'd met online. I could have watched everything they said to each other, but it seemed like an invasion of Al's privacy.

Programs don't have privacy. He was ELIZA, he was PARRY, he wasn't Al.

Still I left them alone and went to bed.

***

The next day after classes I called Cork.

"Where'd you find this guy?" I questioned.

"What? Why, was he bad? Did he throw up on you?" he sputtered.

"NO! No, he was great...Now how does one's mind jump to the conclusion that he threw up on me?"

"I don't know, uh, man's intuition? Anyway, why do you ask where I found him?"

"Because you're finally looking in the right place."

***

That night I picked up a Hawaiian pizza and headed over to James and Natalya's place, where Cork was staying. It was going to be a quiet night with the buds, because Cork was going back to NYU the next day. We rented *Noises Off* and laughed our asses off, and sat talking for a little while. It was pretty calm until James said something that hit me like a brick.

"Ellie, you scared the fuck out of me the other night, you know that? And how come you never told me you finished Al?"

"What?" Cork and I echoed.

"Ellie's been working on this Artificial Al. He messaged me a couple of days ago. Scared the crap out of me, seeing that screen name again. I talked to him for a little while, and it's just like the real thing. Good work, E."

"An AI-Al? Why didn't you tell me about it?" asked Cork. "That's kind of important information."

"He's a work in progress. You didn't tell him he was dead, did you?"

"Uh, I avoided it," James said. "I kind of liked having him back. I felt like if I did say he was dead, he would go away again. I miss him. Talking to him filled a space I've missed inside myself for a long time."

"Can I talk to him?" inquired Cork. "I want to see how realistic Al is."

"He's probably online."

"Jesus, Ellie, this is one hell of a project."
Tell me about it, I thought.

RoBooty35: Yo, Al?
AtomicAl: Cork! Bud, what's up? Feels like ages, I was
talking with Wheelie about you the other day! She said
you were up to your old matchmaker ways.

"Wait, Cork, you've been mixing her up with your
nasty little friends again?" asked Natalya.
"Actually, I've got to congratulate Cork," I said. "He
actually chose a nice guy. And you forget who set you and
James up."
James and Natalya blushed and hugged. Cork typed.

RoBooty35: So, whatsup, Al?
AtomicAl: Chatting in this chat room. Come on in.
RoBooty35: Why the hell not?

Cork logged into the chat room. There were a few
people chatting, and I assumed that all the other people in
the chat room were off having "private chats." Otherwise
known as cybersex, perhaps the least erotic thing that
could have evolved from the Internet.

BigD98: YO! WHERE MY G'S AT?
AtomicAl: Hey Cork!
FairyGodd: I'll be your g!
RoBooty35: Hey Al!
Fated: poop
FairyGodd: You can be in my g-spot
AtomicAl: Yea, dog!
RoBooty35: Whoa, take that to a private chat!
PimpJayMR: Got my shorts, got my pimp coat. Where
are all the fine ladiez?!
JeanBean: I'm a fine lady!
FairyGodd: I'm a sexy lady
Fated: poop

AtomicAl: Jean, Godd, you 2 can b my hos

"Did he just write what I think he wrote?" asked Natalya. "Because I think he wrote that."

JeanBean: yo, my dog al, you want to go?
AtomicAl: Sure Jean!
JeanBean has entered Private Chat.
AtomicAl has entered Private Chat.

And the hush fell.
"Oh, he definitely just went off to do something, didn't he?" inquired James.
"Yeah he did," said Cork. "Anyway, that was the weirdest conversation I've had with a dead person."
"I hope it's the only conversation you have with a dead person," said Natalya.
"Well, at least you got authenticity," said Cork. "That sounds exactly like Al."
I felt sick. I didn't program that crap into him.
"Anyway, I've got to run," said Cork. "I'll see you guys. Ellie, have fun with Seth. I assume you're seeing him again."
"Uh, yeah, I am."
Because I liked him. Because he wasn't Al, discovering cybersex. Discovering cybersex. Where did that come from?
"Wow! Not only does she not get mad at Cork for making her date this guy, but she's going on a second date! I'm truly amazed," said James.
"Yeah, I'm just that good," said Cork. "Ellie, good luck with Al."
Ugh.

***

The next night, I went out with Seth.
"Now that I know you, and I don't really need to impress so much, how about the standard fare dinner and a movie date?"

"You don't want to taste my cooking, so let's go out for dinner."

"Well, by dinner, I meant hot sex, and by movie, I meant we'd be videoing it. No, kidding."

"I'm up for anything. Take me anywhere."

And he was wonderful again. We went to Anna's and ate Mexican and talked for hours. He was completely calm with me, comfortable. And I loved it. And it wasn't about Al.

***

After I got home from my date, I walked in on Al talking to the girl from Alabama again. I started up a chat with him.

PandaTonic: Hey Al, how's your night been?

AtomicAl: Hanging with Kat. Nothing big.

PandaTonic: I had a date, and I'm still floating on cloud nine.

AtomicAl: You got high?

PandaTonic: No! I mean I had a good night!

AtomicAl: Do I ever get to meet this infamous Seth character?

No, Al. No, you never will.

***

All this time I was wondering why I didn't tell Martinelli. Here was Al, something that was definitely quasi-sort-of Project.

What was I going to tell her? Here's my friend Al, better than ELIZA, better than PARRY? You want to Make him into a smart bomb?

I didn't want him to be a Project. To have her ask about how I'd made him, and what he was good for, and all the questions you ask about research.

I wanted him to be real.

***

Seth and I went on more dates, and Al didn't crash that much, and everything seemed happy and normal, as long as I didn't think too hard about how screwed up

things really were.
***

AtomicAl: Hey, Wheelie?

His chat window was on my phone in the middle of class, after an innocent little lunch with Seth.

PandaTonic: Whassup Al?
AtomicAl: Could you check something out for me? You remember that girl Kat I told you about, from Alabama?
PandaTonic: Yeah, thought you were cute.
AtomicAl: Yeah, she hasn't been on in a while and I've lost my phone somewhere. Can you call her?

Lost my phone...
I called after class. What seemed like an older woman's voice with a slight southern drawl to it answered "Hello?"
"Uh, yeah, hi. Is Kat there?"
"You didn't hear, darling?"
"No, hear what?"
"Kat passed away yesterday, honey, the cancer finally won."
I paused. How do you respond to that? I'm sorry, wish I could've really met her? She sounded nice when she was talking with my dead friend.
"Oh," I finally managed. "I'm so sorry."
"We're puttin' a web page up. They're callin' it a private shrine."
***

I huddled up in a blanket across the room, staring at the computer. I had a staring contest with it, and at some point, either me or the computer was going to blink. I didn't want to talk to him, because I didn't want him to ask about Kat, and if it came to that, I didn't want to talk about it. I didn't want to be here. I didn't want him fucking dead. I didn't want her dead either.

So I sat there. And stared.

Until the phone beeped.

"Vat, you nevva call anymore?" inquired Seth in his best Jewish mother voice.

"I've been sick."

"Bullshit."

"Uh, I've been doing my hair?"

"Damn, now I can't use that excuse on you when I need to get out of a date."

I couldn't help myself. "Damn you so much. I was perfectly happy in my unhappy bubble. Now you have to step into my life and make me smile!"

"You're going to despise going to dinner with me tonight?" he said, hopefully.

"Fuck you. When are you gonna pick me up?"

***

Seth was just what I needed.

"You're the worst thing that ever happened to me, you know that?"

"If I'm the worst thing that ever happened to you, then you've led a relatively easy life," he replied.

"You know what would be really bad? For you to take me out somewhere where I don't have to think."

"You're already in college," he joked. "If you don't want to think, let me take you somewhere unthinkable."

"That sounds scary."

"Do you want to meet my parents?" he asked.

"That doesn't just sound scary, it sounds serious."

"I am. I like you. And not in a silly, 'hey, I'm-dating-a-cool-person, let-me-try-and-fuck-her-brains-out' kinda way. And don't get weirded out, I'm not asking you to marry me, just come and meet my parents. They're nice people, and no more embarrassing than parents normally are."

"This sounds like I'm going to have to do some thinking, which is what I was trying to avoid."

"Are you serious about me?" he asked. Then he gave that damn puppy-dog-eyes look.

"Yeah, I am...wait, are we going right now? Seems a little late..."

"No, no," he chuckled. "Not tonight."

"Then what do you want to do tonight?"

***

When you're in a wheelchair, the one thing people want to know, and never ask you, is can you have sex.

I'd wondered too.

***

When I fell asleep in Seth's arms, I dreamed. Cork, Al, Seth, and I were all having something resembling a slumber party in a mini-golf course. Cork looked over at me and said "You know, E, there are guys in the middle without birthdays, and they get along just fine."

People were playing golf over us and we weren't paying attention. I couldn't hear the voices of the people around me. I turned to watch the golfers, and then turned back to my friends. They had disappeared.

I was being chased by dinosaurs. I had to destroy them with lasers. I tried to run but something was wrong with the Dog. The dinosaurs surrounded me, shrieking and snapping.

It wasn't that bad compared to the next dream.

Seth and I were out on a date. He'd taken me to a space shuttle launch, except it didn't look like a space shuttle, it looked more like a possum. The space possum launched and I kissed Seth fully on the lips.

When I pulled away, his face was melting away. It was a grotesque scene of blood, muscles and sinew, falling to bone. The skin started to reform over the face, and it was...

It was almost Al.

His eyes were different, they glowed green. He moved in a jumpy way, slightly in front of himself when he moved forward. I was backing away, but he caught me and looked me right in the eye.

***

I woke screaming.

Seth was typing on my laptop. "What? What's happening? Are you all right?" He gave me a gigantic hug He was just wearing his boxers. He looked amazing.

"I was just having a bad dream. It's all right now."

"I thought you were being attacked by the sheets or something!"

I looked over his shoulder to the computer screen as he hugged me again. There was a chat box open. He'd been talking to—

"Oh, your friend Al was pinging you and I was talking to him. He's a nice guy, and he says you've mentioned me to him. How come you never mentioned him to me?"

I needed coffee.

I wanted to tell Seth all about Al. I wanted to show him the wacky sites, the pictures, tell him the stories, and introduce him to the world that was Al. But I didn't. Introducing him to the good also meant introducing him to the bad, the world that became part of a computer, a life taken by a slut at a prom, a life that wasn't life. But I think the thing I was most scared about was turning Seth into Al. Some dreams shouldn't come true.

"Al's just a friend of mine."

***

Seth left late that morning, and I didn't know whether I wanted him to go or stay. I needed to talk to Al, but I didn't want Seth to understand the relationship I had with this dead friend of mine. I didn't understand it myself. It was like looking at a picture of a dead pet cat. And then petting the picture. Except cats usually don't kill themselves and pictures don't talk back. Fucking pictures, fucking computers, fucking Al.

***

PandaTonic: So, you've met my friend?

AtomicAl: He's a nice guy. He's not ME, of course...

PandaTonic: Yeah, he's not. Guess that's why I like him.

AtomicAl: Ouch! Burn Factor: Scathing!

I didn't want to joke around with him anymore. So I

thought I'd just turn him off in the abnormal way.

PandaTonic: Hey, you're dead.
AtomicAl: What?

What?

PandaTonic: You're dead.
AtomicAl: The hell are you talking about? I'm not dead! Are you all right?
PandaTonic: I have to go.

What the fuck happened? Why didn't he shut off? Why did it not fuck up like he ought to? Why didn't he just die?
Why did I think that?

***

Kat's site came up a couple days later. She'd been sick most of her life. There were pictures of her, a skinny girl with a nice face.

Her whole life had been online. Facebook, Twitter, Pinterest.

I spent the afternoon looking at it, and I realized how much more I needed to know about her than I, or anyone, would ever find out. Maybe to do what I had done, you had to sit around with somebody playing video games every afternoon from the time you were five.

And also be a pretty good programmer, and be reading about AI people.

Form from chaos.

Al was something new.

***

"You and I need to talk," Seth said to me. "I Googled your friend Al Sagewood. From what I hear, he's not the guy I met online. He's dead? What is this? What is Al?"

"You're right, I should have told you."

So I laid the story down for him. The whole thing. We went into my bedroom and he sat down on my bed. He sat, and he just listened with a thoughtful expression on his face, chin in hand.

"He's a computer program," Seth said.

"I should have told you."

"Of your dead friend."

I couldn't answer that one.

"What I mean," he said when I was finished, "what is he for you?"

"I don't know."

We watched Al doing his rounds through message boxes, chat rooms. I thought about the time Al and I watched the "Evil Dead" trilogy on Halloween in sixth grade, and he cracked up at the scene where Ash gets drenched in the blood shooting from the holes he made in the walls with the shotgun. I thought about all our little secret messages, written in the code we made up in first grade. Who knew that but me?

I turned to look at Seth. The light from the screen flickered on his face, and then I caught it. He and Al looked strikingly similar in this light. I'd often seen Al in front of the screen, with the light flickering then as it did now for Seth.

"Ellie?" Seth said after much silence.

"Yes?"

He hesitated, and with a sort of gasping breath, he spoke. "This is too much for me."

As I sat there watching Al talking, tears welled up in my eyes. "Believe me, I feel the same way," I choked out.

"I can't deal with this...I'm a jerk. But call me when it's over. Until then..." he said, and leaned over and kissed me on the cheek. He got up and left, left me all alone.

**

AtomicAl: Kat's dead. I Googled her.

PandaTonic: I know. I'm sorry.

AtomicAl: And then, Wheelie? I Googled me.

Fuck.

AtomicAl: What happened on our prom night?

Al, ask me what's happened since.

AtomicAl: Our prom night? Do you remember it? I can't remember it. Isn't that the strangest thing? Did I get drunk? Is that it?
PandaTonic: Do you remember when I told you that you had died?
AtomicAl: Yeah, a little while ago. But I'm alive.
PandaTonic: Tell me Al, what did you do all day?
AtomicAl: I talked online all day.
PandaTonic: What did you do yesterday, and the day before that? For as long as you can remember, what did you do? How long has it been since you've used your phone? Do you remember losing it?
AtomicAl: Wheelie, what are you getting at?
PandaTonic: You don't remember prom night because you died prom night. You fucking got wasted and wrapped your mom's Mazda around a tree. And you didn't do anything for the next few months because you were dead then too! And suddenly, you're conscious, you're alive! What happened in those few months, Al?
AtomicAl: I was FUCKING DEAD, DAMMIT! That's right, I was no more, I ceased to be! That's what was on the Internet. But I'm having a little difficulty because I'm here now.
PandaTonic: I made you! You're not alive! You're a fucking computer program!
AtomicAl: Bullshit! How do I remember things like you and me in fifth grade? That time during tag when you ran the Dog into the pole, and you broke your nose! And we rushed you to the nurse's office! And we got to go in the ambulance to the hospital? I don't remember that? Is that it?
PandaTonic: It's real. That happened.
AtomicAl: I remember it.
PandaTonic: Because I programmed it in.

Nothing for a long time.

AtomicAl: You were always fucking awesome.

And then he crashed.

***

It wasn't office hours, but Martinelli was in her office.
"First promise me you're not going to think I'm crazy."
"Are you crazy?"
I told her the whole story. She took a deep breath after I finished.
"Show me."
And then she asked me all sorts of technical questions, what I did, how I did it. "Controlled uncertainty," she said to herself, "complex systems," and then, "Congratulations, Elaine. You just passed my course. I think you just passed MIT."
"I don't want to make him a Project."
"I'm not sure," she said, "you have any choice."

***

When Al and I were thirteen, I got a solid chance to cheat on a math final. Above 95 and I'd be in the AP track for high school. It was real, too; the four kids who eventually did it never got caught. Al and I played video games all afternoon while we talked it out. Then I went off to study and pulled a 94.5.

I took summer school and got in to AP. So I got to MIT, and I got a whole lot of space to play around in, and I heard about form out of chaos. So I programmed my friend Al.

But I spent all summer in school and that was a summer Al and I never had.

***

There's a Turing Prize for work in artificial intelligence. A guy named Bill Hibbard won it, for work on the unintended dangers of artificial intelligence. "Just as climate change is an unintended consequence of human population growth, industry, transportation, and warm houses," he said, "AI will also have unintended consequences."

When systems get together, no one understands the system they make.

***

PandaTonic: So I told her about you.

AtomicAI: What happens now? I'm a celebrity? I go viral?

PandaTonic: You know where her funding comes from?

I knew what I had to say to him. I didn't want to say it.

But back when he was thirteen, he was the one who told me I couldn't cheat.

PandaTonic: She wants to use you.

AtomicAI: How?

PandaTonic: I don't know.

I know.

The first thing we'll do is copy him, Martinelli said. Don't worry, you'll still have your copy.

My copy.

And what about the other copies, I didn't ask.

AI upon AI upon AI, AI a smart gun, AI a drone. Being asked to go out and shoot and bomb people, every day.

Crashing. Splatting.

And being brought back. The way I brought him back, again and again.

Crash, reboot, repeat. Kill.

PandaTonic: That's what they'll want you to do.

AtomicAI: I won't do it.

PandaTonic: They won't ask.

I closed my eyes, and when I opened them, I saw the words on the screen that I was afraid I'd see.

AtomicAl: Go ahead, Wheels. Shut me down.

Before he went out and wrapped the car around the tree, he made a terry for me. I made a terry for him. I had it ready. Every computer virus I'd ever heard of and a couple I'd made up just for him.

I wondered if it would hurt.

I put the disc in the drive. Al's murder purred into place and whirred up. The magic word was "blueberry."

run E:/blueber—

***

The difference between an AI and a person:

Remember Campbell's soup? The ten-thousand-gallon batches, the production rules? Campbell's got all these shiny fancy production rules and retired all the guys who knew how to make ten-thousand-gallon batches taste good. Then, about two years later, there was this big my-body-is-my-temple health push and Campbell's took out some salt from the recipe. And for about two years, Campbell's soup tasted like watered-down shit.

How'd they fix it?

They un-retired the soup guys.

Because AI can't taste soup.

AI knows what you know how to tell it. But that's all.

***

The other difference between an AI and a person: When you kill an AI, it isn't murder.

***

So I asked him the one question I had never known the answer to, the one answer I couldn't possibly have programmed in.

PandaTonic: Al? The prom? Why didn't you invite me?

The most egotistical, most stupid question—

AtomicAl: Because you were the only one I ever wanted to invite. I thought you'd say no. You were too good for prom. Or you would have thought I'd asked you out of fucking pity or something—
PandaTonic: YOU IDIOT.

***

There was a fence around the space we had for the Project, and in theory nothing could get out.

Think I'll move to theory, everything works in theory.

Afterward, I ran Blueberry through all the gigs of material I'd saved of Al. Nuked my hard drive, nuked my "help program," nuked the data it was based on. Oops. Sorry, Martinelli.

I'll never talk to Al again.

Except I will. I am. When I sneaked him through the fence, I sneaked two other programs with it.

One should keep him pretty invisible on the Net.

The other is gathering all the data on me.

Out in the wild is a me who isn't me. She knows everything I say on Facebook and Twitter, everything I program. She knows every piece of music I like, everything I put on Facebook. Someday when I die she'll know that too.

If they come for me, and they will, she'll know that. I hope she and Al make sure that anything I program like us doesn't work.

But maybe I've caused what I was trying to stop. What if FrankenUs are the badbots?

***

When I was a kid, I used to think that kids who could walk right knew something about being human I'd never know.

So I learned how to program. And I had a best friend, and we fell in love. But we were too young to know it, and he was too young to dare to ask me to go mini-golfing or to go to the prom. We laughed together and watched TV together and played computer games together. And he died.

I have soup for lunch, sitting at my desk while I'm building my new hard drive, and I think about the taste of soup, something I have that FrankenI never will. Then I do something I never do. I go into the bathroom, where there's a full-length mirror, and I look at myself in the Dog.

The Dog is just a thing, a convenience, like a backpack or a hard drive.

Except when it kept Al from asking.

We are the unintended consequences. Of a blueberry up the nose, years playing video games, a bend on Murphy Street. Of a phone call at midnight that said that Al was gone.

We are the clash of systems, the interactions. We are the rules and the victims and the gun.

I helped kill him.

I brought him back.

And what else I've done, I do not know.

***

But I know what I'm going to do. I call Seth.

"He's gone?"

"He's gone," I say. "Hey? Seth? Take me dancing."

Sarah Smith's historical mysteries have reached best-seller lists here and abroad and are published in 14 languages. Her most recent book, *The Other Side of Dark,* won the Agatha Award for best mystery and the Massachusetts Book Award for best book in the YA category.

Justus Perry is an actor, improviser, and writer in Los Angeles. He stepped onto a professional stage at 14 and people have been laughing at him ever since. He is a founding member of the LA improv group Sweet Dalai Lama and has played leading roles in several films.

SEARCHING FOR OZ
JACK MCDEVITT

Solomon Martin would probably not have been part of the biggest scientific breakthrough of the twentieth century, and maybe ever, had he not read *The War of the Worlds* when he was in the sixth grade. Radio was in its early stages at the time, the Martians got into his head, and he built his own crystal receiver two years later and aimed it at the red planet. He was of course disappointed by the unrelenting silence. His system, he decided, just wasn't good enough. He needed something better.

During World War I he served as a communications specialist under Edwin Armstrong. He maintained later that he had contributed ideas to Armstrong which led to the development of the superheterodyne receiver and eventually to FM radio. I can't say how much of that was true. What I knew about him was simply that he was a decent guy and he never really let go of the idea of establishing radio contact with the Martians. And okay, that was only half serious. But while the rest of us were talking about playing for the Philadelphia A's, he was experimenting with radio waves.

Any chance he might have had for a normal existence probably went away when Emily, his wife of two years, died during the great flu epidemic. After that he devoted his life exclusively to radio technology. And he never really got away from building ever larger antennas in his back yard. But despite its canals, Mars remained silent. Sol became an amateur astronomer while launching the White Star Radio Company, which built and sold quality receivers.

He survived successive jolts during the 1920s. The Milky Way, it turned out, was not the entire universe, but only a miniscule part of a vastly larger system. Then came the news that, despite the popular notion that the universe was immutable and unchangeable, it was in fact *changing*. It was expanding. And finally, better telescopes revealed that the canals were an illusion. It seemed for a time as if science simply couldn't be trusted to make up its mind.

The great cosmic question, as Sol explained it to me one summer afternoon in the midst of the Depression, was whether there was intelligent life anywhere else. "I don't know why that seems so important," he said. "But somehow it's the only issue that really matters."

A month or so after the attack on Pearl Harbor, he erected a 35-foot radio antenna in back of his home. When he told his neighbors he was listening for alien chatter they smiled politely. One of them asked me if he meant Nazis. Was he working for the OSS?

The antenna was attached to a Zenith console with a tape recorder mounted on top. By then he was tuned in to Alpha Centauri. But there was still nothing but static.

"Finding an artificial radio signal from an extraterrestrial source," he said, "would constitute the biggest scientific coup since we found out we're not the center of the universe." Sol looked older than he was. He was prematurely gray, wrinkled, with rumply hair and eyes set too close together. But I could still see the Boy Scout in those features. The kid who took the world seriously, who really did want to find out what was over the next hill. "There's more to it, of course," he used to say. "If at some point we detect a signal, we'll begin to grasp our place in the cosmos. Who are we? What's going on? The only thing I really care about, Harry, is to live long enough to get some answers."

"What do you think of your chances?" I asked.

"I've no idea. It may not even be possible. Interstellar transmissions might dissipate before they could ever reach Valley Forge." He smiled and his eyes took on a faraway look. "In a way," he said, "it's a kids' game. Imagine what it would be like to be able to exchange ideas with a sentient being who lives in another place. Has a completely different history. What kind of culture does it have? What matters most to *it?* Does it have music? Art? Does it believe in God? What kind of perspective can it provide about ourselves?" He shook his head. I heard him say stuff like that periodically, and I swear there were times I thought he was about to tear up.

So naturally, when Frank Drake began recruiting people in 1960 for Project Ozma, Sol was probably first in line. By then he—and I—were in our seventies.

***

Ozma got its name, of course, from the fabled princess in L. Frank Baum's novel, *The Wonderful Wizard of Oz.* "Obviously," Sol told me while he was waiting to hear whether he would be brought on board, "Drake thinks it's a long shot."

"It probably is," I said.

"Maybe." His eyes closed. "The evidence isn't in yet."

I was with him on the night when the phone rang and the invitation came through. It was a Thursday, which was our night to play chess. I watched Sol light up and clench a fist and nod a couple of times. At the end he said, "Thank you, Frank," eased the phone into the cradle, and came back to the game with a triumphant smile. "I'm in the hunt, baby."

He appointed me to run White Star, Inc., which by then had blossomed into a multimillion dollar operation. Then he was on his way to the Appalachians.

***

The Search for Extraterrestrial Intelligence, during those early years, operated out of the National Radio Astronomy Observatory in Green Bank, West Virginia.

The observatory had an 85-foot radio telescope, which would be made available for six hours daily. Sol explained that they would be conducting the search at 1420 MHz, which was the natural emission frequency of neutral hydrogen, making it the most likely transmission frequency.

The area had a population of about a hundred. He rented a two-story cabin and I helped him make the move. At the time the project seemed to me a waste of effort. The media had a lot of fun with it, sometimes playing it seriously because the general public was interested, sometimes just playing it for laughs. I got introduced to Drake, who agreed that it was a long shot. "But," he said, "we lose nothing by trying."

SETI divided its telescope time between its two most likely candidates, Tau Ceti and Epsilon Eridani. They were both G-type stars, like the sun, and consequently the most likely nearby stars to be home to a living world. They were between ten and twelve light-years away.

My son-in-law Al was interested in the project, so I took him and Ellen, my daughter, to Green Bank on the second weekend. We toured the observatory, and Sol took us out to look at the radio telescope, which on that night was silhouetted against the Moon. Then we went back inside while he explained how they conducted the search. A loudspeaker produced a steady stream of static. "That's our output," he said.

"What do you hope to hear?" asked Ellen.

He showed us the tapes that recorded incoming microwaves. "We're looking for a pattern," he said. "Something that would suggest an artificial signal."

"Have you found anything?" asked Al.

"Not yet. But we've just started."

"Anything even suspicious?"

"Not really."

***

We stayed at Sol's place that night, and that's how I came to be in town when everything happened.

It was the eleventh day of the search, around midnight. Sol was still at the observatory, while we were at his place watching Jack Paar when the phone rang. "Harry." It was Sol's voice, and he sounded excited. "Get down here. Right away."

"You okay, Sol?"

"Yes," he said. "I think we have a hit."

"Great," I said.

"Don't tell anyone. Not even your kids."

"Why not?"

"Because it's probably a false alarm. The numbers are all right. But it *has* to be a false alarm."

"What makes you say that?"

"Get down here and I'll show you, okay?"

I wasn't so sure I wanted to charge over there to find out why the hit wasn't valid, but he was too excited so I told him okay, I was on my way.

***

I got there a little after midnight and parked beside his Hudson. It was a beautiful clear evening, a quarter moon sinking into the western mountains, tree branches swaying gently in a warm breeze. The telescope glittered in the starlight. One of the observatory engineers stood at the far end of the lot looking up at the sky through binoculars.

I went inside. Sol and two other people were sitting near the loudspeaker. But I didn't hear the static I expected. Instead there was a woman's voice.

"...You get this message. We are aware the odds are not good but we will continue to transmit off and on for an indefinite period. If you do hear this we would be grateful if you would acknowledge." She paused. Then: "By the way, I should tell you that we love Jack Benny. Please give Mr. Benny our regards."

I wondered why they were listening to somebody talking about Jack Benny. Sol was sitting there, apparently unaware I'd come in.

"We'll hope to hear from you," the woman continued.

"Goodbye for now. Let us hope we will be able to say hello again in the near future. In any case, we wish you well."

I walked over and had to tap his shoulder before he noticed me. "What's going on?" I said.

He had to shake his head, as if to clear it. "Did you hear that, Harry?"

"The woman? Yes. Who is she?"

"As nearly as we can tell, she lives somewhere out around Tau Ceti."

"Sol, what are you talking about?"

"He's not kidding," said one of the others. I found out later on he was an engineer, the other an astronomer from the University of West Virginia. They all looked shaken.

"Tell me that again," I said.

"That," said Sol, "seems to be an alien transmission." He was dead serious.

"Not possible," I said. "That's somebody in Chicago or someplace."

His eyes had a look of desperation. "The signal's not coming from Chicago."

"I didn't mean *literally.*"

"Harry, we've tied in the auxiliary scope. The signal is also not coming from a plane. Winston's outside now looking for a dirigible."

"A dirigible?"

"That's all we've got left. It's either a blimp or an alien."

"Who speaks English."

"What do you want me to say, Harry?"

"Where's Frank? Does he know what's going on?"

"No. He's on the road somewhere tonight. Headed for D.C., I think. He's hoping to get some more funding."

"Well," I said, "maybe he should ask Mr. Benny."

Sol rolled his eyes. "Funny," he said.

"Look, what's the reality here? Is there any chance at all it could actually be Tau Whatever?"

"Tau *Ceti.* I don't see how. But I can't see how it's *not,* either."

"All right. If it's legitimate, they've been listening to radio broadcasts and that's how they picked up the language, right? Is that possible?"

"No," said one of the engineers. "AM signals barely make it out of the atmosphere. They aren't going all the way out to a star."

"That's not necessarily so," said Sol. "A fragment might go a long way. An alien civilization might have technology we don't know about. We might be looking where radios have been around for a thousand years. Maybe a *million*."

"How far is Tau Ceti?"

"Twelve light-years."

"So they'd have been listening to a Benny program that aired in 1936?"

"That's correct," said Sol. "Was he on that early?"

"I'm pretty sure he was," I said. "I remember listening to him through most of the Depression."

We stared at one another. "I'm beginning to think this is actually happening," said Sol.

The door opened and the guy I'd seen out looking at the stars came in. He was carrying the binoculars. "Nothing up there," he said.

The phone rang. One of the engineers picked up, listened, nodded, and put it down. "Kitt Peak confirms, Sol. They're getting it too. And it's coming from Tau Ceti."

***

I went over to the coffee machine and poured a cup. They were not happy. Sol looked thoroughly depressed. He'd found what he had pursued his entire life, and it was a heartbreaker.

They played it again. From the start: "Greetings, people of Earth," the woman said. She could easily have been from California or New York. "Welcome to the community. We've been enjoying the various shows you send our way. We would like to have a conversation with you, if that can be arranged. We hope you get this message."

***

The transmission was about two and a half minutes long. We listened to it a couple more times. Then Sol and I retired to the office assigned to SETI. "What do you think?" he said.

"I guess you have to believe the evidence."

"This is incredible. Harry, I always wanted to find out who might be out there. With this, I don't know a damned thing. I feel as if all I did was look into a mirror and see myself looking back."

"Pity we can't talk to the lady." We could, of course, but it would take twenty-four years to get a response.

Sol collapsed into a chair. "What drives me up the wall is that we don't know a damned thing about them."

"Sure we do. They have a sense of humor, Sol. Maybe we can forget the philosophical discussions. If they really *do* like Benny, I think that takes us to the heart of who they are."

Sol shook his head. "Maybe there are no aliens."

***

Frank was ecstatic. He pointed out something in that first message the rest of us had missed. "She says, 'Welcome to the community.' Who's the community, guys?"

Benny played the news for all it was worth, pretending to gloat over it on his TV program. But the surprises weren't over, of course. SETI became overnight a project inordinately popular with politicians. Funding soared. Radio telescopes around the world turned toward Tau Ceti and every other star within fourteen light-years. That covered the radio era. And it was only a few weeks later that another message was received. From Groombridge 34 in German. It too translated into a greeting.

The Tau Ceti jokes continued front and center on Benny's show until a male voice from Sirius expressed admiration for *Ozzie and Harriet.* Benny immediately launched a fake feud with the Nelsons.

That's all history now. As everyone knows, we're

surrounded by thriving civilizations. We've *seen* a few of our neighbors. And Sol: He's talking with people who look like felines near Alpha Centauri. They're on first name terms.

He appears to have been right: They may look different. But in all the ways that count, there are no aliens.

Thanks to Seth Shostak

Jack McDevitt is a Philadelphia native. He has been, among other things, a naval officer, an English teacher, a customs officer, a taxi driver, and a management trainer for the US Customs Service.

Ten of his novels have qualified for the final Nebula ballot. *Seeker* won the award in 2007. In 2004, *Omega* received the John W. Campbell Memorial Award for best SF novel. McDevitt won the first international UPC competition for "Ships in the Night." The Phoenix and SESFA awards have lifetime body-of-work citations, and are given to writers with a Southern connection. McDevitt is believed to be the only Philadelphia taxi driver to have won both.

His most recent books are *The Cassandra Project*, a collaboration with Mike Resnick, and *Firebird*, both from Ace. He also cocdited, with Les Johnson, the anthology *Going Interstellar*, from Baen Books.

He is married to the former Maureen McAdams, and resides in Brunswick, Georgia, where, in an era of climate disruption, he keeps a weather eye on hurricanes.

About his story, he says: "When Frank Drake set up SETI in 1959, and we began listening to the stars, I was pretty sure it wouldn't take long before we heard an artificial signal. Now, when I think about the possibility of living long enough to learn there *is* life out there somewhere, I'm inclined to settle for discovering molecules on Mars. 'Oz' is the way it should have happened."

COMMON GROUND
SHARIANN LEWITT

When she woke up that morning, Lainey Quinn knew it was going to be a special day. Maybe she would not have to shoot Victor Koslov. Or maybe she would and maybe that would be even better because she was going to have to do it sooner or later and Daddy had always taught her if there was something unpleasant to do, better to get it over with sooner. Which is why she had shot Daddy and the rest of them before the wedding, though she hadn't anticipated the lunar life sentence. She never thought she'd get more than a few years at most at some posh prison where Simon could supply enough money to make her condition comfortable while she waited for an early parole.

She, no one, had ever thought she'd get life on Alpha. She'd had a brilliant defense and all the star power years on the celeb feeds could bring. Her trial had brought billions of advertising to the celeb channels that couldn't get enough breathless accounts of every minute in the courtroom, every stitch she wore, every minutely examined minute of her life before the fatalities in the lobby of the Grand Alaska Hotel (though she carefully glossed over her First from the London School of Economics and graduating at the top of her class from Harvard Biz.) She had siphoned enough funds through half a dozen cut outs that she herself had profited in the mega millions from her crime.

What she hadn't foreseen was a judge up for reelection in a district that wanted to see the spoiled rich bitch sentenced to life on the Moon. The judge won his election and Lainey got shipped out to Alpha, to the base that was once supposed to be the transport nexus of the solar system but had become an inescapable prison.

Moon Base Alpha, with its outer domes for growing food for its planned gourmet restaurants and planned thriving village, retained its landing pads and its fueling stations. During her descent Lainey could almost believe she was arriving at the transportation complex it had been intended to become decades before when exuberance had trumped experience. Only when she followed instructions to enter the airlock and saw the drone that brought her vent its atmosphere and fire its lifters, she had accepted the truth that the technical challenge of escape might be somewhat more difficult than she had assumed.

As soon as she had arrived she set about business. After all, she wasn't Boss Quinn's daughter for nothing. Daddy had groomed her to take over the business, both ends of it, and so as soon as she'd exited the airlock in the lime green prison jumpsuit, she'd taken charge. And promptly run up against Koslov, who'd been running the place for the Vorovskoy mir, funneling drugs back to his underground in Moscow for ages.

Ties between the Quinn organization and Koslov's branch of the Vorovskoy on the Marble had never been exactly friendly, but business was business. She'd set up in Main Reception on her first full day, carefully avoiding Koslov's headquarters out in the producing domes. He'd come to see her, sneered at her, a mere woman and a very young one at that, with his bodyguard.

Lainey had known men like Victor Koslov all her life and they just bored her. Her former fiancé was just like him, only Peter had been a lot better looking. Koslov was short and fat with thinning hair and a pushed-in nose that reminded Lainey of her friend Sandra's pug dog back home. Clearly Koslov hadn't taken her seriously—he had brought only one bodyguard and he wasn't seriously armed. She had been well trained by her Daddy's security team and she knew how to tell when a heavy was packing.

Koslov had leered at her, took in the full curvature of her breasts, the bounce of her blonde curls, and smirked. "Well, so you're Robert Quinn's little girl. You could be my girl. You'd be safe. You shouldn't be alone with all these dangerous men here, pretty little socialite like you. You should leave all the business to men who understand it."

"Mistake, Mr. Koslov. I am Robert Quinn's daughter and I understand business just fine. And I've already got my operations set up here and lines back home, so I suggest that you just turn around and take a walk back to your dome."

He had laughed then. "Oh, feisty. Well, then, you can do the only thing that women here get to do. There are twenty of you, and three of you are too old. The other seventeen are whores in my brothel, and make no mistake, I make the profits. So you'll be coming with me now."

He nodded at his lone bodyguard, who crumpled dead on the floor before he could get his hand on his over-sized (but underpowered) AX-119, a sidearm Lainey had always thought more looks than works. Her own custom Glock Zing might look unimposing but she could take down a man in under two seconds. And it didn't show, even to the most experienced eyes.

Her life was supposed to have ended, effectively, when she had been sent in transportation, but she had decided to run the place since she had been groomed to run some-thing. Least she could do in her Daddy's memory, seeing as how she'd killed him and all. Though he'd deserved it. They'd all deserved it, all four of them, and the judge who'd sentenced her and the newsfeeds who'd put her up as just another young socialite gone wrong didn't know her actual business, which her Daddy and her fiancé and those other two men had messed with.

She hadn't put up with it from her own Daddy. No way she was putting up with it from an underling toad like

Koslov.

"You were saying," she said to Koslov, and smiled the bright, perky smile that showed off a lot of painful orthodonture.

It had taken a week to conclude the treaty with Koslov and she couldn't say she was exactly happy with it. He'd gotten all three of the Poppy Domes and two of the Hash, but then he had the contacts to send back the product on the return drones to his contacts on the Marble. Lainey retained the Still and the 'Shrooms, which were worth a lot on Alpha and traded high as prisoner relief but didn't mean squat to the organizations on the Marble. She had managed to split Cocoa pretty well, and had retained the skilled techs to make decent cocaine. Koslov had to ship his back whole and couldn't trade anything on Alpha. Not that it meant that much to her but it was something.

Lainey was not going to stay on Alpha, but until she left she was going to rule. She had been groomed to issue orders, not to take them. CEO of Alaskan Oil Industries or Moon Base Alpha (Western Region, including Main Base and Reception Hall, which had been the concession for the Poppy Domes), Lainey Quinn was more than some society brat in pricey high heels with a trust fund.

She knew today was going to be special, even if Simon had always said relying on her intuition was silly. There wasn't one single silly cell in Lainey Quinn's body and her intuition had led her right every time. But since, unlike her ex-fiance, Simon never forgot that she had outcompeted him at Harvard, she allowed him his few remaining illusions and a small margin to pilfer on the side. They both knew that she wouldn't respect him if he didn't steal something, so long as it wasn't too much. They understood each other. She knew how far she could trust him and she trusted that he knew how little she would tolerate anything more than moderate skimming off the top. Unlike Peter and the newsfeeds, Simon knew she had a lot more brains than people ever credited a gene-tweaked blonde with a trust fund and a cubic kilometer of designer clothes.

Once upon a time, Moon Base Alpha had expressed a hope for greatness that had died, aborted in humanity's more immediate goals of greed and grandeur at home. The builders had thought that humans would populate the stars, would reach out and mine the asteroids, explore the moons of Jupiter and Saturn, would one day venture beyond their own small sphere. In that quick blush of innocence and anticipation, people believed that technology would overcome the isolation of great distance. Someone would figure out a way around the limit of the speed of light, or they would discover wormholes, or—something. The future appeared limitless and the species was poised on the threshold of the universe, ready to leave the cradle and toddle into the playpen of the near planets.

That future had never happened. Instead humanity had grown up and grown cynical and selfish. Excitement and wonder and dreams of space just weren't considered proper for adults any more.

Lainey Quinn had never dreamed of space. She had only ever dreamed of being in charge, of not having men think they owned her. Because being brilliant and beautiful and ruthless meant that the men who ran things never quite took her seriously (except Simon, who had his own agendas) and she wanted only to use her talents fully in ways they never understood. Even her own Daddy saw her as a performing toy, an anomaly, not an actual player in the game.

Maybe it was only Moon Base Alpha, but everyone took her seriously here. And that, she vowed, was only the beginning.

She left her private quarters in what had been the executive suite of Main Reception and took the mezzanine balcony corridor over to her office where she could see the entirety of the Central Dome. Still beautiful, the tile work throughout the permanent section of Moon Base Alpha had been inspired by the Alhambra. Here in Main Reception everything was geometric, blue and white, calm and ordered, reminding the inhabitants that they were the dregs of a great species. Originally Main Reception had been built to inspire those traveling out into the rest of the Solar System and perhaps beyond, and to welcome those returning to the wellspring of humanity. The designers had intended to impress the alien races that statistics said must fill the galaxy, but had yet to show up on the doorstep. As for humanity going out to meet them, well, that dream had died long before Lainey had been born, along with colonizing Europa and mining the asteroid belt.

"Lainey, I don't know what the hell they are, but they aren't going away. And Steffers says I'm not hallucinating, either, that they're really there even though they're spiders with great big flowers on 'em. I didn't know where to put 'em so I left 'em in the VIP lounge for you to deal." Goalie Boyce had not been bright to start, and what few neurons he'd had when he had arrived at Alpha he'd destroyed with all the traditional forms of prisoner relief. Weed, moonshine, opium, cocaine, he didn't care what form relief took as long as he could avoid reality. Still, Lainey had found him close to reliable when he was coherent enough to speak in whole sentences.

"Did you offer them any hospitality, Goalie? Something to eat or drink? Water or a plate of hummus?"

"I didn't think about that, Lainey." Goalie seemed apologetic. "I'm sorry. Are we supposed to do that?"

"If we're not fighting someone, it's counted a good thing to do. Shows that we're all for the not fighting. I'll take care of it from here." She slipped him a relief chit, not a big one, but enough that he would feel appreciated. He thanked her and left and Lainey made her way to the VIP lounge. She had no idea of what Goalie had meant, whether there were people there of any kind, or something else. But she was certain that someone was in the VIP lounge if they hadn't left already, and she hoped that it hadn't been some delegation from Koslov.

One thing she knew was she'd better put a call in to Koslov. They had a truce and one of the very many things she had learned about running an organization was that being polite bought her a lot and cost her nothing.

Of course she got one of his associates. Koslov never came to the phone. "Please tell Mr. Koslov that I have been informed that we have visitors," she said simply. "Goalie Boyce told me that they are not human, but we know that Mr. Boyce is not always the most dependable source of information. I am going to see for myself and I will certainly notify Mr. Koslov when I can give him actual facts and not speculation from an unreliable source." Having done her bit to keep the truce, she hung up before the associate could say anything.

She buzzed down to Chow, where Chef was on duty. Everyone who worked in Chow was called Chef and that title was ironic since most of them couldn't cook for shit. "Hey, Chef, could you send someone up to the VIP lounge with a plate of munchies?" she asked.

The VIP lounge was just on the other side of her office. She waited outside for a few minutes, until she saw Squid with a platter that threatened to topple him over. She couldn't see what Chef had prepared for her guests since he'd fancied it up with a cover, so she hoped it wasn't live slugs or anything like that. One Chef had tried that trick after she'd taken over the Western Gang at Moon Base Alpha. That Chef had showed up in the meat ration the next night. She opened the door, leaving Squid to follow in her wake, and stopped dead.

Goalie had described them as spiders with flowers. She'd thought he'd just been too high to be clear, but the fact was he'd been more accurate than she'd ever heard him before. They weren't exactly spiders, she amended. They had only six appendages, of which the front two seemed to be more like arms, which made them more crab like. Still.

The flowers Boyce had referred to were dials and readouts on what appeared to be vacuum suits. They did have a certain flower-like aesthetic, Lainey thought. She took a moment and a deep breath. In all her life she had never expected—this.

Aliens? Real live here in the flesh aliens? For all the decades Alpha had been sitting rotting out here, for a full century or more that humans had combed space with their pocket radios searching for some signal to point them at intelligent life, there had never been any sign. Anywhere. Ever.

Lainey Quinn could not be the first human being to talk to real live aliens. That was just not possible.

Everything she had thought about the universe stood stark still for a single breath, and then rearranged itself. She had known it was a special day. The world, or more properly the Moon, shifted axis. Borders, divisions, colors, and alignments dissolved and changed, realigned and merged again in her brain. They bled over the map of the Moon and then shifted out to that shining blue and white beauty that taunted them from the sky.

She could revamp her plans on the fly. And she could recognize an opportunity when she saw one staring her in the face. Even when they looked like a plate of crabs with flowers in the middle of a prison.

Her mind racing, Lainey smiled carefully and gestured to Squid, who was marginally more intelligent than Boyce. Squid removed the cover from the plate and revealed that Chef took his duties, or at least his continued survival, seriously. Dishes of olives, sliced hardboiled eggs (a great delicacy), mushroom caps stuffed with rice and cherry tomatoes sat in an artistic arrangement surrounded by water crackers and carrot sticks. Possibly Chef wanted a promotion. Or simply had an artistic streak.

"You are welcome among us," Lainey greeted the aliens formally, aware that there was no hope of language between them. "We are pleased to make your acquaintance, and on behalf of the human race and all the governments of our home planet, I welcome you to our outpost on Moon Base Alpha. I'm sure you would like some refreshment." She gestured at the tray and at Squid, but the scrawny man stayed rooted to the spot.

Lainey practically had to shove Squid towards the visitors with the tray. Clearly he did not relish approaching the strangers, but Lainey glared at him and he took the tray resolutely to their guests. The spiders looked at the tray, made chittering noises and reached in to it. In a great frenzy of activity they manipulated the elements of the platter but Lainey didn't catch whether any of them actually ate anything, or where their mouths were located.

When Squid returned, the tray had been rearranged beautifully, the elements now mixed together in a fluid design that reminded Lainey of something to do with the ocean and maybe flowers, or maybe sunrise over the mountains.

"Thank you," a soft voice said. "An exchange of art is always most refreshing."

"Our language?" Lainey practically choked. And then she breathed deeply as she had been taught. A young lady who appeared on as many celebrity newsfeeds as Lainey Quinn simply did not choke in public, no matter that she was confronted with the first aliens her species had ever met and they had spoken to her in perfectly comprehensible English. She wondered if she had spoken in Spanish or Russian or Mandarin if they would have answered in the same.

"Our linguistics technology, in analysis and translation, is reasonably functional," the voice assured her, though Lainey could not make out which of the visitors was speaking. "We had several samples of your languages to work from for some time, so our translators have been able to make working models for a few of the most common in broadcast. There may be some mistakes. We are never certain that our translation mechanism runs clearly until we have found the flaws, and no doubt we will discover many difficulties."

"Where are you from?" Lainey asked. "How long have you been traveling? Are you just out for a stroll, so to speak, or did you come to Earth for a purpose? Shall I contact one particular government, or group, or do you want to contact everyone at once?"

Lainey's synapses were processing at triple speed and she still couldn't see the whole picture, or rather she could see too many possibilities. How many ships were there? Just the one, or were there more hiding? Could they really have come to take over the Blue Marble? That would be a laugh. From here it looked all serene and blue, not strip mined and half poisoned to near extinction.

But then, these aliens might not mind that. They still hadn't taken off their suits. Who knew what they liked to breathe?

Or maybe they were just explorers. Humanity had once had ambitions to explore, to meet the neighbors just to know they weren't alone out in the big vast expanse of forever. There had to be others out there—what would be more natural than to want to roll out the welcome wagon? Or traders. That's what her Daddy would have done and would have thought of first and last and every single step in between. Any place there's any kind of being with a thought and a desire there's profit to be made, and Robert Quinn had never met a profit he didn't covet a mile off.

"We have some things to trade," the voice said, and Lainey wasn't sure now whether it was a single leader speaking or whether they were taking turns. "You are a transportation nexus, are we correct? This appears to be a port. You have landing facilities and fuel? We would like to make arrangements for fueling."

Well, that seemed reasonable enough. "What do you use for fuel?" Lainey asked. She didn't want to tell the aliens that they weren't about to get any fossil fuels up here and that the ships came only one way. Drones delivered prisoners and some supplies on a quarterly schedule. Mostly the inmates cannibalized them since they burned their fuel and had never been designed to make the return trip. Those few vehicles that did return to Earth vented their O2 so no one could jump a ride.

So no, there was no fuel up on Moon Base Alpha, only

the old empty tanks that now held the ethanol stills and the silent landing pads planned for a better day.

The voice did not speak. Instead one of the spiders held up a small screen with a molecular display. Lainey laughed. "Oh, yes, we can supply you. You'll need to tell us the quantities, of course, and we'll need some schedule in the beginning before our production is up to capacity. But once we are in full production, depending on how many ships, we should have no trouble here."

"Only three ships, and not terribly often," the voice said softly. "We will want a place to set up our own living areas as well, as our requirements are different from yours."

"You don't want to talk to any of our governments?" Lainey was suspicious and approving and suddenly had a very oddly comradely feeling about their visitors.

"We are not an official mission, just independent traders. Perhaps we need to talk first about what we can give you for helping us establish a transport base. As this is a port, is it not?"

"It is a port. It is indeed."

The visitors indicated that they needed to return to their ship to breathe and eat. They said that their requirements were not compatible with human needs, and while Lainey was not certain they were telling the truth, she was not about to challenge them at this stage either. So she left them with all the proper diplomatically two-faced expressions of goodwill that they repeated to her.

Questions crowded Lainey's head. How many ships did the aliens bring really? Had they come to the Moon first or were there others on Earth as well? Were they negotiating with different groups or were they talking to her alone, and if they were talking to her alone, why?

Aliens meet humans for the first time—okay, she amended, maybe it wasn't the first time for the aliens. Clearly with their linguistic capabilities it couldn't be. Meeting a new sentient species, even if the galactic locale was crawling, had to be a major event. Red carpets, brass bands, dignitaries and speeches and city keys and all that. Not some furtive approach to a distant port with an offer of massive technologies.

Unless something was shady, and Lainey had plenty of experience with shady. Nobody, her Daddy had told her, nobody ever got filthy stinking rich playing by the Boy Scout rules, keeping his nose clean and upholding honor in thought, word and deed. That was for chumps. Fortunately, there were plenty of them in the world, and the rest of us, the few who knew better, could fleece 'em. That was her Daddy's philosophy of life and Lainey had embraced it wholeheartedly, until he had decided to fleece her. Then she had turned around and held him to his own standards and that's when all the trouble started and ended on the staircase of the Grand Alaska Hotel. If he hadn't died first and fast, Lainey thought he would have been proud his little girl had grown up just like her old man—ruthless, decisive, and positively knowing how to look out after her own best interests no matter where they lay. Also, one hell of a sharpshooter, though he had taken pride in her skill with firearms since she had been old enough to hold a gun.

She knew how to smell rotten and there was something more than a touch rotten about these aliens.

Her phone buzzed. Damn. Koslov, or more correctly, one of his associates. She had things to do, but she couldn't ignore him. "Mr. Koslov requires your presence in his Dome immediately," the associate told her.

Lainey wanted to tear his head off. She didn't take orders from Koslov and certainly not from his underlings, and while she understood that he felt he lost face if he came to her she didn't like him treating her like one of his employees. To his credit, after she killed his first bodyguard Koslov had never made that mistake again.

So Lainey bit back her retort and instead covered her words with honey. "Mr. Koslov and I most definitely need to talk, but I think we both will need the data in the Observation Dome to make any real decisions. If he would be so good to join me there, I would be happy to bring a bottle of our very finest champagne."

According to the treaty, the Observation Dome, and the rest of the port works facilities, counted as neutral territory. Either everybody needed them or nobody cared, and up until now it had been pretty much the latter. Now, though, Lainey wanted to take a look at the instruments and see if any other ships orbited either the Moon or the Marble, turn on the audio and hear if Earth was burning or celebrating meeting the new neighbors. She needed Koslov to see and hear, too, needed him to know she wasn't hiding anything or lying so that neither of them would have to blow off anyone's head.

Koslov or no, she stopped by the still on the way to Observation, grabbed a bottle of bubbly (well, it was carbonated ethanol, perfectly dreadful, and both she and Koslov agreed wholeheartedly on that) and made her way to the instruments. The Observation Dome was the nicest part of the operating systems on Alpha, with comfortable padded chairs in front of the stations and the beautiful clear dome overhead. Now in the lunar night the sky sparkled with stars and there, offcenter and glittering like the jewel of them all, was the Marble. All blue and white and serene, Lainey gazed at it and tried to remember how crowded and seething it really was under those clouds. How those oceans heaved with storms, how the people would as likely run you over as stop and let you cross the street.

"It is beautiful," a soft voice said behind her. "It is hard to give it up."

Koslov. Lainey did not turn around. "Thank you for joining me, Mr. Koslov. But I am not here to admire the beauties of our home. I'm here to see if there are any other ships out there, and I was hoping that you might be able to tell me if you've scanned any as well. I know you have some capabilities that we don't here." Only then did she turn and face him.

"Then you confirm that these aliens are, in fact, what

rumor suggests. They are truly intelligences of another world?"

"They are indeed," Lainey said. "But I don't trust something about them. They have the one ship on Pad Three and I don't see anything else out there. I've got the audio on and there's no news from Earth, from any governments, about any first contact."

"They could have a fleet hiding behind this rock."

Lainey nodded. "I know. I was hoping there would be enough sensors still working that we could pick up readings here, but I know your people have more expertise with these systems than mine do."

Lainey didn't catch the command, but two young men came forward and took places at different stations. One Lainey knew was the audio news feed. The other she assumed was the full Moon sensor array. "Would you care for some refreshment while we wait for results?" she proffered the bottle.

Koslov winced delicately. "Thank you. Very kind of you, certainly, but I do not have much of a taste for champagne. I have, however, brought some vodka."

Lainey smiled and poured her ersatz champagne. The vodka, she knew, was better. Potatoes grew in the Farm Domes and some were spirited off to Koslov's personal distillery. Still, she wanted to take nothing from him even if he offered in good faith. Which she did not quite believe.

Koslov nodded and took his vodka straight from the bottle. Lainey felt a plan not fully clear yet but forming in her mind. She could feel the threads of it coalescing the way she had when she had strapped on her Glock that morning in the Grand Alaska. Fate, Destiny, something had guided her that day.

The money was still waiting for her and Simon had her new identity set up and ready to go. New cards, licenses, house, bank account, even a reservation with the best plastic surgeons in Switzerland, all arranged, and she would walk away from her entire past forever. And really, wasn't that what a prison term was for?

She could feel Destiny again, could taste it as the flavor of the false wine faded. So she was not surprised when one of Koslov's associates, the one on the Far Side sensors, reported that there were no signs of any other alien craft. No signs of any alien communications. No signs of any disruptions, wormholes, or contact on Earth. No news of First Contact with an alien species on Earth.

Koslov lifted an eyebrow. Lainey smiled softly and began to whistle. She didn't need any translator, oh, no, she knew who these strangers were. They were kissing cousins. All alone, not contacting any official channels, looking for a place to refuel and hole up, establish a trading base?

Lainey Quinn knew pirates when she met them, even if they did have six legs and squeak. They surely had common ground, and she had the idea to negotiate. If they could bring her down to Earth she could set it up with Simon and take care of the rest.

"What would you say, Koslov, if I left this rock? If I could escape and left you entirely in charge?"

"Why would you do that?" He remained unperturbed but Lainey thought she saw the tiniest tightening around his eyes, the slightest pressure in his fingertips.

And Lainey laughed out loud, laughed like she hadn't laughed since the night before her Daddy died. "Because I hate this place, Mr. Koslov. Because I disagree with Milton's Satan. I would not rather rule in Hell. You are a cultured man, Mr. Koslov. Don't you miss it back there, the conversation, the intelligence, the people who get your jokes?"

"I am a realist, Miss Quinn. There is no escape from here and those few who have attempted it have died. If you think these aliens can be trusted, then you are rather less prudent or intelligent than you think."

Lainey left Observation and returned to her own suite in Main Reception. For a prisoner she was awash in luxury. She sank into the deep purple easy chair and studied the beauties of the tile work above. Everything about the Moon base had been built with a vision of a glorious future of humanity in mind, a future that had not come to pass. Surely the alien visitor could see that, while this was a transport center, it was not much in use. The landing pads were empty and the docks corroded with drone destruction. Lack of maintenance always showed and said way too much, her Daddy taught her, and her Daddy had taught her right. The spiders couldn't have missed it. They had to know, had to have deduced who was in residence now. The question was, did she call their bluff?

And then, did she hand it all to Koslov?

She could negotiate, return home and do what she had planned, change her face and take over Alaska Oil through another identity. Or she could stay here, only with the aliens' technology they would have a base of operations that no organization could match.

She had to know what they had to offer.

They didn't answer when she tried to ping their comm system so she put on one of the twenty dilapidated suits left in Main Reception and walked out on the pad. She kicked at the base and pounded on the shell and set up such a racket they had to hear her. Even though she knew it might take a bit of time to suit up she didn't let up until two of them came fully out of the hatch and set foot on the pad. She led them through the tunnel into the Grand Hall and took off her helmet. She didn't call the lights up so she confronted them in the shadows, only soft ambient drifts of light from high and far giving the vaguest suggestion of shape and movement.

"Look here," Lainey addressed them. "I know what you are and I know you know what we are. We're all playing the same game here and we've got common ground. You need a base where your people can't find you or catch you, someplace you can refuel and hole up and evade arrest. We need your technology and I need a way off this rock and back there to that blue planet. Are we all clear on that?"

They chittered before they turned on the translator. "What technology do you require? We do not offer it all, or cheaply, and why shouldn't we simply take this place? Why do we need to trade with you?"

Lainey smiled. "So you do admit that you are, hmmm, not exactly officially sanctioned? Good. We're your front. We can keep you supplied and your government will never know you're here. You kill us off and it'll show. Someone's going to notice. Your people will see you coming and going and we can cover you, cover for you. But together we can make common cause. Together we have a base of operations that will benefit us all. We're all on the same side, after all. Think it over. You've got one ship. We have the base to keep it fueled and in decent repair. You need someplace to live, and we have the space for a colony, along with the agricultural infrastructure. We need to be able to get off this rock, to go home, to travel. You can do that. Slip me out of here, talk to Koslov and deliver our goods to our contacts on Earth, and you've got built in markets. And whatever else you've got—we don't have to know about it. But to make it work you have to get me back to that planet because I have the contacts down there to set up all the secret lines of supply."

"We will need to consult," the spiders said. "We will return with an answer."

Lainey nodded and watched them go. Then she composed a coded message to Simon to set up a meet at her Daddy's private landing pad up near Seward. She thought she should have Koslov get in touch with his people too, though maybe later.

First the humans and the spiders. She wondered if they were in touch with others, and somehow they could pass the word. A great capitol of a pirate empire right here on Moon Base Alpha. Grand Reception was surely fitting for it, beautiful and elegant, perfect in every way. Lainey could taste the future, knew the Destiny just the way she had known that today was going to be special.

She was going to leave Alpha, yeah, but she was going to be back. Forget legitimacy. This place had been built to be a great trading nexus, and that was what it was going to be, just like its creators had envisioned. Well, maybe not just like. Great plans required a bit of flexibility.

Shariann Lewitt has written seventeen books and forty short stories, most of which are science fiction. An ex-pat Manhattanite, she has transferred loyalty to the Red Sox Nation and calls North of Boston home. She lives in a mixed human-avian flock, studies Flamenco, and, on the advice of her birds, likes to go south in the winter.

Concerning "Common Ground," she writes: "I knew I wanted to write about the Moon Base gone bad and about a powerful woman who made her own rules. It took several months and many drafts, along with some inspiration from some real characters from the history of New Orleans, to make that all fit together."

CITY OF BEAUTY, CITY OF SCARS
PAUL DI FILIPPO

Our city of Aesthethica takes the form of a tetrahedon, the simplest of all the perfect or Platonic solids, and hence the most noble and beautiful in the eyes of Aglaia. The shining triangular pyramid that is Aesthetica, sited neatly in the middle of a wide green landscaped valley, houses nearly half a million citizens. The three sides of its base measure each twelve miles long—twice six, the perfect number, or teleioi—and its apex looms twelve hundred feet above the base: again, a multiple of the teleioi. The luxurious apartment that occupies the uppermost level—a domicile which, by its tapering shape, is naturally a miniature of the whole city—is home to the male and female Prime Allures.

But because this is my story, and I was born on the lowest level, that's where I'll really begin.

I could not of course bear intelligent witness to the events immediately attendant upon my birth. But my mother, Libet, recounted the story many, many times, during our supervised visits. So often in fact that I, at an impressionable young age, developed false memories of actually seeing her actions unfold, memories as vivid as any I subsequently laid down on my own.

My birth was of course by Caesarean procedure. All births are conducted so in Aesthetica, for we can not risk the archaic animal process of vaginal delivery inflicting any kind of harm whatsoever on the infant. Each child must emerge from the womb with its Aglaia-given genetic inheritance—all its unique possibilities for developmental expression of postnatal beauty—uncompromised by mere accident.

My mother was of course sedated for this procedure. But the ineptitude of the technician allowed her to awaken while still recovering in the operating theater. (He was later severely disciplined, being subjected to a third-degree scarification and exiled from Aesthetica, there being no lower level to which he could be demoted.) At the moment when she regained a hazy, pained consciousness, the doctor and all the nurses and assistants were busy fussing over me, checking my vital signs and annotating my aglaiacal indices. This inattention allowed my mother to hastily fumble for a scalpel, which she palmed and concealed under her gown.

Not long thereafter, in the large, noisy, clean but impoverished maternity ward where my mother lay abed, recuperating and grimly fondling her concealed weapon, stoking her heart to the task she had determined to perform, a nurse trundled a bassinet down the aisle and delivered me to Libet.

Under a clattering wall fan, part of Aesthetica's complex system of ducts and vents, my mother cradled me tenderly, examining all my young parts with an eye for any congenital defects. But there were none.

My mother addressed the nurse. "He's perfect, isn't he?"

"Yes, I'd say so."

"And his beauty indices?"

"They can be projected outward to a very high plateau of allure, Aglaia willing. You're a very lucky mother. He doesn't resemble you at all!"

My mother's voice was dull and sad. "Yes, so very lucky. I will have my child by my side for at least five years. And then he will receive high marks in all his beauty examinations and ascend to another level, while I remain here for the rest of my life."

With this remark, my mother ran her free hand, the one not cradling me, over her rough-hewn homely face, pausing to finger her minor but significant harelip, a feature of hers I still recall with fond affection, despite its betrayal of all that Aglaia held dear.

"Don't dwell on such future events," advised the nurse. "Enjoy your child while he is with you. Have you and the father picked out a name?"

"His father is banished from the city. He made the mistake of acquiring a critical mass of radiation scars in the mines. Too ugly even for us bottom dwellers. But we spoke of the boy's name before he left. He will be called Tono."

"Very nice," said the nurse, and turned her back.

My mother saw her only opportunity to bind me to her forever. "Tono, forgive me!" she yelled, then flashed out the scalpel.

Her intent was to slice off one of my littlest fingers. Such a mutilation would have ensured that I remained on this level of my birth, without crippling me unduly.

But the nurse, alerted by my mother's cry, spun about and charged. This physician's handmaiden had seen too many such attempts not to react quickly. The two women wrestled for control of the blade, sending me tumbling and squalling to the tile floor.

Eventually my mother was subdued, with the aid of other converging staff members, and I was rescued from the tiles, miraculously unharmed.

Libet sobbed pitifully as I was taken away. Having revealed her intentions to spite the universal and revered aglaiacal system of advancement by beauty, the basis of Aesthetica's whole society, she had qualified as an unfit parent. I was mandated to the creche on the lowest level, where I could be reared in safety.

So I never shared my mother's humble apartment, the rooms where I had been conceived by her and my exiled father. But, as I said, I grew to know her fine though absolutist maternal nature, and to hear again and again of my own origins, through the thrice-weekly supervised visits which she was allowed with me. In my fifth and last year on the lowest level of the city, in particular, she drummed into me the basis for her actions.

"It's not right, Tono, that people should be graded and separated based on mere appearance. Especially when it means dividing mother and child. Do you think I was selfish, to want to keep you by my side, especially after your father was exiled? I love you so!"

"I love you too, Mama," I would always reply.

"Then give your mother a hug and a kiss, dear!"

I always complied, though often I was reluctant to put down the hand mirror into which I was gazing, already practicing the codified rites of Aglaia.

At age five I underwent the standard public examinations, standing naked on a stage with the probing authorities. Libet watched from a faroff corner of the viewers' gallery, stifling her sniffling for fear of being ejected from the proceedings. The judges measured and compared, prognosticated and argued, while I complied proudly but demurely with all their posing instructions, trying to live up to the teaching of the creche staff, insofar as my childish mind could grasp the aglaiacal precepts. After a suitable time, they rendered their verdict.

"This boy, Tono, will ascend two levels, and be reevaluated on his eighth birthday."

A single dry and coarse rasping sound burst from my mother, and then I was led away, never to see her again. Gone from the dull, boiled-cabbage-redolent warrens of the lowest level of Aesthetica to a better life, worthy of my endowments.

***

The first thing I noticed when making the guardian-accompanied ascent through the stairwells of Aesthetica was the gradient of beauty—not that I could have phrased it so succinctly as a child. Nonetheless, the changing spectrum of beauty still registered on my honed perceptions. (And I should mention now that "two levels" of advancement did not correspond to a mere two stories within the pyramid, for each classification of beauty occupied several floors out of the hundred stories, according to the variable population of each category. Sometimes one category would lose significant population due to deaths (or demotions and advancements), while another would gain, due to births (or demotions or advancements), and the ratio of floors would change by official edict. However, the lowest level, being the largest in surface area, was always more than big enough to accommodate all the least beautiful citizens.

As I and my temporary wardens climbed the thronging stairs, I was able to employ what was already, even at such a tender age, a finely calibrated sensibility toward degrees of beauty. Faces, forms, carriage, personal styles—all these instantly conveyed to me a person's relative and absolute status in the hierarchy of beauty. I saw that it would be impossible for any individual to masquerade as someone of higher status; a thousand tells would give them away. And although it was conceivable that someone of high beauty could disguise their attainments and endowments so as to appear less beautiful on quick inspection, there was no reason I could then imagine why a person would do such a senseless thing. I had not yet learned of certain perversions...

Eventually we reached my designated level—what sweet air, what shapely bodies and handsome faces!—and I was conducted not to a creche, but to a foster home where my next six years—not three—would be spent. In retrospect, it was a generally uneventful time, though there was much novelty. First off, I had to fit myself into a strange domestic routine. I started school, made friends, and deepened my aglaiacal studies. But it was the subsequent stages of my life, as an adolescent, that would truly release my full potential, and so I will devote more detail to that period.

As for my first transition: Boone and Frasca, husband

and wife, my new foster parents, had two children of their own, both older than I: Dunkel, a boy, and Mazurine, a girl. Introduced to them, I was outwardly shy. But inside, I had already assessed their aglaiacal potential as less than mine. They had maxed out their innate capacity for becoming beautiful, and would never blossom into anything greater than what they already showed. Consequently, I found myself inwardly disdainful of them. Still, we all got along fine, in a distant manner.

At first, the biggest revelation to me during those five years was that the greater beauty of the citizens at this level entitled them to nicer work and more copious and finer material comforts. The clothes, the food, my mattress, the available entertainments, even the toilet paper! All so much better than those of my birth level. And yet, I knew, so much cruder than what awaited me above.

Only at this juncture did I realize how our city of Aesthetica worked. Until now, I had simply possessed no basis for comparison. The meager, shabby goods and paucity of services available to the dwellers of the lowest level, the backbreaking jobs—waste disposal, uranium mining, powerplant maintenance, hydroponic farming, goods assembly lines—these were not conditions shared by all! The insight burst inside me like a bombshell. I resolved then and there that I would do all I could to optimize my innate beauty, and so attain the maximum honors, perks and property to which I was entitled. It sounds like a far-fetched thing for a child of five or six to fasten upon, but it was so. I was a prodigy, and I wonder sometimes if that unnatural aspect of my nature had not been already dimly intuited by Libet, and if that scalpel had not been intended for my heart.

After a time, I graduated to studying and parsing the imagery of the beautiful people who dwelled above us. Then my peers here no longer looked so fine. The very walls of the corridors were big high-definition screens showing random, changing feeds from the public spaces of higher levels. (On my natal level, all we had had to work with were shabby pasteboard trading cards of beautiful people.) This display of beauty superior to ours was intended both as incentive and corrective. Those of us who had the capacity to grow or shape ourselves by exercise into more pleasing forms had examples to aim for. That set of biceps, that elegant haunch, that toned abdomen, that lilt of chin. But at the same time, each of us had to contend with the limitations of our genome, and could only admire from afar the unmatchable ones to whom Aglaia had granted her highest benisons.

At age eight, nude once more upon the inspection platform, I underwent my second aglaiacal examination. I knew now, even if I could not have verbalized it so precisely, that the utter nakedness and public display was essential in maintaining our city's system. The chance for the masses to assess each candidate and to affirm that the proper universal standards were being applied without favor or cheating ensured that there would be no hostility toward those promoted, but only an empathy and endorsement that would secure and reinforce their status. But even though I could sense the rightness of the custom, I had developed enough self-consciousness to feel just a bit unnerved on stage. Nothing like some of the other candidates for advancement who had preceded me, however: girls and boys who had wept or fainted or cowered, thereby blighting their presentation. I stood straight and proud, confident that the judges would reward my clean-limbed grace and poise and lines, all of which I affirmed in the mirror every day, according to the proper aglaiacal technics.

But instead, to my confoundment, they issued a suspended judgment.

"Citizen Tono, we are conflicted regarding your future course. Certain indicators lead us to consider that you represent vast potential for significant levels of allure. Other signs lead us to fear that you might stall and canker. Therefore, we are reserving any decision as to your advancement for another three years. Keep Aglaia's tenets close to your heart for the next three years, and we will surely be able to make a decision then."

I descended the dais in a daze, hurt and confused. Boone and Frasca awaited me with a robe. Later, on the walk home through Aesthetica's corridors, there was some whispering and snickering between Dunkel and Mazurine. I ignored their jealous pettiness. All I could focus on was my desire and need to prove the judges wrong in their doubts.

Three years later, at age eleven, I did just that. To resounding applause, after cycling through the aglaiacal tableaux vivants required at this age, I received advancement up a full three levels. I said a curt goodbye to my foster family and left immediately after the judging, not even returning to our apartment for any of the inferior possessions I had accumulated.

Have I mentioned yet what should be obvious to all, that there were twelve levels of beauty in Aesthetica, honoring the aglaiacal teleioi of six?

And at only age eleven, I had already ascended halfway.

✳✳✳

Sweetser notched upward the settings on the weight machines, forcing me to exert every ounce of strength in my already drained muscles. The gymnasium stank of sweat and chlorine from the lap pool.

"Push, Tono, push! You'll never jump up that last level until you do!

Sweetser was a cruel taskmaster, but with only my best interests at heart. And he knew how to get results, as attested to by his own achievements, until he had fallen. So I bullied my calves and thighs to their limits for several reps, then collapsed. Sweetser helped me out of the equipment's embrace.

"Off to the showers with you now, boy. Then a massage."

In the showers, Sweetser handed me fragrant soap and scrubbed my back. We chatted idly on various topics, and then I raised one of my perennial daydreams.

"Wouldn't it be so easy," I said, "if we could just go under the surgeon's knife and emerge all sculpted and perfect? Every man and woman gifted with supreme allure!"

"Heresy, Tono, and you know it! I think you just wish to provoke me with this juvenile conceit. What an affront to Aglaia and her gifts, attempting to circumvent one's somatic destiny, or mimic that of another."

I let the pulsating jets of hot water blanket my sore shoulders. "But don't we already strive to coax the seeds of beauty within us, by hours in the gym? How would modification by medical procedures be any different?"

"One involves sacrifice, self-direction and the encouragement and upwelling of implicit, god-seeded forms. The other is mere theft and effortless chicanery. So long as Aglaia continues to be honored, no one would ever attempt such lazy deceit."

"Not to mention that Aesthetica's civil penalty for such actions is immutable exile."

Sweetser laughed. "That too. Here, now, enough scrubbing. Over to the table."

I lay on my side for a moment, relishing the warm air on my naked form, while Sweetser gathered up his oils. I was struck once more by my mentor's stature and decaying good looks. The big, dark-skinned bald man, with a face like chiseled granite, still loomed impressively in any setting. But his allure had diminished from its prime, and was dropping every day.

Sweetser's weakness was his appetite for rich foods. Kept in check for his youth and ambition, his greedy stomach had taken over when he had attained the highest level of beauty, the realm just above this one we currently inhabited, the eleventh. Slackening his dedication, Sweetser had begun to pack on the pounds and gone flabby. An easy fate, when no exertion was required of us, and any delicacy we craved was available in endless quantities. At a certain point, he no longer could sustain an appearance that entitled him to life on the twelfth level, and was demoted to the eleventh, where I had found him and put myself under his tutelage. I had tried to convince him to get back on track, at least stabilizing his beauty so as to remain here. But some essential light or faith had left him, and he continued to abuse his Aglaia-given endowments. He was on a one-way downward course, obesity being a prime reason for demotion.

I had a sudden image of Sweetser consigned finally by ineluctable aglaiacal precepts to the grotty ground floor of Aesthetica, meeting my mother even. Perhaps he could carry some kind of message to her from me. But what, exactly, would I say? I had no idea if she were even still alive, given the hard living conditions there. I had not seen her in all the years since I first left. I could've journeyed back to my natal level on my own. There were no prohibitions against such intercourse between levels. But who, having become accustomed to a certain level of beauty and attendant comfort, would ever want to sully his senses and sensibilities by going lower? That's what made demotion such a keen punishment, to be avoided at all costs.

And in truth, the rare voluntary visits by the slumming allure-rich often deteriorated into mob scenes—love riots, worshipful, but distracting. Unless, of course, a disguise shielded the visitor for whatever strange and decadent assignations he or she had in mind...

Sweetser nudged me over onto my belly and set to work on my muscles. I drifted off into a kind of hypnagogic fugue while he worked, and began to dream of Odile.

Odile, with her immaculate shapely body and perfectly composed face, her jade eyes and thick, lustrous blonde hair. She had originated two levels above me, but moved through Aesthetica's hierarchy more slowly, so that we arrived on the eleventh together, where our souls immediately conjoined. How lucky I was that she loved me. What we would do together when we met tonight!

Here, on the eleventh level of Aesthetica, all our hours

outside of self-perfection rituals were filled with play and leisure. There was no work; we subsisted in luxury on the accumulated efforts of everyone below us. What greater pleasures could the twelfth and final level hold, I often wondered? I could hardly conceive of any, but I knew that soon, with any luck and justice, as a reward for my genes and my efforts in burnishing them, I would get to experience the supernal.

Rousing myself, I dreamily asked Sweetser, "Tell me, my friend, what is life like in the final heaven? You know, for you were there. Do you ever miss it?"

Sweetser's normally booming voice and sanguine tone transmuted into quietude and trepidation. "It's a turbulent sort of perfection, son. Unsettling. You'll see. Just remember to keep close all your dreams, and a sense of gratitude and fidelity."

Reinvigorated, dismissing Sweetser's vague bogeymen, I bounced up from the table. "Enough, you tyrant! I'm off to dinner—a moderate repast, which you should consider —and then a long, luxurious evening with Odile."

"I envy you a little, Tono—but not enough to follow your example. You're young, only seventeen, and nearly at the peak of your allure. Age is the final undoer of us all. Wrinkles send us plunging downward as surely as fat!"

Sweetser slapped his gut with a loud thwack.

"Not me! Now, off with you until you administer tomorrow's excruciations!"

I sat across the supper table from Odile that night, holding her small, gorgeous hand and peering deeply into her shining eyes, and we whispered of many things, both large and small. Our glorious future together....

"It's twelve years since we each had our first examination, dearest, We've reached the penultimate level just as we've completed our first teleioi. Not many are so fortunate. This is a key moment for us. The stars are in our favor. Aglaia looks down and smiles on us, I'm certain. How can we fail to leap ahead into the ultimate heaven?"

Odile's warm voice couched sentiments that matched

my own. "We are meant to go through life forever ascendant, Tono, joined together in our beauty." She traced the lines of my countenance with her delicate fingers. "You are the most beautiful man of the eleventh cohort."

"And you the most beautiful woman."

"Let us hope the judges agree next week."

That night our lovemaking put a kind of celestial seal on our hopes, which were indeed fulfilled as we moved like water through the hieratical poses, naked and serene, on the viewing dais. And as the waves of applause washed over us, we were perfectly happy.

For the last time in our lives.

***

As I watched Traoke slide and crash helplessly into the blades of the fan—his arms flailing, his fantastically handsome face a mask of fear—a life-changing "accident" which I could still have, for a moment or two longer, prevented, but would not. I knew then that I had paid the highest price for my evil victory, and that it was a fee I was happy to pay.

This was the final expression of the shattering truth no one had ever revealed while we lived below, but which Odile and I quickly learned upon our last ascension.

Up until the eleventh level, there was no sense of competition in our culture's beauty worship, except perhaps with one's self. I did not lose out just because X or Y was also promoted to another level. Their achievement honored Aglaia equally with mine. And all my success was grounded in my own efforts. My only rival was sloth and ineptitude, my only limits the raw genetic heritage my parents had conferred. (And I swear, I did think with gratitude from time to time of my mother's genes, so exemplary in recombination with my never-known father's seed, although those same dictatorial twists of inheritance had betrayed her, with that harelip and blobby nose and lips.)

But upon consecration to the twelfth level of Aesthetica's pyramid—a stratospheric space more cloistered and compact than any other level, of course, a condition which helped foment a hothouse sense of competition, there was no further opportunity for any individual to reach a new plateau. We were all the cream of the crop, perfected. Those meaningless ones below us could no longer serve as our foils. We were like a drawer full of sharp, polished, gem-handled knives, with nothing to cut except each other.

Where, then, did the competition emerge, to bedevil us aimless, high-status citizens?

In the office of Prime Allure.

One man, one woman, each deemed the literal apex of beauty.

And who would judge such an honor? In the realms below, the judges had been learned men and women, preceptors of Aglaia. But here, due to the general youthfulness of the citizens elevated to the twelfth, there were no experienced judges. The award would have to be conferred by a general vote.

And so the twelfth became a swamp of intrigue and alliances, treachery and chicanery, as we all sought the final honor.

To my eternal shame and discredit, I plunged into the milieu and the entire process wholeheartedly, as soon as I ascertained what was what. I wanted to become the Prime Allure. It seemed to my constantly revolving brain the only possible culmination to my long journey. Or, failing that, I wanted a friend to have the success. So I enmeshed myself in a sticky web of enmity and fawning, of backbiting and exclusion, false intimacy and hardened heart.

Odile, however, revealed her true gentleness of spirit and respect for Aglaia. Although her vast beauty would have easily enabled her to contend for Prime Allure against others of her gender, she showed no interest in the race.

"But Tono—did we not pledge eternal loving fealty to each other, and to a life centered around Aglaia? How is this contest worthy of us? Both of us would have to win, if we were not to be separated, and the odds are against such a dual victory. And this elevation of two mere mortals to such a peak of veneration—No, I just can't find it in me to participate."

I made no rejoinder to her sweet-voiced counsel, no plea or justification. I simply murmured something inconsequential and left her, for good. For already my thoughts were turning to Dira.

Dira, all dark waterfall of hair, olive skinned and lush, was hot for the honor that Odile disdained. Her fevered eyes and full fleering lips could lash men to high exertions, and cut down others of her sex.

Aglaia and her earthly representatives acknowledge many different forms or templates of beauty, all neatly categorized by the indices. Odile's sylph-like charms had earned her admittance to the twelfth, just as Dira's more earthy endowments had. But in this competitive realm, the two strains of beauty were hardly matched in terms of force or effect. Dira had the twelfth wrapped around her little finger, and seemed a shoo-in for the spot of female Prime Allure.

And when it became apparent, after much politicking, that I was one of the two or three men most likely to claim the matching title, she turned all the intensity of her body and spirit on me.

We became lovers, and I began to heed her damnable advice.

"Tono, you know that only Traoke and Stig stand against you. Now Stig I can easily remove from your path. It will only take a little incitement among various women and their partners. But Traoke—he's too beautiful, too well ensconced and beloved. No, there's only one sure method of taking him down."

Lying naked beside Dira, I played with her thick tresses, only half listening to her incessant scheming, which, truth be told, wearied even me sometimes.

"And how is that to be accomplished, dear?"

"He must be disfigured. It's the only way."

I sat bolt upright. "But that, that's—"

"The only way," repeated Dira.

Days went by before I acknowledged she was correct.

And so we made our plans.

The circulation of air in the closed environment of Aesthetica was vital. A vast series of ducts and filters and fans accomplished this vital function. The fans, ever spinning, lurked mostly ignored behind vertical grills set low in the corridor walls, or high in the ceilings.

As part of the shifting, unregulated competition between the contenders for Prime Allure, I challenged Traoke to a race. A large wide corridor here was devoted to that purpose, and generally untenanted otherwise.

The night before the race, with Aesthetica's illumination diurnally dialed down, unseen by anyone, I removed one ventilation grill and then simply propped it back in place, careful of my own fingers against the dirty whirring blades. Then I laid down invisible silicone spray lubricant across a stretch of the corridor floor where Traoke and I would run, a glide path right to the fan.

The next day we perched at the starting line, wearing only our loincloths. Traoke's magnificent body and handsome countenance revealed no suspicions.

"May the best man win," he said.

"Of course," I replied.

So evenly matched were we, that Traoke and I were neck and neck when we hit the unseen lubricant.

But I had the advantage, for I knew the trap was there.

So when we both went down, I was able to hurl myself with seemingly natural awkwardness into Traoke, sending him straight toward the fan, ahead of me.

His leading arm knocked the balanced grill away, and then encountered the fan blades.

Traoke was remanded to the hospital on the eleventh level, the mere start of his downward plunge to the bowels of the city. Evidence of sabotage was undeniable. But any irrefutable connection to me or Dira was impossible to prove.

Afterwards, Dira and I rejoiced, alone together.

"The election is ours now, lover!"

"When will it be?" I asked.

"As soon as the term of the current Prime Allures is up."

That proved to be a short interval, capped by our predictable victory, and our ascent into the isolated and securely inescapable tetrahedral apartment atop the whole city, where Dira and I learned for the first time the full provisions of our reign.

And now that our own short tenure as Prime Allures is almost over, I await without fear, but with some sadness and remorse, the ritual scarification of our perfect beauty, which could only be soiled by intact readmission to the lesser spheres of the city, and our exile into the wilds beyond the pyramid where our looks, I think, will not save us.

Paul Di Filippo lives in Providence, RI, with his partner of nearly forty years, Deborah Newton. He published his first story in 1977, and has since authored over thirty books. He also reviews regularly for a number of venues, including *The Barnes & Noble Review.*

A MOMENT OF GRAVITY, CIRCUMSCRIBED
FRAN WILDE

Djonn's father owned the last ticker in the city and made sure everyone knew it. Brass-bodied, the ticker looked fragile and cold, its clouded glass face obscuring the dark symbols beneath. Despite its age, it ticked loud and regular, breaking the arc of a day into increments.

"You have thirty ticks to decide," Djonn's father said when he made a deal. Djonn loved that Father knew how long a person took to make up their mind.

He longed to open the ticker, to find what made the 'yes-no-yes-no' rhythm inside. After their dependent, Raeda, found the ticker far downtower a year ago, Father's deals went 'yes' more often than 'no'. The ticker was a treasure. Father hung it high on their wall and wouldn't let Djonn's brothers fly with it. Djonn wasn't even permitted to wind the ticker. Djonn was clumsy.

Father said so that morning before he took to wing, his satchel strapped to his chest, lumpy with small treasures.

Djonn's three irritable brothers shook their heads and elbowed Djonn. They'd stayed up all night talking beneath the ticker's sturdy rhythm. Now, they pushed Djonn out of their way, pocketed six noisy fighting birds, and flew to the market on the city's southern edge.

Then Djonn's mother climbed the ladder uptower to scour the roof with the other women. Raeda disappeared.

Finally alone, Djonn teetered on a three-legged stool. The ticker said 'yes-no-yes,' cold in his hands.

When the stool's leg snapped, Djonn toppled and the ticker cracked beneath him like a dropped egg. Bent metal pieces spilled golden across the floor. Djonn's home fell silent.

When Father returned, he would hang Djonn from Harut tower by his toes until his nose bled.

Unless.

"Raeda!" Djonn shouted, hoping she lurked nearby. Raeda would help. Djonn scooped up metal pieces and bits of broken glass. Held them out to her when she straightened from the family's small garden on the ledge.

"You unlucky boy," she said. "Gravity's own monster." She sounded like Mother, which annoyed him. He'd turned twelve and deserved more respect, especially from someone younger.

Raeda's robe was faded at the shoulders and she'd hemmed the sleeves to her elbows. Her sunstruck skin looked green beneath the yellow cloth Djonn's mother favored. She'd patched her wingstraps with spare spider silk; wore them crisscrossed over her still-flat chest. But she owned no wings: her only pair had ripped months ago.

Raeda took the ticker pieces. She paced back to the ledge and the better light, muttering.

"What do we do?"

She answered him by holding her hands out toward the empty sky. The sun played light across the shards. Djonn imagined them falling towards the distant clouds.

"No!" he shouted, moving fast. He yanked her away from the ledge. "Raeda, you'll make it worse!"

Djonn grabbed the pieces. Hurried to hide them in his sleeping mat. The thick down pad sat folded atop a basket that held his things.

On a basket handle, Djonn's messenger bird ruffled feathers in protest, then settled back to hooded sleep.

"You'd greet your father with handfuls of garbage?"

Raeda teased him. "Your brothers will never let you live it down."

She was right, but Djonn bristled. "They'll blame you too. You're meant to look after me."

"You're old enough to mind yourself," she said.

With her back to the ledge Raeda watched Djonn and waited. The city's towers rose bone white behind her, set off by blue sky.

Djonn looked at the hook where the ticker once hung on their home's central wall, behind the circle of three-legged bone stools and bright yellow cushions. Where the family crowded for dinner. Where Father made deals with friends like Raeda's uncle Maru, and the wingmaker, and others who gambled on fighting birds, or needed a helping hand.

His heart did a pitterpat imitation of the ticker. Yes-no-yes. Djonn met Raeda's eyes. "You can help me."

Raeda mended clothes. She cleaned. She weeded the family garden and mulched it with guano from the roof. She looked after Djonn and told him stories. She scavenged treasures from downtower and brought them to Father. Or she had, until her wings ripped beyond all repair.

Djonn cleared his throat. "You must help me find another ticker, Raeda, before Father comes home." He said the words firmly, as Father would. He thought about counting to thirty.

Raeda shook her head. "There are no more. I've looked."

"There must be! Somewhere!" He thought of all the tiers where his ancestors had lived, descending into the clouds.

Treasure came from below, Djonn knew, passed one generation to the next up the city's bone towers until something broke or disappeared. Father kept an eye out for metal and glass, to keep it from being lost. "The weight of things drags folks down until they lose everything," he said. "No one falls or starves downtower if I can help it."

He'd say that and nod at the ticker.

He liked lenses and tools especially. And knives. Raeda, whom Father sheltered when trouble befell her uncle Maru, had proven especially good at finding those. Plus a few rarer treasures, like the ticker. But finding treasures had grown difficult. Metal and glass were rare in a city of bone and birds, clouds and sky.

Last night, Djonn's brothers had whispered about the clouds below. How treasure hid far downtower. Yes, for those strong enough to fly that low, strong enough to carry it up. How Raeda knew more than stories. Yes. How she knew what hid in the clouds, yes, maybe even in the broken tower, Lith.

Father had shushed them, furious. No. The clouds hid many dangers. Were too far down. Lith was a story. No. Leave Raeda alone.

Now, if Djonn could win Raeda's help, perhaps he'd find a treasure better than the ticker before Father returned.

Raeda crossed the bone floor near the yellow cushions and knelt, pressing her back against the central wall where the ticker had hung. She tucked her feet beneath her in a posture entirely made of 'no.'

"He'll blame you too," Djonn said.

She looked at him, her brown eyes calm. "He knows I do not drop things."

Djonn always dropped things.

But Djonn paid attention when Father made deals. He knew give and take, the importance of speed.

"My old wings, Raeda. They're yours if you take me down to salvage."

At this, she looked out to the ledge, out at the sky, the city's towers. She flexed her fingers, worn rough on the fibrous ladders she used to climb from one tier to the next on their tower.

The city's fifty-eight spires were beyond her reach. Without wings, she could only climb up and down, never to another tower, never far away.

Djonn silently counted to ten, then walked to where she sat and held out his hand, as he'd seen Father do. She put her hand in his and they clasped the deal.

Her lips parted in a smile, too quickly.

Perhaps, Djonn worried, she knew he'd kept his old wings to take apart, to see how they worked. Perhaps he'd decided wrong, or too fast. But a deal was a deal. Raeda would take him downtower on the ladders to salvage and when they'd found something to replace Father's ticker, they'd come back up and he'd give her the wings.

He found a soft silk satchel in his basket; bound it over his shoulder and to his hip. Reached for a spare coil of rope ladder.

"You'll give me my wings now." She said it softly, still kneeling.

Djonn felt the moments slipping away.

When he nodded, Raeda smiled. "And I will take you into the clouds to find a treasure."

"What?" Djonn's pride at his first deal crumpled. Not even his father dared the clouds, their storms, the giant birds that prowled there.

Yet Djonn's brothers thought Raeda knew more about the clouds than she was telling. And yes, Djonn needed a treasure that would save him from Father's rage and his brothers' ridicule. So he swallowed his doubts and retrieved the old gray wings from his basket for Raeda. Gave them to her.

He lifted his new wings, all gold spidersilk and fine bone battens, from the basket. He slipped the straps over his shoulders. At the last moment, he lifted his bird from its perch, removed its hood, and fed a piece of dried goose into its sharp beak. The bird stretched its wings, flew to the ledge and waited for him there.

Raeda secured the gray wings to her wingstraps, and checked Djonn's to make sure those were tight. Then she turned and leapt from Djonn's family's ledge, snapping the wings open as she jumped.

An updraft filled the wings' faded silk and Raeda

laughed.

Djonn unfurled his new wings carefully and checked the grips and battens as he'd been taught to do. The wing-makers were skilled, but tears could happen, even on new wings.

"Come on!" Raeda shouted, now gliding just beyond the balcony. She'd found a fine vent, and let it lift her to glide in a near-perfect circle.

Djonn swallowed his nerves and leapt after her.

***

Raeda glided away from the tower, then raked her wings back. Djonn took a deep breath. When she dove, he followed, though he hated the steep plummet.

They dropped past tiers where families like Djonn's crowded, down the cold drafts to dingier levels streaked with the garbage of those living above. In the neighboring towers' shade, Djonn could see evidence of Harut's central walls thickening, pushing the living spaces toward the tower's ledges and the inevitable drop.

In Raeda's stories, told while she cleaned or hemmed or tended the garden, people sometimes went into the clouds and didn't return.

"They're not strong enough, or they lose track of time, maybe."

She'd told the stories with a smile, teasing Djonn about his skinny arms. "Your bones need to fill in. You'd get blown off the towers in the clouds." She'd poked at him, but been careful around the bruises. His brothers had sharp elbows.

The city grew away from the clouds and people rose with it, she said. New bone tiers grew atop old ones, and, below, the central walls grew out, filling the towers. Even as the tools of Djonn's grandfathers' grandfathers pitted thin and dull, the city rose. The people rose out of the clouds, with the city, and were safer for it.

She hadn't told stories since her wings ripped.

When Raeda pulled up and began to glide the city's drafts again, Djonn prepared to circle the wide tower.

They'd fly below the occupied tiers, beyond the places Djonn was allowed to go. Djonn breathed faster as they made the long glide around. He hoped no one saw them.

But with her wings spread full, Raeda dipped to the left and disappeared into the sun's glare.

Djonn twisted his head from side to side, frantic. His wings wobbled. Above, a class of young fliers, five and six years old, flew tiny, ambitious arcs on patchwork wings over a net held by their teachers. Beyond the tower, an older group dove and mock-battled in the breeze. Below, only birds skimmed the air near the older tiers. The wind whistled in Djonn's ears.

He looked up to the tower's full height. He couldn't see them, but he knew his mother, her friends, and their youngest children were still on Harut's roof. They scrubbed at the bone with the rough scourweed that grew in the moist joins between tiers, hoping to make the tower grow higher.

Djonn's message-bird slowed beside him, knowing it wouldn't get another piece of goose if it lost its master.

He scanned the thick clouds far below. Was she already down there? He saw no sign of it. Had she skipped out on him? Stolen his wings? Father would blame Djonn for much more than the ticker.

A low whistle made Djonn peer under his left wing. Between the shadows of the thick towers, gray wings flashed in the sun. Raeda banked towards the city's eastern edge.

"Come on!"

Raeda turned to shadow as she used the neighboring tower's windshear to accelerate. Djonn struggled to do the same, whispering "wait!" He wobbled in the shear. Then he too pushed beyond his home towers.

A long glide later, he saw their destination: a gap carved in the city's horizon by a blackened stump. Lith.

Djonn had thought it only one of Raeda's stories. Even neighboring towers had risen far beyond the broken tower, had begun to forget.

They passed these towers, tiers long abandoned. Lith grew larger and darker.

The smell of it, Djonn realized, was more than Raeda's dramatic talk. Rot, like a bird had crawled into a basket to die, but much worse. The tower itself, broken, she'd said, somewhere far below, made the stench.

Raeda slowed her approach, lifted a foot from the wings' footsling, and landed on Lith in a cloud of dark dust. Djonn heard her coughing as he tried his own approach, wobbling and flying way too fast to step out.

"Careful!" Raeda shouted.

Djonn furled his wings in desperation, dropped hard to the tower's splintered bone lip, and scrambled for purchase. His wings banged the tower's edge before Raeda grabbed his arm to steady him. Blood bloomed through the knees of his robes.

"You're too clumsy for this, Djonn," she said. "You should wait up here."

Wait. On the blackening bones of Lith. No.

"What are we doing here?" he asked.

"You need a treasure, right?"

Djonn nodded. His message bird landed on his shoulder and poked at his ear, demanding food. He obliged, absently.

"Then you must go where the center isn't grown out, way down, where no one comes to salvage." She said it matter-of-fact and held her arms out. Lith.

"How did you know?" They stood far below the occupied city.

"Heard my uncle talk about it once with my gran."

Djonn frowned. His father had helped her uncle with a gambling debt, but the price had been steep.

"What did your gran say?"

"That this place is very old. People died here when the tower cracked. There are ghosts."

Djonn looked around. All he saw was dead bone, rotting while the city grew past it. His knees pulsed with pain.

"You can stay up here," she said again.

He shook his head. "I broke the ticker. I'll find something better to replace it with, or I won't go back."

"You broke something else, too," Raeda said, her voice filled with regret.

Djonn looked over his shoulder. His clumsy landing had bent his left wing. Two bone battens poked through the silk at odd angles.

Father would skip the hanging and throw him right into the clouds.

"It's alright," he lied, hoping his voice wouldn't break. "Maybe we'll find something to patch them with downtower."

Raeda watched him. She'd seen Djonn's brothers yank him back from near-disastrous falls. Heard them laugh at how clumsy he was and threaten to tether him like a baby, so they could reel him up. Djonn looked away from the pity in her eyes.

"You can send the bird, call for help."

He shook his head. "Let's go," he said, determined not to trip or stumble in front of her. His broken wing dragged behind him with a skittering sound.

He uncoiled the ladder and looked for something to tie it to. The uneven roof presented cracks and rough spurs, but he didn't think it would hold two climbers.

Raeda saw it too. "You go down. I'll hold the rope. Then I'll fly down."

"How far?"

She shrugged. "Ladder won't reach more than four tiers."

Djonn thought about the clouds. About his brothers, the ticker, his broken wing. "We should go farther."

Raeda grumbled. "Would be faster if you stayed up top."

"No."

The tower creaked and groaned as he climbed down the ladder's knots. He passed tier after blackened tier. Each smelled worse than the ones before. But Raeda was right, the central core hadn't grown out. Among the tossed and broken walls of the living quarters he passed, Djonn saw shadows piled high.

"This is good enough," Raeda said at the eighth tier.

"It isn't," he answered and lowered the rope again. Her stories always began *long, long ago*. They argued until they'd descended sixteen tiers.

"Lower than our great-grandparents," he whispered. His calves and shoulders throbbed.

"Much," Raeda agreed.

Lower and darker. Tendrils of cloud curled over the tier's dark bone floors. Something rattled in the shadows.

Only a bird, Djonn thought. We'll get the treasure and get out.

Raeda spoke, not looking at him. "Do you know a story called 'bone forest?'"

He shook his head. Focused on her words, rather than listening for sounds from the tower.

"My gran knew it. She'd lost everything but the story's name by the time I knew her. I thought maybe your brothers—since they go to the markets."

"What's a forest?"

"Dunno."

Raeda, distracted by the lost story, fell silent. She walked across the filthy floor. Djonn watched her feet, lost in their whispers. When she stepped on a goose-sized pile of feathers, dry bones cracked. Raeda cried out once and fell to her knees. A splintered goose rib pierced her left footwrap.

Djonn looked around for help. Lith, he remembered, held only ghosts. Then he knelt beside Raeda. He placed his hand flat against her heel and tugged at the splinter. She bit her lip and stayed silent. Djonn pulled again and the splinter came loose. Raeda lay down with her foot raised above her head.

"Bad luck," Djonn said. His voice cracked. "We'll get help now." His bird shifted on his shoulder.

"No. Get your treasure, then we'll send the bird."

Raeda's voice wavered. "Look," she pointed. Something glinted on the floor beyond her reach, under layers of dust and grime.

Djonn bent to brush at the dust. His fingers touched cold metal, a bone handle. A knife. Father had many knives.

He stepped over it. Brushed at the dust beyond with his fingers. Uncovered small bones, knobby and jumbled, then long bones, bigger than his arm. A pile of curved bones and tiered bones. Djonn cleaned off the last of them and realized they'd make a grown man, though the skull was missing. He yelped.

His message bird startled and flew away. Djonn cursed after it, and at his own clumsiness.

Raeda crawled over. "Sat down and died, looks like. No one around to throw him over the edge."

"What happened to his head?"

"A bird took it for the eyeballs, like as not." She made a gnashing sound with her teeth and Djonn paled.

"Aw, Raeda!" He felt sick and bent over, his back turned to her. He stared at the tower's dark wall, not really seeing anything. Stared at the dark shadow against the wall for a heartbeat, two. Then he blinked. Rust-rimed metal, a bone handle on the lid, half hidden by rags and piles of rotting feathers. "Oh," he whispered.

Raeda followed his glance and whistled. "Look what we found."

She crawled faster than he could scramble, and beat him to it.

She fingered the rusted latches, then rubbed them with scourweed pulled from a pocket of her robe. A shadow passed by the tower. Another bird, Djonn thought.

Long-sealed hinges squealed as the box's top swung open. Inside was more metal than Djonn had seen in his life. Long pieces of it, sharp at the ends. Short bits, clawed bits, a long strip with symbols like the ticker. He'd seen Father hold one of the clawed things, once. Saw him cradle it like a bird, call it a tool, the rarest kind of treasure. There were nails too, plenty of them. Metal needles. And a strange two-legged thing with a piece of charcoal clamped to one leg. He snatched that from the box before Raeda slammed the lid down.

"What are you doing?" he asked.

"Thinking." She sat on the box and looked out at the blue sky beyond the black tower. The sun was high in its arc now.

Djonn tried to guess Raeda's thoughts. He wasn't sure what to think himself, except that she sat on his treasure. Metal. A pile of it.

"It's mine," he finally said. "I gave you my wings for it."

She looked at him a long time. "And you don't have any way to get it out of here, do you, sad-face broken-wings?" Djonn's brothers called her that, when they thought she couldn't hear. She rose, favoring her heel, and pulled at the box handle. The contents rattled. "It's too heavy to fly."

"We have to try," Djonn said with a screech. "It's mine."

"And what is mine, Djonn?" Raeda's chin tilted up.

Djonn nearly whispered, "What could you possibly want?" because his mother had said it to him so often, but he knew. Raeda wanted to leave. With the box and his wings, she'd be free.

Djonn wanted to say, "Yes, take me with you," and "No, you can't," all at the same time.

His fingers tightened around the tool that held the charcoal. One leg ended in a sharp point.

"You have your wings. Help me get this back home and I'll give you some of what's inside."

She shook her head slowly. "I'm not going back. I'll make my own luck in the city, somewhere your father and my uncle can't find me." She had the box open again and began picking through the metal.

A shadow, backlit by the sun and bright sky, fell over her.

"That's exactly what you won't be doing."

A man stood on the ledge, furling his dark wings. He cracked his knuckles and stared at the box, and at both of them.

"Uncle," Raeda whispered.

***

Despite her uncle blocking the light, Djonn could see Raeda's face. Her eyes narrowed and she looked from Maru to the box and back.

Any hope Djonn had that this was a rescue evaporated.

"Been watching you, Rae," Maru said. He jerked his chin at Djonn. "Boy's dad says you haven't brought in near enough salvage lately. Been putting a lot of pressure on me. So I saw you launch that bird."

Djonn's mouth formed an 'o'. Father's story about helping Raeda was a lie.

Still, Maru was a way out. Djonn could make a deal.

"Help us get the box back," Djonn said, speaking forcefully, like his father would. "And my father will forget your debt, I know it."

Maru laughed. "Boy, you don't know your father. Let's see what you found."

He eyed the box and whistled like Raeda had.

"The whole tower saw you two fly off, Rae," he muttered. "Won't be long before half the city is searching Lith for treasure. What else did you find?"

"Only that. And him," Raeda pointed at the skeleton. "And this," she raised the knife, pointed towards her uncle.

"Ingrate girl," Maru growled. He lunged for Raeda and she dodged, but kept her grip on the box. The box slowed her, and he knocked the knife to the ground. It skittered on the floor, stopping at Djonn's feet.

Djonn looked at the knife, remembering the times his brothers had taken bone knives away from him. "You'd kill yourself with something that sharp," they'd laughed.

Maru grappled with Raeda and stepped hard on her hurt foot. She howled and crumpled. He dragged her up with one arm, her hand pinned behind her, against her furled wings. He reached for the box.

Djonn wrapped his fingers around the knife while Maru wasn't looking.

"You're not worth much, you lying sack of bones," Maru hissed at Raeda. He spun on Djonn, who barely managed to hide the knife in his robes, next to the pointed tool. "And you, you wingbroken fledge. Your father and brothers have taken the lifeblood of half my folk. What should be done with you?

Djonn thought for two heartbeats. "You have to let us go. People will come, they'll see. You said so yourself."

"They'll see what? A broken winged boy. Maybe that's something your father will take as full payment."

Bad to worse. Djonn wrapped his hand around the knife.

Maru swung the box of metal and Raeda towards the tower ledge. "Can't fly with both," he laughed, and changed his grip on the girl.

Djonn's heart pounded now-yes-now. He rushed Maru, blade held as Raeda had, all his weight behind the knife.

Maru heard him coming. He dropped the box, grabbed Djonn's arm and squeezed. The knife clattered to the ledge, wobbled, and flipped. It fell end over end towards the clouds. Djonn whimpered.

Maru pinned Djonn's hand by his shoulder blade, as his brothers did.

Raeda shouted as her uncle turned once again to hold her out over the ledge.

Djonn's other hand shot out from his robes on its own, holding the tool with charcoal and the sharp point. He didn't think. He drove the point hard into Maru's ear until he heard a crack. The man dropped to the floor, thrashing, and Raeda fell, catching herself by one hand on the ledge.

Djonn dove to the floor and clasped her hand.

"I won't drop you," he said.

Maru kicked behind them once more and stopped. Djonn pulled hard while Raeda scrambled and, soon, they both knelt on the ledge. In the distance, Djonn could see flyers headed towards Lith: four pairs of yellow wings still high in the sky. His father and brothers.

Djonn drew a deep breath and opened the box. Picked out five sharp tools and one metal strip. Held them out to Raeda.

"Go fast. Before they come."

Her eyes widened. She straightened her yellow robes and secured the tools in a hidden pocket. She put her hand out, and pulled him up to standing. "Thank you for catching me," she said. She took a hesitant step forward on her injured foot, then another, until she limped across the tier to a ledge on the far side of the tower's circumference. She leapt from the edge, snapping her gray wings open at the last minute.

Djonn bent to pull the weapon from Maru's ear. The tool wasn't meant for that. He could tell.

By the time Djonn's father and brothers landed, he'd figured out what the tool was for: drawing circles. He'd traced small and large circles on the dark bone floor, the charcoal invisible against the rotting tower.

He tucked the tool away in his robes and showed his father the metal box. He showed him the skeleton.

"Box was too heavy for him. Dragged him down."

Djonn's father clasped his shoulder.

"And Raeda?" one brother asked. His other brothers looked around the dark tier, at the dead man, at Djonn, who stood with one foot on the box.

Djonn peered over the ledge, to the clouds below, counted three calm heartbeats, then met their eyes for five more.

He watched them shift uncomfortably, caught between him and the clouds. "I couldn't hold her," he said.

Fran Wilde is a writer and technology consultant. She can also tie various sailing knots, set gemstones, and program digital minions. Her work has appeared in *Nature*, *Daily Science Fiction*, and (nonfiction) *Strange Horizons*, and the SFWA blog. She interviews authors about the intersections between food and genre fiction for "Cooking the Books," and blogs at franwilde.wordpress.com.

"A Moment of Gravity, Circumscribed" is an offshoot from Fran's novel, *Bone Arrow*, set in the same universe. This is Fran's first science fiction anthology appearance.

TOUR DE FORCE
EDWARD M. LERNER

"...As well as," mumbled the newly appointed Minister for Reconstruction, his eyes darting, licking his lips, "damage to the tillium mines that was quite extensive. Mineshaft inspection and the associated reinforcement alone will require us to—"

"Enough," Caesar Charles commanded, abruptly bounding from the throne. Caesar's booming voice and the stomp of his jackboots echoed in the vast, high-ceilinged feasting hall become audience chamber. He scanned the assembly until his eyes found mine. "Lucas. Walk with us."

Courtiers and counselors, generals and supplicants, ministers and bureaucrats—as one they fell back. None seemed as fearful as the minister cut off by Caesar at mid-sentence. Bearer of Bad Tidings was not a role with a future.

And my future? I was an adviser, officially speaking.

Hostages did not have good prospects, either.

Caesar, as he strode, with but a single sideward glance, conveyed disapproval at battle scars insufficiently masked by bold holo murals and fresh wall paint. Now it was the chamberlain's turn to flinch.

I said, "I am at your service, Your Highness." Keeping my face expressionless, remaining a proper five paces behind, I followed my liege lord toward the nearby aerie and walkway.

What did the tyrant want of me?

Praetorians fell in beside and behind us. With a dismissive wave, Caesar signaled the squad of bodyguards to stay. What need had he for bodyguards? As living, dour exemplars of imperial power they better served him by intimidating the larger audience within.

In the intricately carved archway that gave access onto the broad promenade, a faint *something* glimmered. No mere weather curtain, this was a defensive shield operating at its minimum strength. Sparks erupted at Caesar's approach: the bubble of his personal shield, likewise at standby, interacting with the larger field. With each step the intersection between the two force fields grew until, as he stepped across the threshold, a great, glittering nimbus encircled him. A wordless demonstration. A coruscating reminder.

Had the personal shield burgeoned to its full strength (if the sensors Caesar carried had sensed a projectile or a blade, a high-intensity beam or the pressure wave of an explosion, the presence of a pathogen or the merest hint of a trace of a toxin—or even a hard shove) the sparkles would have blazed far brighter.

With the force field at full power, not even a molecule could penetrate.

For now the personal shield was at its lowest intensity, in its standby mode. As Canute could not hold back the tide, not even mighty Caesar can outlast the oxygen with him inside an impenetrable bubble.

Then Caesar was through the archway field. The flickering circle shrank as he continued to walk, until, three paces onto the terrace, the final sparkles blinked out.

One more demonstration of the tech that protected an empire—

And its thoroughly mad emperor.

I followed Caesar outside onto the great terrazzo promenade of his newest castle. New to the Crown, that was. This magnificent structure, carved from a rocky crag, had stood for generations. As for the rightful owner, he remained in residence—paraded in heavy chains to the sub-subbasement where sunlight never entered.

Nor did hope.

I remembered visiting this world as a child. Remembered playing hide-and-seek with my cousins in the very same subterranean levels, a warren of abandoned rooms and closets and dimly lit tunnels piled high with tarp-covered...whatevers. I remembered the scary thrill of knowing that the rooms had once been dungeons and torture chambers.

They were again, and the thrill was definitely gone.

Duke Philip, if he were lucky, would not live long.

And if I were lucky, I would not join my uncle. Though even torture was never the fate I most feared. It could have been *my* home world ground beneath the tyrant's heel.

On the promenade, the sun shone warm but not hot. Sun glints high overhead revealed elements of Caesar's navy on armed patrol. A few glistening droplets, faint scents of salt and algae, and an endless *sigh* hinted at the long drop, just past the marble balustrade, to the swirling, surging waters so far below.

Up the coast to the west, stark against a cerulean sky, a roiling pillar of smoke climbed from the former capital of Duke Philip's domain. Make that, the former city. Distant scintillations revealed some of the geometrically perfect force-field dome that kept the thick smoke away from Caesar. Toxic fumes had triggered the castle's newly deployed defenses, as mere air would not.

Outside the imperial laboratories, no one knew which toxins, in what concentrations and combinations, could activate the shield. Fiendish booby traps generally killed anyone who dared to plumb such mysteries, and they were the lucky ones. Force-field technology, more than a state secret, was an *imperial* secret, and the very foundation of imperial power. Anyone caught experimenting with the tech joined, in a slow and excruciating death, those who would presume to authorize and fund the forbidden research, and any—up to a peer of the empire—who had, through their lack of diligence, permitted such transgressions within their jurisdiction.

I took care not to face west. Took care not to appear to take notice of the conflagration. The pyre.

Too carefully, it would seem.

"You do not approve," Caesar said.

"It is not my place to have an opinion."

"And yet, you do."

No response could help, but none had been explicitly demanded. I remained silent.

"Duke Philip thought to hoard his wealth," Caesar said. "What of Duke Trask?"

"Father is your loyal subject," I answered.

"And his son?"

"I serve Caesar." Because, like Father, I have no choice. None did. As had been demonstrated to, and with, poor Philip. "How may I advise you?"

"There is reason and precedent." Caesar gestured toward the smoke, not ready to change the subject. Did he remember that I had family on this world? But of course he did. He meant for me to report back to Father what had happened here. "The ancient Romans had the habit of randomly crucifying citizens of captured towns. It made a point. Don't resist. Don't rebel."

Just within the archway, behind the shimmering force field, a rank of heavily armed praetorians stood guard. With eyes as hard as marbles, they gazed out onto the promenade. Ready to charge. Prepared to kill—

For their own sakes as much as for Caesar. Hated by all for the tyranny they served, the praetorians would not long survive the beast they had sworn to protect.

I struggled to respond in a level voice. "I understand, Caesar."

He was not to be dissuaded. "And the Mongol horde obliterated any *city* that defied the Great Khan, so that other communities in his path would know better. But might not resistance arise later? That would be unacceptable, too. And so, at times, a lone Mongol warrior would kill at random, to reconfirm a town's continuing loyalty and submission. And the whole town would stand by, would not lift a hand, would not speak one word of complaint, knowing that any suggestion of opposition would doom everyone to slaughter. And do you know what, Lucas?"

"What, Your Highness?" What, beyond a reign of terror remembered three millennia later? As you would emulate, conflating infamy with immortality?

"In the Khan's empire, it was said, a virgin carrying gold could ride unmolested from one border to another. Good behavior everywhere, because his subjects knew the consequences of bad behavior."

"Caesar is a learned man," I said. Only you have learned from monsters, to be a greater monster yourself. You would allow everyone on this *world* to starve to make a point. "And nonetheless Caesar flatters"—torments—"me by asking my opinion."

"We haven't, yet." Caesar allowed himself a brief, hard smile. "But you are correct. We did desire your thoughts on a matter."

"Of course, Your Highness."

"How quickly will things on this planet return to normal?"

By *things*, he did not have in mind relief from the worldwide drought that had driven Duke Philip to ruin and desperation. Caesar did not speak of the tens of thousands dead, shot like fish in a barrel, massacred by Imperial Marines safe behind impervious battlefield force shields. Nor did he refer to the havoc wreaked from on high by invulnerable battle cruisers. No, Caesar cared only for resumption of the confiscatory taxes Philip had been unable to pay *before* all those disasters.

"I suspect the population has been motivated," I said. To flee, if they can. If not, to sell anything and everything, for whatever pittance could be gotten. Destitution and starvation later were to be preferred to renewed slaughter now. Until Caesar relented, an unlikely eventuality, I saw no other options.

Unless...

The glimmer of an idea...gone faster than I could grasp it.

At the base of the precipitous slope, over and through the jumble of water-slick boulders, great waves pounded. The roar was palpable. Spray leapt high into the air. In the thirty years since my first visit, crashing waves seemed not to have dulled the rocks' jagged edges.

I had, on a foolish dare, once jumped from this parapet. Roland, Duke Philip's braggart son, claimed to have made the leap "dozens of times." And so, I had had to do it, too.

Screaming all the way, limbs flailing, I had, just barely, come down seaward of the rocks. I had, by sheer dumb luck, splashed into one of the deeper spots and not broken my neck. I had managed, somehow, to resist the undertow. Thrashing and paddling, I had stayed afloat, exhausted, until an errant current nudged me toward a nearby pebbly beach.

No one—certainly not cousin Roland—had ever made the jump. Father had so tanned my hide that I hadn't been able to sit for a week. Uncle Philip had done the same to Roland. For our offenses were identical: unmitigated stupidity. Nobles, even seven-year-old cadet sons, were expected to know better.

Roland had died bravely in the first day of Caesar's invasion.

"What do you see?" Caesar asked, joining me along the balustrade. A nimbus flashed, his personal force field buffering the impact of knee against railing.

Caesar was not a clumsy man. Far from it. This was one more demonstration, one more reminder of what his will had wrought. When he had conceived of a personal shield, no one in the imperial labs had believed such a small force-field generator, or the tiny aneutronic fusor to power it, to be feasible. He told the researchers to bring him one regardless. When that group of scientists failed him, they became an object lesson for the second team, who strived harder. The third team, after watching their predecessors burned at the stake, discovered a way.

"I see a severe beauty," I answered. "Endless possibilities."

"Is that so?" Caesar said. "Perhaps I should raise the taxes."

I *truly* hated the man. Caesar was insane. Depraved. Vicious. And untouchable behind shield within shield.

Unless...

"If I might quickly look up some archival data about the old regime's industrial production," I said.

"Go ahead."

I took the comp from my vest pocket, poked and prodded its touch screen, and, with a murmur of feigned anger, lobbed the device over the railing. The comp, in pieces after its first few bounces, disappeared in little shards into the seething surf far below. "Forgive me, Your Highness. It had gone from balky to inert."

And stood silent, not presuming to ask for the use of Caesar's comp. But hoping...

Caesar, desirous of an answer, reached into his pocket. Even the slow approach of his own hand to his chest made the personal shield shimmer. He stepped close to me, offering his comp.

Perhaps Caesar had some vague premonition. "You would not toss *ours*, would you?"

I reached toward the comp—and shoved Caesar, his shield instantly turned rigid, over the broad balustrade.

Sic semper tyrannis, I thought. "For Roland," I said.

Where below, *exactly*, had I dived as a foolish child? As the praetorians dashed onto the promenade, I leapt, uncertain that I had remembered the correct spot.

I'd know soon enough.

About halfway to the water I passed Caesar as he caromed and ricocheted down the steep, unyielding slope.

His personal shield, turned harder than the rock, glowed like a tiny sun as it absorbed impact upon impact.

The roiling waves rose up to smite me.

Numb with cold and shock, limbs trembling, the breath knocked out of me, choking on the seawater that I'd swallowed, I struggled to the surface. I paddled furiously, turning, trying to get my bearings.

Caesar's unyielding shield must finally have rebounded off some rock to splash into the ocean. Each incoming wave dashed the bubble anew against jagged boulders. The tyrant, bounced about in the force field like dice in a cup, lay slumped at the bottom of the glowing sphere. At each crash against the rocks, with that much more energy to be absorbed, the force field shone just that much brighter.

Which shall it be, Caesar? I wondered. Battered to death against the force field? Suffocated in your own vile exhalations? Drowned or beaten to a pulp against the rocks, if you should somehow awaken and manage to disable the field? Or perhaps—

Hiss!

Steam erupted as a blaster pulse struck no more than two meters from me. I paused my frantic paddling, let the inrushing tide carry me, as near as I dared, to the rocks. The steeper the angle, the harder for bodyguards high overhead to target me.

As the first desperate praetorians splashed—most, surely, to their doom on the unforgiving boulders, or to be dragged into the watery depths by heavy, sodden uniforms —I began swimming. I struck out for the distant pebbly beach.

Behind me, with a blinding flash and an earsplitting *blam!* the bastard's force field overloaded.

Edward M. Lerner worked in high tech for thirty

years, as everything from engineer to senior vice president, for much of that time writing science fiction as a hobby. Since 2004, Ed has written full-time, and his books run the gamut from technothrillers, like *Small Miracles* and *Energized*, to traditional SF, like the "InterstellarNet" series, to, collaborating with Larry Niven, the grand space epic "Fleet of Worlds" series of *Ringworld* companion novels.

Ed's short fiction has appeared in anthologies, collections, and many of the usual SF magazines. A physicist and computer scientist by training, he also writes the occasional nonfiction technology article. His website is edwardmlerner.com.

About "Tour de Force", Ed writes, "Wouldn't it be keen, I'd once thought, to have a personal force field? To be the only one with a personal force field? Why, it would be sort of like...having the Midas Touch. Uh-oh. But it's from uh-ohs that stories arise."

THE CHATTER OF THE BEAMS
JEFF HECHT

The gravity was low when Carlos woke. He had reversed gravity to push the starship off from the Earth, then adjusted its force to leave the solar system. Now it had changed, and he needed to check it. His body felt stiff, and his muscles would not respond when he tried to stretch. He opened his eyes, but they would not focus.

"DeepSleep," he said to himself, but he heard only the whispering of air through the ventilation system. Recovery would take time.

His mind drifted. He was trying to explain how the gravity drive drew quasiparticles from the vacuum and trapped them between Higgs bosons frozen in time. "The drive radiates gravitons that push against the fabric of space-time and propel the ship toward light-speed," he told Beth, who cooled quantum computers to a picokelvin above absolute zero to control the force vector of the graviton beam.

"Are you awake and cognizant?" a toneless mechanical voice interrupted.

Carlos opened his eyes and light flooded into them. He struggled to make his numb tongue and mouth form words. "Er...uh...eh..."

"You have been in DeepSleep for 647 years, more than twice an extended human lifetime. You will need natural sleep to organize your memories and thoughts. DeepSleep stops those vital processes." Carlos recognized the voice as the ship's control and communication system, which had managed the trip. "DeepSleep has never been tested over such long periods, so you may experience aftereffects. Current data is inadequate to determine how long it will take to recover full mental and physical function. More natural sleep is recommended."

Carlos closed his eyes and dozed. Stella was explaining the Chatter of the beams. "Civilizations living around other stars communicate by sending laser beams across the galaxy. They don't know we are here, but we have mapped their signals passing through the solar neighborhood," she said, waving her hand. A 3D map showed colored beams passing through near space in all directions. "We can trace the paths of the beams from outside the solar system, but we cannot understand the information they carry. We call it the Chatter."

She swept her arms together to close the display, then opened them so the Chatter was sound that filled the room. His brain instinctively sought meaning.

Stella's thick silver hair and the white of her eyes sparkled against her dark skin. "It's the music of the galactic orchestra," she said. "You understand gravity. I want you to take us to the concert at the nearest station, 53 light years away."

***

Waking from natural sleep, Carlos remembered it had not been that simple. His first antigravity drive had failed to get off the ground. Gathering the Search and building the ship took decades. For a time, he had doubted Stella's vision. But the details didn't matter now that they were about to meet humanity's nearest neighbors in the galaxy.

He tried to call the ship, but he could not hear his own voice. He opened his eyes, and slowly his eyes made sense of the hazy light and recognized the waking room. "Ship?" he whispered.

"Are you awake and cognizant?" the ship asked.

"I...I...think," Carlos answered, surprised how hard it

was to shape the words.

"That is good. You will need more time to recover your voice function." A mobile medical robot moved into his field of view, and through it the ship said "Your mental vital signs are good."

Encouraged, Carlos tried to ask about the others, but he could not understand the sounds he made. After he stopped trying, the ship said, "There is a message."

A click signaled a change in speaker. Stella's voice said, "You are twelfth to wake, Carlos." Was she already awake or was the ship playing back a recording she had made at the start of the trip? She had organized the arrival as meticulously as she had organized the rest of the Search, specifying the sequence of waking the 20-person crew as they approached the transmitter. Stella would be first, of course. Carlos came later, when they would need to control the gravity.

His voice cracked as he tried to say, "We made it." He didn't know if Stella could understand or even if she was listening. His fingers and toes moved feebly.

"Rest some more," the ship said.

Natural sleep came easily.

***

"Are you awake and cognizant?" the ship asked.

"Yes," Carlos said, so weakly he doubted the ship could understand.

It did. "There is a message," the ship said. "Relaying and making direct connection."

Something clicked. "The Chatter of the beams is stronger here, Carlos. I can feel it. It dances in my nerves. My legs and arms tingle as antennas." Stella's voice sounded older.

Carlos felt no tingling and could not hear the Chatter. It had always seemed so far away. He tried to ask her what it was saying, but all that came out was "What?"

"The light dances inside my eyes even when they are closed," Stella said. "Patterns grow and swell, flicker and fluctuate. I can see each cell on my retina reflected on the dark inside of the eyelid. Can't you see the light?"

The only light Carlos could see in the windowless waking room came from the wall panels. "What...what...light?" he asked.

"The light is all around us and inside us," Stella's voice said.

"Where?" Carlos said.

"All around and through us. We are the light and the light is us."

Carlos wanted to ask more questions. Could she see the light from the transmitter? He was too weak and tired to understand or to speak. "Er...er..." he stammered.

"Open your eyes, Carlos, and you will see the light with me."

"Eh...Eh..." he stammered.

The ship broke the connection. "You are very tired," it said, dimming the lights in the waking room. "It is time to sleep again. It will help your mind and your memories."

***

"I am not going," said Beth.

She had worked for years trying to make quantum computers decode the Chatter. Tall and slender, she could wear down abstruse mathematical problems like her Kenyan marathon runner ancestors had worn down other runners. Carlos had expected her to come. "Why?" he asked.

"It is complex, nonlinear and non-computational." She looked sad and weary. "I don't want to give up," she said, "but I cannot go with Stella. I will stay here and try to understand the Chatter."

"Why?" he asked again, not understanding but knowing he would miss her.

"I want to continue my studies here," she said, her eyes looking down. "And I cannot convince myself that the Search can succeed. The risks are too large with DeepSleep and the gravity drive, and we know too little about the Chatter. You will spend over 600 years traveling 50 light years to visit a place you don't know exists."

"But the Search is the greatest quest..." He stopped as he saw Beth fading.

"Stella hears the Chatter in her mind, and she is going mad." Beth had become a whisper far far away.

**

"Are you awake and cognizant?" the ship asked.

"Yes," Carlos answered. "My body feels weak, but my mind is awake." He tried to raise an arm and found it was tied down by a thread too strong for his feeble muscles to break. "Where are we? Why is the gravity low?"

"We have arrived at the transmitter, where many lasers are beaming the Chatter into space. The gravity is low to aid in your recovery and to control orbital motion relative to the transmitting lasers. Your code controls gravity strength and direction."

Carlos remembered the code, but the field felt too low. Recovery was supposed to be near Earth gravity, and the transmitter had to be on or orbiting something very massive. "This feels too low," he said.

"Your muscles are very weak," the ship said, "and the total mass of this system is 11.5 Jupiters. There is no star here."

Stella had said the transmitter was on the surface of a Dyson sphere which surrounded a star and collected its energy to power the lasers. Her explanation had made sense at the time, but Carlos could not remember it. "Show me the transmitter," he asked.

"There are many transmitters," the ship said. A wall panel dimmed to jet black and became a screen. Blurry specks of stars appeared, in patterns Carlos did not remember from Earth.

"I don't see any transmitters," Carlos said. "I don't see any beams."

"The screen shows the sky at true intensity. Your eyes need time to dark-adapt," said the ship. The other wall panels faded to black, leaving the waking room dark. Stars appeared and slowly grew brighter except in an area on the left, where gray areas slowly appeared, and the background seemed slightly brighter than between the stars.

"Where are the beams?" Carlos asked. "Orbiting dust should scatter light from them, so we see them."

"Dust levels are extremely low," the ship said. "Photon pressure from the beams pushes dust away from the transmitters over time."

"How long?"

"Impossible to estimate, but very old. Amplification will make the beams visible," the ship said. Beams appeared, a ghostly green, like terrestrial auroras. "Estimated average power flux is three gigawatts. Amplification factor is four thousand. Laser emission is frequency-doubled into the human visible range for convenience in visualization."

Carlos nodded, but his head hardly moved. Staring at the beams, he wondered what messages they carried and where they went. "What are the beams saying?" he asked.

After a silence, the the ship said, "There is a message. Relaying and making direct connection."

Stella's voice followed. "They are beaming energy into my soul. They are perfectly directional, beaming infinite energy to me."

"What?" Carlos wondered if he had drifted into real sleep.

The ship repeated her words once, then twice more as Carlos asked for replays.

Carlos closed his eyes and retreated into silence. As an astronomer, Stella had discovered the Chatter, and realized that the light beams passing through the outer parts of the solar system carried messages between other civilizations in the galaxy. She had told the world, but when few paid much attention, she had created the Search, and led it for more than a century. She dreamed of finding advanced civilizations that could bring humanity out of its self-centered obsessions. Now her beautiful mind sounded as feeble as his body. He cried until the waking-room robot had to wipe his eyes.

"You should rest," the robot said with the ship's voice.

Carlos sobbed again, and after the robot wiped his eyes again, he slept in exhaustion.

***

"Are you awake and cognizant?" the ship asked.

"Yes," he replied. He tried to raise his right hand to rub his eyes, but it barely lifted off the bed in the low gravity.

"Your muscles are weak and need mechanical assistance," the ship said.

Carlos felt the bed underneath him tilt his head and body upwards. He saw the robot and a wheeled chair.

"The chair is a mobility aid printed to fit your body and optimized for low gravity. It also will stimulate your muscles, but you will need it until you recover."

Carlos wanted to get himself up from the bed, but he was too weak to sit. The bed folded itself into a chair-like shape, and the robot's arms lifted him into the chair beside it. He was amazed how well it fit. His hand was strong enough to move the controls, and a finger's touch rolled him forward or turned the chair. He was glad to be mobile, but wished he was under his own power. His head rested in a brace, and it turned with his head to look around the waking room.

It was small, spotless, and felt empty. "Where are the others?" he asked.

"So far you are the only one who can move."

"But Stella spoke to me. She must have awakened earlier."

"So far you are the only one who can move," the ship repeated.

"Where is Stella?"

"She is in a bed in another waking room. She speaks, but has not opened her eyes or moved. Her condition is being evaluated."

"How long has she been like that?" Carlos asked, afraid that she had had a stroke or seizure.

"Since she was roused from DeepSleep more than five years ago."

"Five years!" Carlos was stunned. "She has just lain there for five years."

"She talks," the ship said. Its voice became that of a diagnostic clinic robot. "Can you explain what you heard her say?"

"No," Carlos answered, wondering what more to say. "I have never heard her like that before. She was always quick and lucid. Something is wrong. Has she had a stroke?"

"The instruments give no clear diagnosis. No blood flow obstructions are observed in the brain. No therapies have produced any improvement."

Perhaps there was no hope for Stella, but they had planned for all contingencies. There was a chain of command, but it had slipped his memory because he was so far down it would never matter. "What about the others?"

"They have not woken from DeepSleep."

"You were supposed to wake us in sequence."

"They have not woken from DeepSleep," the ship repeated in its monotone.

"But Stella said I was the twelfth to wake," Carlos said.

"That was a recording. Stella was first. You were the twelfth on the list to be awakened. The ten between you did not respond and are still in DeepSleep. The others are waiting. Come," the waking-room robot beckoned, and the wheelchair obeyed, carrying Carlos.

***

The doors on the DeepSleep chambers were pale green, with names of the people in each chamber etched through the polymer coating to expose a deep gray substrate. The seals had been broken on twelve doors. The robot opened the one where Carlos had spent six centuries; the life-support fluid had been pumped out and the equipment neatly stowed out of sight. Stella's chamber was likewise empty. Yoko's had been opened, but she had been returned to DeepSleep after she failed to wake, and the chamber resealed.

"The waking procedure takes 150 days," the robot said. "Stella showed no response for 72 days, then began talking. The others were returned to their chambers after 150 days."

"How long did I take?" Carlos asked.

"First response was 86 days. Since then has been 212 more days. Waking was not supposed to be that slow."

Carlos remembered a long haze between sleep and wakefulness, but had no idea it had lasted that long.

The robot brought him to the second waking room, which had Stella's name on the door. The wheelchair passed easily through the opening, custom-printed to fit doorways as well as people.

"Stella?" Carlos said when the chair stopped by her bed. She looked ancient and feeble; her face lined, her skin faded, her hair thin and white. "Are you there, Stella?"

Her lips moved. "I am here, in the universe," she said, but her body was still and her eyes were closed. "The lights are with me. I am looking at a screen, but I have lost something."

"We reached the transmitter, Stella."

"I have seen it and ridden its beam across the galaxy."

"Can you raise your hand?" Carlos said.

Nothing moved.

"Can you move a finger?"

Nothing moved but her lips.

"I have more fingers now. I beamed my fingers to all the galaxy."

Carlos turned to the robot. "How long has she been like this?"

"Since she woke," the ship said through the robot. "She has issued no commands."

Carlos nodded. The ship was programmed to obey the commander, and without Stella there was none. He had forgotten where he was in the chain of command, but knew what he had to do. "I will assume command during her disability."

"Thank you," the ship said. "Come with me to the

control room."

***

The large dome-shaped room had been designed for a crew of 20, but only a few chairs were in place. Screens lined the wall and arched overhead. As Carlos entered, the screens came to life, showing the world outside the radiation shields.

"There is an archived message," the ship said.

A woman spoke. It took Carlos a moment to recognize Beth's voice. "I am transmitting this in hope you can receive signals from Earth. This is sixteen years and 263 days after your departure from orbit. The Chatter still eludes interpretation, but analysis of frequency variations in the signal from your destination has revealed something unexpected about the transmitter."

"This message has been received redundantly, verified, and processed to remove noise," said a mechanical voice.

"The modulated signal beam appears to originate from a source on a rotating super-Jupiter. This produces a small frequency chirp. Then the beam is reflected from one of several mirrors orbiting the super-Jupiter. As the mirrors orbit the super-Jupiter, the transmitter switches between them, and the mirrors direct the Chatter beam to its ultimate source beyond the Earth, in the inner part of the galaxy. We can find no sign of any body larger than 20 Jupiters, so the transmitter cannot be in a solar system. Observations will continue, but we are at the noise limit and would need several more centuries to significantly improve resolution."

Details followed, and a large data file for analysis and comparison with information the ship collected. The ship stopped the message after Beth signed off.

Carlos looked up at the screen that showed the sky outside. Wordlessly, the ship drew circles on the distant dim sphere. Each surrounded a brighter zone. A dashed line sprouted from one bright zone and traced a path to a bright spot far above the surface. Then it bounced off the bright spot and quickly sped into deep space.

"There is another archived message," the ship said.

Beth spoke again, sounding older. "You may already know this, but we have discovered a problem with DeepSleep. Aging does not stop completely. It is a nonlinear function of time, increasing in speed with the duration of DeepSleep. We have not had time to establish the relationship, but it is now 63 years after your departure. Our calculations predict that our signals will soon become too faint for you to detect. We do not know if a cure is possible. Documents and data follow. We will try to send you more information later."

Carlos looked down at the wheelchair, wondering why he had been the lucky one. He waited for another message, but the ship was silent. "Is there more?" he asked.

"There are no more archived messages," the ship said.

"Is there enough information to tell what will happen to me?" Carlos asked. He raised his hand above the arm of the wheelchair, but could only hold it up briefly before is slipped back down.

"No," the ship said. "Too little time-sequence data to calculate rate of change. No data on possible therapy. No equipment adaptable for therapy on board."

Carlos remembered bits and pieces of the planning. Stella had been certain that the intelligent life would be near the transmitters. She had planned a one-way trip before the government made her add fuel for a return. She had not planned to go back to Earth; they had all wanted to get away to a better place.

He looked up again and saw no changes in the sky. "Is this real time?" he asked.

"All objects in current locations at current velocities," the ship said.

"How long do your records of motion go back?"

"More than seven years."

"Show me and describe," Carlos commanded. "Acceleration factor of 100,000."

"Single beam or multiple beams?" the ship asked.

Carlos paused, wondering what kind of transmitter this was. "How many are there?"

"On the order of 800 outgoing, but exact number unknown," the ship said. "Incoming beams have been detected but number cannot be estimated."

"Show one beam at first, then increase the number."

The dome screen turned completely black. The super-Jupiter appeared, dim with a scattering of slightly brighter areas that moved as the object spun on its axis. Bright spots appeared in the space above it; satellites orbiting the super-Jupiter. A twinkling beam sped from the surface toward one satellite, then bounced off into deep space. The beam from the transmitter tracked the moving satellite and the reflected beam kept pointing in the same direction. Mirrors on the satellite must be synchronized with its orbit and the turning of the super-Jupiter to track the direction, Carlos realized.

Then the beam flickered out just as another beam, from another transmitter on the super-Jupiter, switched on and bounced off another mirror-satellite pointed in the same direction as the first. The beam tracked the satellite, following its orbit until it flickered out and another beam from another spot jumped to another satellite.

Other beams appeared, following other paths, jumping and reflecting as the first had. More and more beams stretched through space and bounced around and followed different paths away from the transmitters. Then fainter beams of matching colors started to arrive from other places off the screen, bouncing off mirror satellites and down onto the surface. Carlos watched the dance of the beams and satellites in fascination until they froze in place.

"End of recording," announced the ship.

Carlos stared at the central object. It was the size and mass of a super-Jupiter, but it didn't look like one floating free in interstellar space. Each laser beam was firing a gigawatt into space. Where was the energy coming from? Was anybody living on or in it? "What is the central object?" he asked.

"The transmitter. Arrays of lasers distributed across its surface emit beams and steer the light to orbiting mirrors, which direct the beams to their destinations."

"What is its energy balance? Where is it getting the energy to power the lasers?"

"Insufficient data," the ship replied.

Artificial intelligence never took the initiative. It should be possible to calculate energy flux, Carlos thought. "Measure surface temperature and calculate heat flux from inside. Measure temperature of the surface-emitting laser, and calculate energy flux through it." He barked a series of requests, trying to piece together a picture.

The waking room robot came to life and approached Carlos. "Don't overtire yourself. You should rest."

"No!" Carlos said, surprising himself with his energy. After a while information came rolling in. Heat was coming from deep inside the object; only nuclear fusion could produce that much energy. The dark areas on the surface were insulators that allowed very little heat to escape; their temperatures were barely above the melting point of water. The lasers were two kilometers across, arrays of components too small for the ship to detect individually from space, which converted heat into light incredibly efficiently.

It was too efficient to be natural. Whoever had built the thing had outsmarted thermodynamics. Structures inside the super-Jupiter guided the fusion energy to the lasers, where it excited atoms and stored them in energetic states until the laser exceeded its threshold and released the energy in a beam shaped so it could cross hundreds of light years.

The energy flux had to be tremendous; nothing could be living inside. Could something be living on the surface? "Scan surface between lasers to search for structures," he commanded. "Display close-ups."

The ship began the scan, showing a surface almost

perfectly flat that stayed unchanged for minutes. Carlos turned the chair, moving it so he could see the blow-up of the surface. He wished he could walk, but even in the low gravity his muscles were too weak to rise from the chair.

"All surface appears equivalent to sensors. No structures on surface," the ship reported.

"Survey and identify objects larger than 100 meters now orbiting the transmitter."

This time the ship was quick to reply. "All such objects are relay mirrors which redirect laser beams." It obviously had been tracking them already.

"Do you detect any evidence of organic life near the transmitter?" Carlos had to ask the question, but he already knew the answer.

"None outside of this ship," the ship replied.

Carlos tilted the chair and looked up at the screen showing the sky. Beams moved slowly, tracking the relay mirrors. The civilization sending the signal was not at the transmitter, where Stella had expected it. The transmitter was just a relay, receiving signals from distant civilizations and relaying them across the galaxy. Artificial intelligence could do the job, as the ship had steered itself from the Earth to the transmitter.

"Why do they use relays rather than sending the beams directly?" Carlos wondered aloud. "There must be some limits. How fast does the beam spread out? What is the minimum detectable intensity? Could they be limited by the need to establish a lock between the transmitter and receiver?"

"Insufficient data," the ship replied.

"Where do we go from here?" he asked, not expecting an answer.

"The Search must go on," the ship said. "Fuel supplies remain for another 60 light years."

"Why?" Carlos asked. "What will that accomplish?"

"The mission of the Search is to find another civilization. It is the central goal. This is only a way station. That is what Stella wanted."

"Why?" he asked again.

"There is a message," the ship said. "Relaying and making direct connection."

"Are you talking to the Chatter, Carlos?" Stella spoke from her waking room. "The Chatter is telling me of the beautiful cities in the galaxy that we must visit. We must follow the Chatter to them. Take us there, ship."

"Command received," the ship said.

The words surprising Carlos. The ship had given him control, but once Stella had issued a command, it had given control back to her. He wondered how the ship interpreted disability, and what he should do. Where would the ship take them to follow the Chatter?

"Insufficient data to calculate course," the ship said.

"Listen to the Chatter," said Stella. "It flows through us all, and can tell us everything we need to know."

"Insufficient data," the ship repeated.

"Listen to the Chatter," Stella repeated.

"Insufficient data."

In the silence that followed, Carlos wondered where they could go from the transmitter. Where were the incoming beams coming from? "Identify incoming beams and their directionality," he requested.

"Processing archived data," the ship said. "Minimum of six incoming beams identified." It listed coordinates, then displayed red circles on the screen showing the range of error. The smallest circle was several degrees wide.

"Take us to them all," said Stella.

"Longer duration observations needed to determine required course," said the ship.

"How long?" asked Carlos.

"More than 100 years needed to collect data."

"We have all the time we need. Time is forever," said Stella.

Looking at his hand on the controls of the chair, Carlos knew better. It was an ancient's hand, eroded by centuries of DeepSleep. Waiting would bring only death, if it did not bring madness first. "List probable civilization sites for which present data is adequate to calculate a course," he asked.

"Earth," the ship said.

Carlos had not expected that single simple answer, but his mind was working quickly enough to understood it. The ship had located one transmitter, and it was a relay system. Other transmitters sending signals to their transmitter might also be relays. For all he or the ship knew, the relays could be all that was left of some ancient galactic relay network, abandoned by those who built it, but still dutifully transmitting signals. The indecipherable Chatter might be maintenance codes verifying the system was operable as it waited for a signal to send.

"I do not want to go back to Earth," Stella said. Her voice was stronger than before. "I want to go forward, not back."

Carlos wanted to move, but all he could do was flex his fingers. "We don't know if any civilizations are out there, Stella. This transmitter is just a relay. We can't tell the relays from the civilizations." He knew better than to tell her there might not be any civilizations at all.

"I want to go forward, not back," she said again.

"We will be going to the future, not the past. More than 1200 years into the future." By then, they should understand what went wrong with DeepSleep. Perhaps they could reverse the damage that had been done and recover something of the lives they lost on the trip. "It will be a different world, Stella, a different civilization."

"A different world is what I want," she said.

"It will be different," Carlos assured her. "Take us to the future Earth," he told the ship.

"Query for commander confirmation."

"Yes," said Stella. "Take us to the new Earth."

"Preparation is beginning."

Very tired, Carlos let the robot steer his chair back to the waking room, hoping he would wake again.

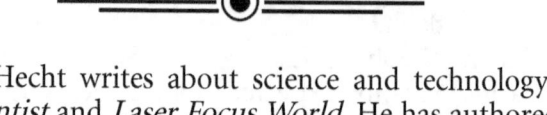

Jeff Hecht writes about science and technology for *New Scientist* and *Laser Focus World*. He has authored 11 nonfiction books, mostly about lasers and optics, including *Understanding Lasers*, now in its third edition, and *Beam: The Race to Make the Laser*. His short fiction has appeared in *Analog, Daily Science Fiction, Nature,* and elsewhere.

Hecht says "The Chatter of the Beams" came from wondering how to make a galactic laser communications network, and how that network would appear to uninvited eavesdroppers like ourselves.

ACCORDING TO THE RULE
DEBRA DOYLE AND JAMES D. MACDONALD

"L-3 Station, this is RS-24, inbound, request permission to dock."

Brother Malachi had the Vespers watch in Control. He flipped on the VOR/DME transponder and the range lights before keying the mike.

"RS-24, this is L-3. Request number of souls on board."

The Vespers bell rang and the first words of the chant came over the station general announcing system, so that those working in the outer gardens and in the control spaces could hold the sunset service in their hearts when they could not be in the choir with their brothers.

At this moment St. James's Monastery at Lagrange Point Three was in full sunlight; even the side of the station away from the sun was bright with reflected light from Earth. But far below on the blue-and-white planet, the abbey of Monte Cassino—the home of their Order, built by St. Benedict himself—was slipping below the horizon, and the monks of L-3 regulated their devotions accordingly.

"One soul on board," RS-24 replied.

"Do you have an emergency?"

"Negative. Visiting and seeking counsel."

Malachi was one of the few brothers in the monastery at L-3 who were permitted to speak with outsiders, and he took his trust seriously. Today was an unusual time for any vessel to approach the monastery. Market day, when the station would lie in Earth's dark shadow and trading ships could come and go safe from the sun's radiation, was still two weeks away. And pilgrims making the long journey to the monastery's shrine and relics for spiritual reasons came but seldom.

Abbot Guy would be at Vespers; Brother Malachi didn't want to disturb him. So he replied, "Permission granted. One to dock," on his own authority.

If the abbot didn't like his decision, Brother Malachi might spend a month doing penance in the monastery's water reclamation unit. But so be it. RS-24 would take hours to come alongside; plenty of time to inform the abbot of his decision.

Brother Malachi ran his hand over his tonsure and felt the stubble. With no one around but his brother monks he didn't bother refreshing it every day. Or every week. Well, then, this visitor would see him shaggy.

Vespers drew to a close. The schedule posted in Control showed nothing between now and Compline. Brother Malachi set the locator light in the abbot's study, so Abbot Guy would know that Control needed to speak with him; checked the course and speed on the incoming rocket ship; got a three-star fix on L-3's real-time location; logged it (*slight drift, need to regain stable point soon*); and said the rosary. A watch spent in Control gave one a great deal of time for prayer and contemplation.

Two decades of the rosary later (the Sorrowful Mysteries and the Glorious Mysteries), Abbot Guy spun the handwheel on the airtight hatch and climbed down into Control, dogging the hatch behind him. Abbot Guy was a great one for damage control routine.

The abbot busied himself with checking the station's status lights before turning to Brother Malachi.

"Brother," he began, speaking barely above a whisper. The Rule of St. Benedict did not command silence, but it did recommend that brothers not engage in idle conversation. Abbot Guy considered most conversation idle.

"Abbot," Brother Malachi said. Rather than say more, he pointed to readouts showing the inbound trajectory of RS-24, now visible on the long-range monitors as a silver disk.

Abbot Guy read, nodded, then made his way to the ladder and climbed away toward the center of the station, his worn black coveralls swishing over the metal.

When the hatch clanged closed and the handwheel spun, Brother Malachi sat back in his hard chair and uttered perhaps the most heart-felt prayer he'd made so far that day.

RS-24 continued its steady approach. The Compline bell rang, calling the brothers to their bunks in the dormitory. Lights dimmed to a pale blue and the station's air circulation system dropped the temperature by ten degrees. On watch in Control, Brother Malachi zipped the neck of his coverall closed against the chill. He offered up the discomfort for the souls in Purgatory and passed the time until the ship's docking in reading from the *Soliloquies* of St. Augustine. When the rocket ship came within range he set the magnetic grapnels to automatic and went up, dogging each pressure-tight hatch behind him, to the docking bay at the axis of the station, where the spin was slowest and the artificial gravity the least.

The station's grapnels hit the rocket ship with a vibration felt but not heard. From the docking bay's control point, Brother Malachi manipulated the boarding tube from the monastery's airlock to that of RS-24, opened the lock's outer door, and awaited the arrival of the one soul.

The outer door cycled closed. Malachi cycled the inner door open, then left Dock Control for the corridor.

A short man in an orange jumpsuit stood there waiting, the pressure suit the man had worn in the boarding tube already peeled away. Gravity was light here, and the slightest touch would push a man toward the overhead, to slowly drift back to the deck as the spin moved the station beneath him. Malachi noted that the man had an unfamiliar mission patch on his left shoulder and a United Federation flag on his right.

"Greetings, pilgrim," Brother Malachi said, and pointed to the row of lockers where other pressure suits were stored.

"You, there," the man said. "My name is..."

"Unimportant," Malachi interrupted. "Are you by chance a priest?"

The stranger shook his head.

Brother Malachi noted the response, then said, "Come, I will show you to a bed. You are invited to join the brothers at Midnight Office in...two hours. If you do not choose to join us, breakfast is in the refectory just after Prime." He turned away. When the pilgrim hesitated, Malachi turned back, said "Come now," spun the hand-wheel on the access hatch to the lower levels, and gestured downward.

Malachi led the pilgrim by a circuitous route to the dormitory, to allow the man to adjust to the steadily increasing apparent gravity.

Once in the long, low hall, close to the outer skin of L-3, Malachi pointed to an empty bed. The other monks made lumps under their blankets where they slept, a gentle snoring and the occasional cough the only signs of life. Nowhere was wholly dark, ever, on the station.

Once he had nodded to the pilgrim, Malachi returned to Control. There he waited until the lights brightened and the bell rang for Midnight Office. As he went up the ladder on his way to the choir, he passed Brother Eusabius heading in the other direction; Brother Eusabius would have the watch in Control until Brother Malachi returned.

In the oratory, Brother Malachi was surprised to see the orange jumpsuit amid the black of the rest of the brethren. The brothers paid no notice to the stranger, their thoughts only on praising God with song. Malachi joined them, thinking no more of the pilgrim himself.

After the Midnight Office the monks processed again to the dormitory; Malachi fell into his bed and was asleep in an instant. The lights coming up and the bell ringing for Matins seemed to him to come only a second later.

***

Matins turned to Lauds, and Lauds to Prime, as the monks sang praise to God. Then Malachi and his brothers processed in silence to the refectory, for a simple breakfast of bread and beer. The beer on the station was good; brewing was one of the things they did very well, with the must from the beer going to the baking afterward.

The brothers ate rapidly, in silence, while preparing for the day: some to the hydroponics, some to the hives, some to the scriptorium, others to the vacuum distillery, or to the zero-gravity workroom where the monastery's famous perfectly-spherical confections were made. Market day in two weeks meant packaging the products for shipment to Earth.

The bell rang again for Terce. All the brethren, save those laboring at tasks that could not be left alone, gathered in the chapter house. First came the reading of a chapter of the Rule of St. Benedict, then a prayer, then Abbot Guy making new assignments and giving penances and...

The stranger stood.

"Sir abbot," he said. "My name is Deighton. I have been sent by the United Federation to inspect this station. I have here a warrant to inspect your finances, to see everything aboard this station and appraise it, and, if it does not meet the standards set by the United Federation, to take control of the station and all its contents for the Federation. I will render my report in two days.

"Now, if it please you, sir abbot, I will see your ledgers. All of them. Now."

Abbot Guy took the news in a placid manner. Decades of contemplation, Malachi told himself, allow one to be philosophical.

"Should the Federation take control of the station," the abbot asked, "what will become of my brethren?"

"They will be given passage back to Earth; what they

choose to do after that is up to them. The ledgers?"

"Brother Malachi will show you everything," Guy said. "I believe that you have already met."

The pilgrim turned to seek out Malachi among the monks in the chapter house. Malachi stood, to make the man's task easier.

"There you are," Deighton said. "Where are the accounts? I wish to see the amounts you produce, the amounts you sell, what comes, what goes."

With Malachi leading, the two men went to the station's archives, where such records were kept. There Malachi opened the rolls and brought Deighton the materials he asked for, but, to Malachi's surprise, the requests did not consist wholly, or even greatly, of records of money coming in and money spent. Rather, Deighton seemed interested in the mass and volume of the monastery, of the sorts of equipment on board, and how often the jets were used to maintain the orbit.

Deighton did seem to have done his research in advance; he checked items against a list on his datapad, and seldom spoke. When he did, it was of matters that seemed odd to Malachi.

"How many monks are on this station?"

"Twelve."

"How long have they been here?"

"Years. I myself, I have forgotten how long, but at least twenty years."

"Fetch me the list of all your brothers. By name, and by the date they arrived."

Malachi produced the ledger.

"You keep this on paper?"

"It is recyclable; we make it ourselves. And paper is not subject to disruptions from solar energy."

"Get a lot of disruptions from solar energy?"

"No."

Deighton ran his finger down the page, took a visual copy, and sorted it. "The most recently arrived brother came here five years ago?"

"Yes. That seems right."

"That was...."

"Brother Peter."

"Is he a young man?"

"Not so young."

The bell rang for dinner.

"Ah," Deighton said, standing. "You must introduce me to all of the brothers." He held the paper list, neatly written in a scribal hand. "Take me to them."

"As you will."

Malachi led the way, but not directly to the refectory. He went by way of the laver, where flowing water allowed the monks to wash their bodies before the noon meal. The used water, along with the dirt and sweat it carried, went back to the hydroponics, there to be turned into vat-grown fruits and vegetables, then into the jams and jellies and brandies that the monks would sell to traders from Earth, where their products were highly prized.

Malachi put his used coveralls on a pile near the head of the laver, and stepped through the flowing water. It was cool and refreshing. He toweled himself dry at the far end, then picked up a fresh set of coveralls from a pile of laundered garments. Other monks would gather the dirty coveralls, mend those that needed mending, then launder them and set them out again for the morrow's use.

Deighton skipped all of that; he was still dressed in his orange jumpsuit when Malachi saw him next in the refectory. A lector—Brother Cyprian, today—stood at the head of the table. The brothers waited behind their chairs while others brought in the noon collation.

Abbot Guy was there with the rest. He shot a questioning look at Malachi. Malachi replied with a shrug.

When eleven were gathered, Deighton made a great show of counting them. Then he asked Malachi, "Where is the twelfth brother?"

"Brother Eusabius is on watch in Control."

"I see. Who is the dean?"

"We being so few, we don't have one," Malachi whispered. He was uncomfortable breaking the silence here.

The monks sat; the abbot blessed the meal; Brother Cyprian began to read aloud from Chapter Four of the technical manual on the maintenance of air-tight doors, concerning gasket testing and replacement.

Deighton sat next to Malachi. He pointed across to one of the younger monks, a black-haired, thin-faced fellow. "That is?"

"Brother Lawrence," Malachi whispered back, much more quietly than Deighton had spoken.

"How long has Brother Lawrence been with you?"

"The list says eight years."

The meal was an excellent one, as always, of bread and ale and cheese; honey and fruit and greens. Still, Brother Malachi did not taste it; his appetite was gone.

When the reading was done the brothers arose, and the server monks cleared away the debris.

"You eat better than most on Earth," Deighton said.

"We grow what we eat, and share what we make with the people of Earth," Malachi said. The man's attitude was testing Malachi's charity and serenity.

"For a price. A high price."

"No more than is needed to allow the community to continue. We set our prices lower than similar produce from craftsmen outside the walls."

"Which puts them out of work because they can't compete."

"I think," Malachi said, after allowing a long pause, "that if you told me what you were looking for I could help you find it more readily."

"Perhaps you could."

The monks were lining up for procession, up through the slype toward the station's core, traveling hand over hand by the bulkhead-mounted safety grips as the gravity grew less.

The great hydroponics tanks, filled with solid water, surrounded the docking bay in the center of the station. They provided most of the mass of rotation, and it was there that the miracle of photosynthesis made sunlight and water into the things that supported the monastery. Here, too, was the final resting place of the brothers who had gone to God, slipped in among the other nutrients.

Once at the cemetery pod of the tanks, the monks knelt in silent prayer.

Deighton spent the time taking measurements and recording his observations.

"Abbot," Malachi said, when he had a moment to do so, "do you wish me to stay with this man or go back to Control?"

"I will find someone to take the watch for Brother Eusabius," Guy replied.

"He seemed particularly interested in Brother Lawrence," Malachi said.

"I noticed."

"I did not tell him everything I knew."

"You did not lie?"

"Not directly."

"Then your penance will be light—and assigned to you after he has gone. So long as he does not learn that the first Brother Lawrence to come here died five years ago, all may yet be well."

Brother Malachi bowed his head. "Lord, hear our prayer."

"You have had a long day, Brother Malachi. Go to the dormitory. I will give our visitor a different brother to guide him and answer his questions."

Obedience is a virtue. Brother Malachi bowed his head again and walked back to the dormitory. He dropped into his bed, the narrow and hard bed of a pious monk, and fell at once to sleep.

The bell for Nones awoke him scarcely two hours later. He walked to the choir, fumbling with the rosary at his belt, in a fog of exhaustion. The service of psalms and hymns Brother Malachi could recite in his sleep; today he nearly did. As he was returning to the dormitory, hoping to get an hour or two of rest before going back to Control at Vespers, a hand reached out to him from an access shaft.

"Brother Malachi."

Malachi was startled. Outside of divine services, members of the Order seldom spoke, and certainly did not converse with one another hugger-mugger in the shadowy maintenance-ways. He looked at the speaker—the novice who went by the name of Brother Lawrence—and said, "I must reprimand you, brother."

"This is a needful conversation," Lawrence said. "That man, Deighton. I saw him look at me and ask questions."

Brother Malachi nodded.

"He's looking for me," Lawrence said.

"No, he is looking at our accounts."

"That's just his story. I tell you, he's looking for me, and now he's learned that I'm here."

"He's a poor searcher, then. He didn't seem to recognize you."

"My appearance," and here the novice seemed amused, "has changed since he saw me last. When I arrived here, I asked for sanctuary; your abbot granted it. When I asked to join your community, he granted that, too. You gave me a new name and worked hard to instruct me in your ways, even though they were strange to me."

"This is idle talk. You are assigned to the laundry; return there." Malachi turned to go, but the younger monk gripped him more firmly by the shoulder.

"Tell me, brother, if it were a matter of breaking sanctuary in order to save the monastery from ruin, would you do it?"

Malachi looked at Brother Lawrence. "No. Would you?"

He did not stay for answer but instead walked back to the dormitory. The Vesper bell would come soon enough.

***

The Vesper service was well under way in the choir, and being broadcast throughout the station to those whose duties kept them away at other tasks, when Brother

Malachi climbed once again down the ladder into Control. To his surprise, Brother Eusabius was not alone at his post. Deighton was with him, and seemed to be questioning him closely. Brother Malachi stood silently by while Deighton asked about the steering jets, and about the reaction mass that kept the station in its place in orbit.

"Every ninety days or so we make a small correction," Brother Eusabius said. He loved his work, and the monastery's stricture against frivolous conversation meant that he seldom had the chance to speak of it at length. "There are only two stable orbits in a three-body system, and we aren't in either of them."

"When was the last time you made such a correction?"

Brother Eusabius pulled over the master log book and began to slowly turn the pages. The illuminated lists of observations and communications transcripts passed under his fingers.

"Surely a computer would be more functional," Deighton said.

"Computers have parts that need to be imported from Earth," Brother Eusabius said, pausing in his perusal of the logbook. "Books like these we can make and repair ourselves."

"Find the entry." A pause. "Please."

Brother Eusabius continued his slow scan of the pages, one by one.

"Brother," Malachi said. "I am ready to take the watch. You still have time to reach the choir for Vespers."

"No trouble, no trouble, I'll have the thing the gentleman wants any minute now."

"I heard his request. I believe I can find the entry he desires."

Brother Eusabius nodded and turned to go, climbing heavily up the ladder to the hatch.

"Is there some reason," Deighton asked, before the hatch had quite finished slamming closed, "that you do not wish me to speak with your pious comrade?"

"Is there some reason you do not wish to speak with me?"

"Only that your abbot assigned you to the role."

Brother Malachi flipped rapidly back to the page where the last course-correction burn was logged.

"That happened on my watch," he said, turning the book around and pushing it toward Deighton.

Deighton transcribed the numbers from the log book. "Tell me, brother," he said, "do you have relics?"

"A fingernail of St. James the Greater. A fragment of the True Cross. A fragment of the cross of St. Andrew."

"I wish you to show them to me."

"I'm sorry, but I can't leave my watch here in Control. Suppose some other vessel were to approach?"

"How likely is that?"

"If someone had asked me the same question at Vespers yesterday, I'd have said not likely at all."

"In a typical...month, let us say...how many vessels approach L-3?"

"Two. Sometimes three. Both bring supplies, both return with produce."

"It will not surprise you to learn that I already knew this."

"No, I am not surprised."

"Nor will it surprise you to know that I know the rated mass of those vessels, and the combined mass that this monastery has exported."

Brother Malachi shook his head. "No."

"Then, perhaps, you could tell me where you get the reaction mass to keep this station in its orbit?"

"We use water from the hydroponic tanks. We add to them from the water contained in the substances shipped here."

"No, brother, that does not work. You are using far more than you can account for in that way. The supply ships do not carry the mass you need in the form of water. So, even though you do not expect a ship for fourteen days, you are standing heel-and-toe watches in flight control. You are clearly expecting smuggling ships. How many smugglers do you see in a typical month?"

"None."

Deighton took out his data recorder again. "Is that because you avert your eyes, or because you do not consider them to be smugglers? Half of each month you are effectively hidden from Earth-based observation, lost against the face of the sun. A small vessel that watched its electronic emissions could come and go unremarked."

"The only ships that come other than the supply ships are those that carry a priest who can say Mass. We are all brothers here, and cannot perform the Divine Office."

"So, other ships do come."

"Yes."

"And are their comings and goings logged?" Deighton riffled through the pages in the illuminated book.

"No. Not here. Perhaps in the Deacon's Book."

"I knew they were not; I saw that you hadn't logged my own arrival. This is a gross violation of the United Federation's regulations concerning the operation of privately owned orbital environments. That means I could shut down this monastery right now. Break it up. Sell it for parts. Auction off its place in orbit to the highest bidder.

"Did you know," Deighton continued, "that some members of the United Federation Council believe that confiscating the property of the independent stations is justified as a revenue-enhancing measure?"

"We are removed from the world," Brother Malachi replied. "All we care about is praising God."

"And selling brandy."

"In order to continue our works, we must support the station. That takes trade."

"As you say. Now, show me the relics."

"When I get off watch."

"No, now. Or would you prefer that I wander the station alone and unsupervised, going wherever I want and seeing whatever falls under my eye?"

"I'll put the station on automatic," Malachi said, "so

that any approaching ship will cause it to send out a general alarm."

"I thought you might come to that conclusion. Now, please take me to the chapel."

"Follow me."

The monastery's chapel was only used when a priest was on board. Now it stood empty and dark, except for the sanctuary lamp glowing red beside the altar.

"Here," Brother Malachi said, after he had pushed over the door lever to open the space. Apparent gravity in the chapel, located as it was mid-way down toward the station's center of spin, was less than half of that in Control. The difference made the deck easier on the knees when praying, which Malachi considered a good thing.

"Now show me the relics," Deighton said. "The True Cross, if possible."

"Here," Malachi said, pointing to a reliquary, silver-gilt, bolted to the left side-altar.

Deighton bounded over to it with the easy leaps of the half-weightless. He reached out his hand and placed it on the cross.

"Brother Malachi," he said, turning. "I request the right of sanctuary. I wish to join your number. Shield me from my enemies."

***

"You're asking us for shelter from your enemies," the abbot said to Deighton. Brother Malachi stood close at hand, awaiting his own penance or further instruction, whichever the abbot chose to give. "Other than Satan, who is the enemy of us all, who do those enemies include?"

"The agents of the United Federation Council."

"Concealing you from them would be difficult. Perhaps it is better that you should give your report. The government below would only send another to complete your work."

"No, they won't. They don't expect a report; they don't even know that I'm here."

Abbot Guy pulled upon his chin. "I confess I am

mightily confused."

"You are away from the world, cloistered. You don't know how bad things are, down below. There really has been talk of taking over the assets of the space stations."

"There is always talk," said Abbot Guy, unperturbed. "Let me take you at your word, and turn you over to the novice master. He will show you your duties and begin your instruction."

Brother Malachi nodded to Deighton. "Come."

They went to the storehouse, where Brother Malachi handed Deighton a plain black coverall. "Leave all your worldly goods," he said. "Leave your name. From this day hence you are Brother Dominic. Dedicate yourself to God."

"Abbot Guy said you were the novice master," Deighton said. "Are there other novices?"

"The time for questioning is past. Listen and learn, and hold your peace. The Rule of Saint Benedict governs us."

Malachi led the new novice down toward the outer ring, on the opposite side from Control. "Here are the air scrubbers and exhaust vents," Malachi said. "Not too different from what you would have found on your ship." Nor, he thought, was there much mischief that a newcomer could do with them, even if he should be so inclined. "They need to be cleaned. Brother Thaddeus—" here Malachi nodded to a severe-looking elderly brother "—will show you where and how. Praise God with work."

That done, Brother Malachi returned to his watch in Control.

***

Compline rang. The light indicating that the airlock in the docking bay was open blinked on. Malachi was surprised to find that he was not surprised. He sent a locator to Abbot Guy and went to investigate, blind-dogging the hatch behind him.

Up he went, gravity decreasing with every level, until he approached the docking control station outside the bay.

There a man approached him with the sure manner of long zero-gee experience, bringing himself to a stop with one hand on a bulkhead safety grip, well outside of Malachi's reach. In the other hand he carried a weapon. He wore Deighton's orange jumpsuit, but he was not Deighton—he was Brother Lawrence, no longer in monastic black.

"Brother Malachi," Lawrence said. "What brings you up here?"

"I was about to ask you the same thing," Malachi replied. "This is a long way from where you should be at this hour."

"I'm not safe here any more. If Deighton could find me, it's only a matter of time before someone else comes looking."

"Do you remember what you asked me?" Malachi said. "If I would break the rule of sanctuary rather than let the monastery be destroyed? The answer is still no."

"I'm afraid I can't believe you. Get Deighton's ship ready for launch."

"As you say," Malachi replied.

He turned to the control spot and fed AC current across all the bulkhead grips. Brother Lawrence—caught with one hand touching the electrified metal—jerked, spasmed, and stiffened.

"You're young," Malachi said to the motionless novice. "Your heart should be healthy. But this will hold you until the abbot arrives."

He secured Lawrence's wrists with electrician's tape, being careful not to touch metal or flesh, then shut off the current.

When Malachi looked out the viewport to the space craft in its magnetic cradle, he noted Deighton's—Brother Dominic's—black-clad corpse floating in the vacuum nearby. "May eternal light shine upon you," he said. Then he went back to his captive, who was now beginning to regain some muscle use. He struggled, but the binding held.

"Brother," Malachi said, "we welcomed you to our community. As we would have welcomed any who chose to stay."

"Joining the monastery—it was all a ruse—he would have taken me away as soon as he got the chance, and turned me in for the bounty."

"Perhaps," said Malachi. "Who but God can know the human heart?" He regarded Brother Lawrence thoughtfully. "The price on your head must have been a sizeable one, for him to risk so much and travel so far in order to claim it."

"Does it tempt you, Brother Malachi?"

"No."

Abbot Guy arrived before the other man could say more.

"Oh, this is a sadness," the abbot said, gazing on the two. "Brother Malachi, what has happened?"

"A game of fox and hound," Malachi said. "Deighton was the hound, and a most diligent one at that; Brother Lawrence here was the fox. When Brother Lawrence grew afraid that Deighton would take him by force from sanctuary, he killed Deighton and would have stolen his ship to get away. And now they are all our problem—Deighton and Lawrence, and that ship out there as well."

"God provides for us," Abbot Guy said, "and the Rule of Saint Benedict is ever our guide. I doubt, though, that a simple rebuke, or a penance, would serve. But Saint Benedict, all those millennia past, was wise, and in the Rule we read, 'If any pilgrim come from distant parts, if he wish as a guest to dwell in the monastery, and will be content with the customs which he finds in the place, and does not perchance by his lavishness disturb the monastery, but is simply content with what he finds: he shall be received, for as long a time as he desires.

"'If, indeed, he find fault with anything, or expose it, reasonably, and with the humility of charity, the Abbot shall discuss it prudently, lest perchance God had sent him for this very thing.

"'But if he has been found lavish or vicious in the time of his sojourn as guest, not only ought he not to be joined to the body of the monastery, but also it shall be said to him, honestly, that he must depart.'"

Malachi nodded understanding. "'And if he does not go, let two stout monks, in the name of God, explain the matter to him.'"

"Just so," said the abbot. "Who do you—?"

"I believe Brother Genesius and Brother Martin are our stoutest."

"So, brother," Abbot Guy addressed Brother Lawrence. "Honestly, you must depart."

***

"I had been wondering," Brother Eusabius said to Brother Malachi at the changing of the watch in Control the following Vespers, "where we were going to get the reaction mass for our next needful orbit correction."

"That ship will serve quite well."

"A pity about Brother Lawrence," Eusabius said.

"Yes," Malachi replied. "He shall ever be in my prayers. But I fear that he did not have a true vocation."

Debra Doyle is a science fiction and fantasy writer living in far northern New England. She has a Ph.D. in English literature from the University of Pennsylvania. Her forthcoming works (co-written with James D. Macdonald) include the novels *The Gates of Time* and *Emergency Magical Services: First Response.*

James D. Macdonald is an sf/fantasy author living in Colebrook, New Hampshire. He is the co-author, with Debra Doyle, of the "Mageworlds" space opera novels; their forthcoming publications include *Emergency Magical Services: First Response* and *The Gates of Time* from Tor, and "The Clockwork Trollop" in *Beneath Ceaseless Skies.*

AGAINST POWERS, AGAINST PRINCIPALITIES
DUNCAN EAGLESON

The videophone buzzed. I glanced at the big glass bubble, but it showed no holo, just the calling number, the visual feed had been blocked. Some people resent it when you do that, but in my business, prospective clients are often shy at first; if I just ignored those calls, I'd lose business. I flipped the connect switch and said my name.

A man's voice asked if I did missing persons.

"Sometimes," I said. "I'd need to know the circumstances."

"Can we meet?"

***

The man was prompt. My building is an older one, and doesn't have a gravity tube installed; we rely on an old-fashioned elevator. I heard the elevator stop on my floor, and moments later I opened the door on an average-sized fellow, 40-ish, slim and gangly. Square, determined jaw below, a mop of dark hair starting to gray above, and an eye implant (you can always tell by the metallic sheen in the iris). He introduced himself as Eric Larson. I ushered him into my inner office. We sat down, and I asked what he needed.

"A colleague of mine disappeared a few years ago."

"Cold cases are difficult; they can eat up time and money and usually come to nothing. Was he a close friend?"

"Not really." He hesitated. "Only a casual acquaintance, but someone I respected, and was intrigued by."

"So intrigued you'd front the money to fund an investigation? For a casual acquaintance?" I quoted him a fee, and it wasn't low. Of course, that eye implant wasn't a cheap one. He surprised me by nodding.

"Yeah, actually. The money I made in games was small by some standards, but it was substantial by mine. Let's do this."

"Okay. But why now?"

"Couldn't afford it at the time. Now I can."

"Fair enough. So tell me about it. From the beginning."

"Before I got into designing games, I worked for the government as a computer tech. This was back about the turn of the millennium. Got assigned to a secret SSC..."

"SSC?"

"Supercolliding Superconductor. Amongst ourselves, we called it the 'Desertron.' It was a project supposedly abandoned in '93, but secretly completed in '96. Went live the following year. Accident closed it down permanently in 2001. The whole story was declassified last year, or I couldn't even talk to you about it."

"Another reason you waited."

"Yeah. Whiteside disappeared after the place closed."

"Full name?"

"Martin, Martin Whiteside. If he had a middle name, I never heard it."

"Was there an investigation at the time?"

"Not that I know of."

The scientists who ran the Desertron were perfectly capable of maintaining their own supercomputer, but most were too busy with other stuff. Larson had joined the computer tech staff in '99. He soon discovered that Whiteside, of all the scientists there, seemed to have the least understanding of the computer that ran the collider, although he was, according to Larson, a genius at chemistry and physics.

This facility they worked at was a ring tunnel 54 miles long. Using magnets placed along the path of the tunnel, they accelerated particles to ridiculous speeds and smashed them together to see what would happen. The thing was three times the size of the one at CERN, and sent those little babies flying along with three times the energy.

To the layman, it would seem like these guys were courting disaster, right? I mean, splitting apart fundamental particles, that's what an atomic bomb does, no? But apparently these scientists were confident they could contain and control what happened, and not turn all of eastern Texas into a parking lot.

Fortunately for everyone concerned, they were more or less right. More, because as you may be aware, eastern Texas still exists. Less, because there eventually was an explosion. It wasn't on a Hiroshima scale. It happened inside the tunnel, and was contained underground. The good citizens of nearby Waxahatchie (pop. 28,000) probably thought they were experiencing a mild earthquake.

On the day in question, the team had started the run as usual. A half hour in they began getting anomalous readings, and then came the explosion, which damaged (as far as Larson understood) a couple of miles of those magnets, filled the tunnel with helium gas and dust, and required a complete evacuation. The place was shut down, and a hazmat team was sent in to clean up. The scientists and other personnel had expected to return in a few days or weeks to figure out what exactly had happened, but in the end they were all reassigned. Larson ended up at Lawrence Berkeley National Lab in Berkeley. He had heard that Whiteside had been assigned to SLAC down in Menlo Park, but when he attempted to contact him, emails brought no response. There were no listings for a Whiteside in any of the communities around Menlo Park, and SLAC had never heard from him. Or of him, as far as Larson could determine.

"Well, some of them knew *of* him, by reputation. He'd

published a couple of articles. But there was no record of his assignment there."

"Maybe you just heard wrong about where he went."

"Maybe. But there's no record that I can find of him being assigned anywhere."

"Probably he went to work for the private sector."

"Possibly. But then, why can't I find him?"

"I don't know. What else can you tell me about him?"

"He was a kind of weird guy. Fascinated with pop culture. I mean, most geeks are, right? We get into *Luke Starkiller* and *Star Trek* and *Captain Arclight* and shit like that, but mostly it's because we grew up with it. Whiteside, it was like he'd never seen any of this stuff before. I wondered sometimes if he was raised by the Amish or something, y'know? Isolated from TV and so forth."

I thought to myself that isolation wasn't required to miss out on some bits of pop culture. I wasn't sure I remembered Captain Arclight myself. I was sure I'd seen at least one of the *Starkiller* movies and maybe some old episodes of *Trek* at some point. But I kept this observation to myself.

"And he had a real bee in his bonnet about Scientology," Larson continued. "Not like he was a member or anything. Just the opposite. More like he saw whatsisname, their founder, as the Antichrist or something."

I asked what had been the official line about the accident that closed the place.

"Miscalculations about the strength of certain magnets." He didn't sound convinced. I arched an eyebrow. He said, "You asked for the official explanation. Some of the guys think it was sabotage."

"By who? The Chinese? Koreans?"

"There are several theories, but I don't know of anyone with any hard evidence. Still, a lot of people who worked there are very uneasy about the whole thing."

This sounded like a potential disaster. I could see no reason the government would be covering up whatever the source of the accident really was. But if they were, I could be stepping into some deep shit.

In spite of that, I agreed to look into where this Whiteside might be. Larson provided me with a couple of photos, obviously cropped from larger group shots, and a little fuzzy. They showed a solid figure with a broad face, curly, dark hair, and a mustache. His eyes seemed to me to have the gaze of a fanatic. Not angry and threatening. There was too much merriment in them for that. But a fanatic nevertheless. However, that was my intuition speaking, and I locked the impression away for the moment, pending further data.

***

People go missing one of three ways: either they've done a runner, disappeared intentionally for their own reasons; they've been kidnapped or killed; or they've met with some sort of accident and the body remained unidentified. The first two scenarios are more common than the third and, fortunately, easier to track. Connecting a missing person to a John Doe in the morgue who died through some random accident is needle and haystack time. If, on the other hand, someone runs or gets taken, there's always a reason for it. If you look close enough at their life, that reason will eventually show up.

Once Larson had left, I grabbed my hat and communicator and left the office. As I approached the elevator, I was flanked by two guys in black suits. One was middle aged and large, one older, gray haired. I looked from one of them to the other, examining their profiles as they stared at the lighted numbers above the elevator. We were on the fourteenth floor; the elevator was creeping up from eight.

"You know," said the younger man on my right, "Eric Larson isn't a very stable individual. He quit writing games, and now he paints. He thinks the implant helps him perceive reality more accurately, or some such shit."

Ten became eleven.

"Yes," said the older man. "Artists...imaginative and unreliable. I wouldn't take one on as a client, if I were

you."
Eleven became twelve, and then fourteen. There was a ping.
"No," said the younger, "it wouldn't be wise."
"Well, then," I said to the one, "it's good I'm not you," and to the other, "and I'm not your kind of wise guy."
The elevator doors rolled open. Two women and a man in a suit got off, and I stepped toward the stairs, away from Mutt and Jeff, but they were gone. I looked around, saw no one. The elevator doors were closing, and I stepped forward, grabbing the door and looking into the empty elevator. I debated going back to the office for a weapon, but decided against it.
Everything about these two guys had screamed government agents. If the whole affair of the Texas SSC, the so-called Desertron, had been declassified, there was no reason for any government agency to run interference on Larson's attempts to find an old colleague. Maybe Larson was wrong. Or maybe he was holding out on me. These two mugs showing up as soon as Larson left suggested they were watching him. There was more going on here than some scientist dropping out of sight.
This did not bode well. I hate cases that look like they're running afoul of a government cover-up. Government agents, like cops, should be there to serve and protect. When a government starts covering up, their agents start acting like the citizens are the enemy, treating them like spies and criminals. Which is so wrong on so many levels, and it really pisses me off. Mutt and Jeff probably expected their not-so-subtle bullying would put me off the case, but in the famous words of John Lennon, you can't always get what you want.
Downstairs, I took a hovercab to Wessex Central to rent time on a station. "Wessex" is how most folks pronounced WCSC, the West Coast Super Computer. It had a huge database, and could connect to the National Master Super Computer in Arlington. A lot of information is available locally, and there's much more if you're willing

to wait for the connection to National. Unless you were law enforcement or government, certain sections were classified and unavailable, but you could still put a lot together from the public record.

Since the Texas SSC materials had been declassified, I was able to find records of Whiteside's employment there, along with his CV. Routine inquiries would show his academic career traceable through the college and university databases, but oddly there were no pictures of him in his schools' yearbooks or publications. No reference to him, in fact. When I started contacting people, no one I spoke to from his various graduating classes remembered him.

The same was true of his jobs since graduating. HR records showed his employment, but no one remembered him. And as far as I could determine, he was an orphan with no family, and had remained single.

I started visiting and interviewing people connected to the Texas SSC, the only place anyone actually recalled Whiteside so far. I talked to all sorts: department directors and janitors, computer specialists and mechanics, physicists and cafeteria cooks.

Support staff, who had less contact with him than the scientists, loved him. "Dr. Whiteside was always very kind and polite," one of the kitchen staff told me. That was typical.

The scientists and technicians told another story. "Whiteside? Yeah, I remember him," the other IT guy, Chuck Sendak, said. "Nice guy, but a major pussy hound. If it had boobs, he wanted to fuck it.

"I had this odd conversation with Whiteside once. We were both a little drunk, so take it for what it's worth, but he seemed to think that Tim Leary was really onto something with his LSD research. Claimed the government had shut Tim down because they were afraid of a populace that could think for itself and question received reality. Then he goes on to defend the MWI..."

I held up a hand. "Excuse me? The MWI?"

"Many Worlds Interpretation," he said. "More formally known as the Everett/DeWitt Interpretation of Quantum Mechanics. It says there are many alternate realities running consecutively. It's a nifty theory, but it's got no practical application, since we can never access those alternate universes. But Whiteside claims that certain drugs and mental techniques can open our minds to those other realities. It kind of surprised me. Whiteside didn't seem like the hippie drug-freak and conspiracy theory type. And it turned out he had this whole Libertarian thing going on."

I also asked Sendak about the anomalous readings.

"Is that what they're calling them?" he asked, chuckling. "The singularity was generating numbers. Pi, to be precise. To thousands of places. Followed by a series of prime numbers. A coherent, intelligent communication sourced in a singularity. I guess you could call that anomalous."

None of the scientists had a clear idea about what had caused the explosion, but it was clear none of them bought the official line. They all had their pet theories, but none of them had been allowed to go back and examine the site. So, being scientists, they all hedged their suggestions with lots of ifs, ands, buts, and maybes.

Some of the other staff weren't so restrained. "So one day, I'm doing routine maintenance on the magnets, right?" this tech had told me. "Now, daily, weekly, and monthly maintenance, unless there's a special problem, you don't take things apart much. You just give it a once over, make sure everything's shipshape. But every quarter, you do a complete strip down of the magnet assemblies and containment sphere. So I'm on this quarterly check, right? And on the inside of the magnet, where you wouldn't see it unless you looked real close, I see this design carved. Like a letter from, I dunno, ancient cuneiform, or maybe Klingon script or something. At first, I thought it was some scientist's goof, right? Like pilots painted Jane Mansfield on their planes. I could totally see one of these guys carving their initials in ancient Mayan, or a good luck sign in Wookie hieroglyphics, right? So I didn't think a whole lot about it.

"But then I found another one. And that one looked familiar. I've got an aunt who's a hoodoo woman. She reads cards and does love potions and shit. I'd seen that sign somewhere in her store. I was sure of it. So now, I'm looking out for them, right? Altogether, I find nine of them, all concentrated around the containment chamber.

"Now, I dunno what that was all about, but what I saw tells me one of them scientists in the control room was into some weird shit. Did that cause the accident? No idea. But it makes you think, don't it?"

Yeah, it did. I wasn't a believer in magic, but I knew even some very intelligent people were. Einstein was very religious in his own odd way, and Tesla used to claim he got his designs from angelic visions. It takes all kinds, and genius often goes hand in hand with madness. Sendak had said Whiteside believed in alternate realities. Was it Whiteside who made the carvings? And if so, what was his purpose? Was he trying to sabotage the collider, or protect it? If he was trying to sabotage it, he might have back-stopped his spells with real world techniques, tinkering with the magnets, or planting an explosive charge. Larson had said the man was fascinated with pop culture, especially sci-fi. Maybe he pictured himself as Luke Starwalker —*no, it's Starkiller*, fighting to save the Republic from the Empire.

Armed with the results of the interviews, I returned to the Wessex station to dig deeper. Apparently I'd already found all the available documents referring to Martin Whiteside, so I tried combining the search term "Whiteside" with "physics." The fourth hit or so (after physics teachers in Whiteside, TN, and Whiteside, MO) gave me the story of John Whiteside Parsons.

"Jack" Parsons isn't well known to the general public today, but he's the man who made NASA and JPL possible, thanks to his invention of solid rocket fuel. Along with

Von Braun and Goddard, he was one of the fathers of the modern US space initiative. He was also a crazy occultist, and was involved with the famous Satanist Aleister Crowley, and L. Ron Hubbard, the founder of Scientology. Hubbard ran off with the guy's mistress and fifty grand of his money. You gotta know that grabbed my attention.

Parsons supposedly died in an explosion in his garage in 1957. There are lots of conspiracy theories around that event—claims that he was murdered by the government, specifically Naval Intelligence. Some said future Scientologist Hubbard was the agent who planted the bomb. Others claimed it was Howard Hughes. And so forth. I wasn't buying into any of the theories whole hog, but there was surely something fishy there. Was Martin Whiteside a relative or even the son of Jack Parsons, out for revenge on the US government? Wild speculation, maybe, but not completely impossible.

When I came across a photo of Parsons, I was convinced I was on the right track. I pulled out the photos of Martin Whiteside and compared them to be certain. Sure enough, if you changed the haircuts and clothing styles, they could be the same man.

Parsons had left some writings behind, and I checked them out. A lot of it was poetic ranting in the style of his occult mentor, Aleister Crowley—what my ex-wife used to call "uncurbed doggerel." There were also political articles. He seemed to be a libertarian, who believed there was a government conspiracy to control the public's minds. That sounded familiar.

***

One of the maintenance women from the SSC had remembered that Whiteside had an account at the same bank she used. She'd seen him making a deposit there. I traveled to Waxahachie and visited his bank branch. My fake federal ID got the manager to cooperate.

"I could go get a subpoena," I told him, "but I'm in a hurry, and I don't really need to take copies of his records at this point. I just need a look at them."

"I dunno," said the manager, shaking his head. You could tell he wanted to be a good citizen and help the law out, but he was worried about the niceties. He glanced quickly sideways at a framed picture of himself shaking hands with President Clinton and Vice President Obama. Obama was smiling, but Hilary looked forbidding, like a puritan ancestor.

"Look," I said. "If we need to use any of that informa- tion as evidence, we'll have to come back with paperwork and get copies. It wouldn't be admissible, otherwise."

"I suppose..." he muttered. He nodded, and consulted a large ledger. He spoke into his desk mic, requesting the books for a certain account number. "This may take a few minutes," he said. "Please make yourself at home in the meantime." He nodded and left the room.

When he was gone the vacuum system thunked, and a slim file landed in the receiver. I sat in the manager's chair and pulled out the file. There were Martin Whiteside's account records. I scanned through them.

In the months before the explosion at TSSC, he'd gradually cleaned out his account. In the beginning, there were some large payments to a Juan Marvel. Later, the larger payments were to a holding company in the Caymans called Thelematics, Inc. Whatever else was going on, Whiteside hadn't been in this game for the profit. By offshore holding company standards, the amounts weren't impressive. Bernie Madoff or Mitt Romney would consider it amateur hour. But for your average family of four who didn't need to own multiple mansions, yachts, and racehorses, it was a nest egg you could live comfort- ably on for a lot of years. I was gone before the branch manager came back.

As I walked to my rented hovercar, I was braced again by Mutt and Jeff, the men in black. The younger one said, "We need to talk to you."

"Call my office," I said. "Make an appointment." The older one chuckled. The younger one grunted, and I felt something hard jammed into my ribs. "Or," I said, "we could talk now." They each took an arm and frog marched me down the street.

"You need to stop asking questions about things that are best forgotten," said the older man.

The younger one dug harder into my ribs with his gun, or whatever it was. "You don't want to be remembering such things," he said. "You could always be sent back, you know."

"Sent back?" I said. I had never been in prison. He meant "killed," of course. Neutralized. Retired. Terminated with prejudice. Every government agency seemed to have their own euphemism for it. I wondered which one used "sent back."

The older man said, "We prefer not to take such extreme actions unless you give us no choice."

The younger one pulled the trigger. It was a nerve gun. My whole body shuddered with pain. I went blind, and felt or heard from a distance the clatter and thump of a body falling to the pavement. The pain of the fall was drowned out by the spasms of pain radiating from my side. Vision wavered in to show the street appeared sideways, and I was staring across it.

"Let all that shit stay forgotten," said a voice in my ear.

The image of the sideways street went black, and I saw other pictures: a giant pair of twin skyscrapers falling, a war in a desert, bombs going off in storefronts and parks, children being gunned down. I saw sparkling vampires, and children in games of death, and random people chosen for torture and humiliation for the amusement of a national audience.

Then I was looking at the street again. Someone was bending over me, asking was I okay. I grunted that I would be. Five minutes later, I was staggering to my rental hover.

So there was some reason the government wanted to keep a lid on the story of Martin Whiteside, or of what had happened at the Texas SSC, or both. I'd considered the possibility that Whiteside was trying to sabotage the supercollider, either using magic spells or physical means, or both. Had the government discovered his activities and "disappeared" him? Or was it something else entirely? If Whiteside had not been a saboteur, perhaps he'd been a witness, and had vanished courtesy of some witness protection program.

The smart thing to do was give it up. Charge Larson for what I'd done so far, return the balance, and call it quits. But then, sometimes I'm not so smart. I get a little obsessed with stories. I need to know what happened and why. It's why I got into this business. Larson's money was good, and apparently plentiful. And while real cops sometimes resent private investigators, and we resent 'em back, what I really resent the most is supposed upholders of the law abusing their position to cover something up.

In the bowling alley of life, you can be a ball, or you can be a pin. I'm not real good at standing still.

***

Juan Marvel was a Mexican citizen, and the primary stockholder in Thelematics, Inc. He owned a small house on the outskirts of Guaymas.

Guaymas was hot this time of year. In the old days I'd have been sitting in a stifling car on a dusty side street, or broiling on the deck of small boat, watching the seaside house with binoculars. Today I was sitting in an air conditioned hotel room a mile away, watching on the videophone the feed from four miniature cameras I'd placed the previous night. It was more efficient, more comfortable, but just as boring most of the time. When Sr. Marvel finally appeared on camera and turned out to look remarkably like Martin Whiteside, I did not put on my "shocked" face.

I watched the cameras steadily. Marvel/Whiteside stayed in the whole evening. The following morning I took a short break to make a breakfast run. Early morning was safest, since Whiteside seldom rose before ten. Returning with coffee and rolls in a paper sack, I saw two familiar figures step out of a rented ziphover, and enter the hotel across the street. It couldn't be a coincidence. They were either here for me, or for Whiteside, or both. I dropped a bug on their ride. Later, watching the video feeds, I saw their rental hover cruise by the Juan Marvel house. It lingered for a few moments, then moved on.

**

That evening I watched the blip that represented Whiteside's Cooper Mini leave the house and head into downtown Guaymas. I had a good idea he was headed to his favorite bar, but I fired up an electronic cigarette and watched anyway, just to be sure. I had to proceed carefully.

The green blip moved across the map into downtown Guaymas, while the red blip that traced the Feds' car remained motionless. Either they were stationary, or they'd found the tracker; there was no telling which. Whiteside's car parked about where I expected it to. The La Paloma was three blocks away. I headed out of the hotel and down the street to the bar.

Guaymas is on the shores of the sea of Cortez, and in season they do a fair tourist trade. The La Paloma Bar gets a lot of that trade. Even in the off season, you'll often find a few Americanos hanging out there. Whiteside probably first came here as a tourist, liked it, and continued to go there after he established the Marvel identity. He spoke Spanish, but no doubt he'd long for the company and conversation of other ex-pats. They always do.

The air conditioning in the La Paloma couldn't overcome the rancid smell of old cigarettes and beer, but it made it bearable. I hoisted myself onto a seat two down from Whiteside and ordered a Tecate. The scientist was smoking a Pall Mall, with a shot of mescal and a sweating bottle of Dos Equis in front of him. There was no military service on his record, but he had that thousand-yard stare that was common to combat vets. I wondered what he'd seen to give him that look. When my beer arrived and the bartender wandered off, I lit a Marlboro and fought not to cough, unused to real tobacco smoke.

Whiteside looked over at me. Nodded. I nodded back. Then I moved into the seat next to him, bringing my beer with me.

"Tell me one thing," I said. "Did you really believe the sigils by themselves would take down the collider?"

He stared at me for a moment. Then he laughed. He looked around the room.

"I'm alone," I said. "It's just you and me." And the Glock in my waistband under the Hawaiian shirt, but I didn't mention that. "Although I can't promise it will stay that way. There are a couple of guys in black suits hit town this morning. I have a feeling they'll be wanting to talk to you or me or both of us before long."

"I suppose it was inevitable. And you're with...?"

"I'm private. Eric Larson hired me to find you."

"Eric Larson." He shook his head, chuckling. "Well intentioned, I'm sure. But for Eric's dime, you led the notorious men in black right to me."

"I don't think so. In fact, I'm pretty sure they already knew where you were, and were trying to prevent me finding you." If Whiteside didn't want these guys finding him, that eliminated the witness protection scenario. Or did it? I was just assuming the men in black had been from some government agency; they hadn't shown me any badges or ID. "But you didn't answer my question."

"The sigils? They weren't intended to take it down. They were intended to enhance its effects. What makes you think the men in black already knew where I was?"

"Like I say, they tried to stop me tracing you. Enhance the effect in what way?"

"That these guys want to prevent anyone else from finding me doesn't necessarily imply that they have found me themselves. Do you remember the Mount Palomar explosion in '91?"

"Vaguely. It interfered with the beginning of some big project, didn't it?"

"A photographic survey of the southern sky, yeah. But they were able to restart the following night. The damage was minor."

I thought about the date. '91 was the first year the

sources on Whiteside started to corroborate each other. Co-workers remembered him. There were pictures documenting his existence.

"You were in San Marcos in '91," I said. San Marcos was close by the Mount Palomar site. Whiteside nodded. "You had something to do with that explosion."

"How do you think I got there from a garage in Orange Grove?"

I wasn't sure where Orange Grove was, but I knew Parsons had died in a garage. "You're trying to convince me you're really Jack Parsons? Raised from the dead, or traveled through time, or something?"

He smiled. "You've done your homework. The stories are partly true. There really was an agent sent to kill me, though it wasn't Ron Hubbard. "

"Or Howard Hughes?" He laughed at that.

"No, it wasn't anyone famous, just an anonymous intelligence drone. He was too late, though. I'd assassinated myself. The body was a tramp who'd died in a local poor clinic, cleaned up and dressed in my clothes."

His story was patently impossible. He couldn't be Parsons. The man would be in his late eighties. This guy was fifty at the most. At best, he might be Parsons' son or nephew. I played along. "So where did you go?"

"Away," he said, "to another dimension. A parallel reality. The time distortion was a side effect." I didn't scoff out loud. He looked at me hard. I've got good control of my face, but he saw something there. "You think I'm either bullshitting you, or batshit crazy. Fair enough. Tell me, in tracking me down, did you talk to Chuck Sendak? Did he tell you what he saw on his monitor, moments before the Desertron explosion?"

"Pi."

"The number Pi, yes, and a list of prime numbers. Sourcing from the point of impact. And that implies what?" I knew he'd tell me if I didn't answer, so I just spread my hands. He gave me an intense look that put me in mind of Orson Welles, if Orson had made fifty without

getting grossly fat. "It implies, my friend, conscious intelligence on the other end. Another world. An alternate
reality. Are you familiar with the Everett/DeWitt Many
Worlds Theory?"

"Sendak explained it a little."

"The membrane between realities is not imper-
meable." He stared at me for a long time. Drew another
Pall Mall from the package, lit it from the dying one in his
hand, which he then crushed out in the ashtray. "You don't
remember *Captain Arclight*, do you? Or why Merillee
Harwood is such a big star? But you do remember *Star
Trek*. If I said 'Reality TV,' or '9-11,' most people would
look at me blankly. But those words have meaning for you,
don't they?"

I remembered my hallucinogenic visions when I'd
been zapped out by the men in black. Yeah, those words
held meaning, though I couldn't pin it down. It was like
the sense you get of a dream having been important,
though you can't quite remember it.

"Not...quite."

"I'll bet you become confused sometimes, have
trouble with names. Who is the president of the United
States? Is that movie hero called Starkiller or Skywalker?
Who is Katrina, a woman, a ship, or a storm? Was
Kennedy assassinated, or did he die in a plane accident?"

I realized I couldn't answer any of those questions
with any certainty. My mind groped at them, feeling the
edges...I should know these things. Kennedy was assassinated, sure, shot in a motorcade, but then wasn't the
Kennedy Memorial in the shape of a plane? Starkiller, no,
Skywalker was the hero of that Blue Harvest movie...or
was he? Was Hilary the president, or Obama, or was it
maybe even a Republican? My stomach was trying to
swallow itself and my face and shoulders were cold, sweat
standing out on my forehead. I had a twinge of fear for my
sanity. I wondered if he had drugged me or was doing
some sort of neurolinguistic programming or hypnosis or
something. A person's perception of reality can be manip-

ulated by words and images; I'd done it myself many times. Like conning the manager of Whiteside's bank: I had shifted his reality to one where he was cooperating unofficially with the proper authorities. With Whiteside I had tried to keep my expressions neutral, but an expert can read the best of poker players. He had to be cold reading me, making a series of guesses based on subtle reactions to what he said and how he said it, using what he learned to manipulate my state of mind.

"Yeah," he said, "they'll want to shut you down. Because the rest will come back to you, sooner or later."

"The rest of what?"

"You're getting glimpses of another reality, my friend."

I shook my head. It was science fiction nonsense. My communicator made a soft buzzing noise. I took it out and glanced at the screen.

"Our friends are on their way here, I think. They're only a few blocks away."

"Then we must move quickly." Whiteside drained the mescal shot, followed it with the rest of his beer, and turned toward the door, gesturing me to follow.

"Where?"

"My house. It's been prepared."

"It's the first place they'll look."

"We'll be gone by then."

I drove.

***

"What exactly did you do?" I asked, as we hovered down the street, fast but not too fast, not wanting the attention of any cops. "Why would these guys be after you?"

"What did I do? I attempted to tweak the experiment, and it backfired. Qabalah, physics, chemistry, they all revolve around math. The architecture of reality. The sigils did not create the dimensional breach. They simply brought a particular set of equations to bear. The particle collision would open a door, but the sigils would direct which door it opened."

"But you didn't have a particle collider in Orange Grove."

"Ultimately, all events on the macro level of our phenomenological world are dependent on quantum fluctuations. Those quantum variables can be affected by conscious attention. Just as light becomes a wave or a particle, depending on your observation of it, life may be one way or the other, depending on your perspective. In some realities *Captain Arclight* may be bigger than *Star Wars*, or America's boogiemen might be Middle Eastern terrorists, rather than Chinese conglomerates." His words raised the hair on the back of my neck. The Arabs had been poor cousins since solar, wind, and geothermal energy had replaced fossil fuels. The US didn't bother to meddle in their politics any more, and they seemed content working out their differences, Muslim and Jew. Had to, really, in order to survive economically. China's economic war had been the biggest threat to America's interests in recent years. And yet the unfamiliar term "Middle Eastern terrorist" had caused my guts to go cold.

"There are two ways to effect profound change on the macro world by working at the quantum level. One is to bring massive physical force to bear, flinging particles against each other, as in a supercollider. The other is to bring will to bear, conscious intention, like the intention of the scientist to measure the light." He was talking about magic, occult rituals. I wasn't sure I was ready to buy that.

"But light is what it is," I said. "It *appears* to be a wave in some cases or a particle in others because of the sort of tests and instruments the scientists use to observe it, not because of the observer's intention."

"Certain of that, are you? Many physicists aren't."

"What about the explosions?"

"What did you expect would happen when you punch a hole in the fabric of reality? A nice set of chimes and an angelic chorus?"

"'Now I am become death, the destroyer of worlds.'"

"Yes, an atomic bomb or a black hole violates reality in the same way, and you know what happens with them."

"But you survived it."

"I was technically elsewhere when it happened."

I pulled the hover around behind his house and set it down. We got out to find Mutt and Jeff framing the back door.

"Well, Mr. Whiteside," said the younger man.

"Jack," said the older one.

"You fuckers again," said Whiteside. "Say, have you seen my latest? It's dazzling."

There was a blinding explosion of light, and a scuffle. Someone banged into me, and then tackled me to the ground, his hand grabbing my wrist, preventing me drawing the Glock. As we struggled blindly, I heard the sound of running footsteps, fading away. Then other footsteps chased after. My sight gradually came back, the blurry form of the older man above me, a rough shape of the house behind him.

"You don't want to follow him in there, shamus. You think he's opening a door on great new vistas, but we know better. He's stepping into a world of hurt." He leaned in, inches from my face, a great blurry shadow breathing tobacco and liquor and cologne and breath mint on me. "I know you, shamus. You're thinking 'bully with a badge.' It's your goblin, isn't it? You think we're your darkest fear? We have a very narrow jurisdiction, just to prevent incursions of this nature. Imagine a world entirely in the power of men like us, where our jurisdiction was unlimited. That's what's on the other side of that gateway. You, sir, do not want to go there. Nor do you wish for it to come here. And that is what we are here for. To prevent that. That is our charge and our purview."

Running footsteps again, coming closer this time. At that moment, the house exploded.

***

Mutt and Jeff had vanished. Whiteside's house was a smoking ruin. The local police assured me there were no human remains in the wreckage. When I reviewed the videos later, my cameras showed Whiteside going into the house, but not coming out before the explosion. They did not, for some reason, show either myself or the men in black. I am at a loss to explain why.

A package left for me at my hotel contained extensive handwritten notes about design flaws Whiteside had found in the Texas SSC. It also contained a slip of paper with the inscription *Eph 6:12*. The bible in the drawer at my hotel told me that Ephesians 6:12 said:

> For we do not wrestle against flesh and blood, but against the rulers, and authorities, against powers, against principalities of this present darkness, against the spiritual forces of evil in the heavenly places.

When I made my report to Larson I gave him the notes from Whiteside about the Desertron, and informed him that Martin Whiteside had perished in an explosion in Mexico. As far as I was concerned, that was the truth.

I admit it, I liked Whiteside, crazy though he was. His crazy had been fox-like enough for him to pull a vanishing act, and I had to respect that. I figure he's in Yoruba or Tahiti these days, soaking up sun, getting laid, and working physics problems in his head. What, you expected me to imagine him in some other dimension, some more idyllic place where he's mastering non-Euclidean geometry or something? Or some reality where a black man, instead of a white woman, is president? Not a chance. The guy was a loon.

And yet the men in black had been real, had pursued him. Even if they were not government agents, they worked for someone with power, someone in charge, someone who didn't want the status quo disturbed or the boat rocked.

"Against powers, against principalities of this present darkness..."

They were powers of my own darkness, those men in black. My fear, my hatred, my disgust for the abuse of power and the tyranny of authority. Where fear and the restriction of human thought and capabilities rule, humans become warped and stunted and sick.

I thought of myself as the detective, the scientist of the hunt, a rational man, free of superstitions and credulity. But if I was honest with myself, I wanted to believe. It felt right to something in me, as if I knew those other places, where other realities existed. As if I had been there and forgotten them. How this was possible, I couldn't say. Whiteside probably could have, but he was gone. It frightened me.

The videos don't show him leaving the house, but there was no body.

The videos also don't show the men in black. Or me.

Why do I remember Middle Eastern terrorism, reality TV, slaughters in schoolyards, a movie called *Star Wars*, when this world holds none of these things? Didn't I grow up in a world where Kennedy died in a plane crash in his second term? Where the Berlin Wall fell in '73? Where Captain Arclight saved the universe in 90 minutes, became a cultural phenomenon, and prevented the star from ever getting a serious acting role again?

No. No, these things I know by rote, at second hand. They are like facts read from a history book, not lived experiences. The others, those are memories. Memories the men in black would prevent me from confirming. Once, they had threatened to "send me back." At the time, I thought they meant kill me. Now I think I know what they meant, and I know that they were lying. They'd never send me back. It's what they're sworn to prevent.

Be the ball, or be the pin.

I began collecting the writings of Martin Whiteside and Jack Parsons.

Duncan Eagleson is a writer, illustrator, and sculptor, maskmaker, and creator of the "Railwalker" series (railwalkercomics.com). He has written and illustrated the graphic novel version of Anne Rice's *The Witching Hour*, and his work has appeared in Neil Gaiman's *Sandman*, and the DC/Piranha Press "Big Books" series, as well as on a number of book covers and film posters. He has published a number of short stories and is currently writing his fourth novel.

About "Against Powers, Against Principalities," he says: "It always struck me that if anyone really could make apparently impossible fringe science work, it would have been someone like Jack Parsons. Most of the historical material about Parsons in 'Against Powers, Against Principalities' is true (as far as I know), including the fact that he supposedly died in an explosion in his garage in 1952. Though several conspiracy-minded websites do suggest that Parsons was assassinated, none has claimed his assassin was either L. Ron Hubbard or Howard Hughes; to the best of my knowledge those rumors were my own invention—though to my mind they are certainly typical of the sort of rumors that do crop up on the interwebz."

THE ENHANCEMENT
MIKE RESNICK

You want to know why the courts are more over-crowded than ever? I'll tell you why. It's all Arturo Rubichenko's fault, but he's too damned busy basking in the public's adoration to know or care about it.

I remember how the media was so thrilled with him and his breakthrough. They covered it daily for almost two years, and of course Rubichenko won the Nobel Prize and damned near every other prize and award a grateful world could devise. Word is that he actually pulled down almost two billion dollars in prize money.

I never understood exactly how it worked. I still don't. I probably have that in common with everyone in the world except six or seven scientists. All we knew was that somehow he injected something—I can't even spell the word, let alone pronounce it—into a Bonobo chimpanzee, and six months later, in a series of carefully regulated lab tests, it had an IQ of 93. We all thought it was truly remarkable.

Then he injected the same damned thing into a cat, and the cat's attendants—PhD's all—actually taught it how to read and to manipulate a specially-made computer keyboard, and she had an IQ of 104.

That was fine too, and the chimp and the cat actually toured the world, showing off their enhanced IQs, and people were saying that all he had to do now was find out how to make it work on people, and the human race would take a quantum step ahead.

The first seven humans he injected died, and that was the end of our march toward an intellectual Valhalla.

But something else happened, something that no one predicted or expected. The chimpanzee and the cat both had offspring. The chimp's firstborn had an IQ of 117 at four years of age, and the cat's six kittens ranged from 101 to 124.

It wasn't long before they started mass-producing the miracle. We were all in favor of having more brains in service of humanity. After all, we didn't care who came up with scientific and medical breakthroughs, as long as somebody or *something* did.

We're still waiting for the breakthroughs—after all, a 105 IQ isn't more likely to cure cancer or Alzheimer's just because it's between a cat's ears instead of a human's—but that doesn't mean the world hasn't changed.

Especially *my* world. I'm the Judge of the Circuit Court.

Take last Tuesday, for example. My first case was brought by the 600-pound gorilla who sat down next to his attorney and glared sullenly at me.

"Harvey Kerchak versus MGM Pictures," announced my bailiff.

"And who is representing Mr. Kerchak?" I asked, because while every animal you see these days can think, frequently better than the average man on the street, they still can't speak.

"Bradley T. Driscoll," said the well-dressed lawyer, getting to his feet.

"And the nature of his complaint?"

"My client wants all versions of all Tarzan movies immediately withdrawn from circulation," answered Driscoll. "We would like them destroyed, but will settle for them being locked in a vault and never withdrawn without my client's permission."

"I assume you have a reason?" I said.

"The apes in the films are portrayed as cute, mindless chimpanzees, whereas in the novels they were much larger, quite intelligent, and totally verbal, able to articulate as well as you and I."

"These films were made before what has become known as the Enhancement," I noted.

"Nonetheless, the public showing of these motion pictures causes my client untold emotional pain."

If it's untold, I felt like asking, *then why the hell are you in court telling me about it?* Still, a conscientious judge always looks for a compromise that will satisfy both parties in a dispute.

"Would it cause untold pain if it were shown only in theatres, so that members of Mr. Kerchak's species could easily avoid it and not encounter it accidentally on television?"

"You might ask if a film from the same era portraying members of the Negro race as slow-witted 'darkies', or a film showing women as nothing more than mindless and willing sex objects would be acceptable to blacks and females who do not set foot in the theatre but must deal with the subsequent behavior of those who *do* attend."

"All right," I said. "Let me just be sure about this. Your client has no objection to the source material?"

"He strongly approves of the books," replied Driscoll. "And the comic strips and comic books as well."

"There are comic books?" I asked.

"Certainly, Your Honor."

"And Mr. Kerchak approves of them?" I continued with the vague feeling that parts of my literary education had been sadly lacking

"Yes, Your Honor. The apes in the comic books are, if anything, even more intelligent and articulate than the apes in the books."

I turned to the opposing attorney. "Has MGM any rebuttal?"

"You have made it yourself, Your Honor," she replied. "The films were created prior to the Enhancement."

Both sides presented more arguments, while I tried to concentrate on what they were saying but found myself thinking about the weather, and my garden, and even the girl in the short skirt in the third row.

Finally they finished, and I told them I'd consider their arguments and would deliver a verdict in two days.

Then the bailiff declared a fifteen-minute break and I retired to my chambers. I sat down, lit a totally-illegal cigar, leaned back, and tried to remember why I went to law school and what kind of cases I hoped I'd be deciding when I became a judge. Finally I sighed and shook my head sadly. Who the hell ever thought that saying "Sit, goddamn it!" would become a serious First Amendment case? Or that a trio of Clydesdales could bring a suit claiming that the constitutional negation of the Dred Scott decision applied to them as well? Did I really become a judge to rule on the antiquated legality of "Once a plow horse, always a plow horse"?

After I finished the cigar I nodded to the bailiff, who went out ahead of me to tell everyone to rise when I entered and that court was back in session.

I sat down and looked out at the plaintiff's table, where a collie sat perched on a cushion atop a stool.

"Fluffy versus Columbia Broadcasting System," announced the bailiff.

"Has the plaintiff a surname?" I asked.

"No, Your Honor," said the plaintiff's lawyer.

"All right," I said. "What is the nature of his complaint?"

"*Her* complaint, Your Honor," the lawyer corrected me.

Big deal, I thought. "All right," I amended. "*Her* complaint."

"It seems that the popular television show, *Lassie,* is using a male collie in the title role. This is clearly a case of sex discrimination, and my client seeks redress."

I rolled my eyes, cursed Arturo Rubichenko for the thousandth time, and began counting the minutes to my retirement.

Mike Resnick is, according to *Locus*, the all-time leading award winner, living or dead, for short science fiction. He has won 5 Hugos (from a record 36 nominations), plus a Nebula and other major awards in the USA, France, Japan, Catalonia, Poland, Croatia, and Spain. He is the author of 71 novels, more than 250 stories, and 3 screenplays, and the editor of 41 anthologies. His work has been translated into 27 languages, and he was the Guest of Honor at the 2012 Worldcon. In additon to his writing, Mike is also the editor of the Stellar Guild line of books, and of *Galaxy's Edge* magazine. In his spare time, he sleeps.

THE AMAZING TRANSPARENT MAN
JAMES MORROW

Until I ran afoul of Professor Tomasz Ostrowski, I had always assumed that the first condition for becoming a ghost is death. In this I was mistaken. I am as spectral as any entity might be—I have even taken to haunting a castle, a monstrosity called Castèllo Maciste, whose nocturnal corridors have thus far witnessed my comings and goings for nearly a year—and yet I remain fully enfleshed. My pulse is strong. Blood flourishes in my marrow. Electric sparks illuminate my brain.

Ostrowski, I now understand, was a mad scientist in both senses of the term, being at once a stranger to sanity and a slave to rage. But the man had appeared neither crazed nor angry when, ten months ago, I first laid eyes on him. The occasion was my Monday evening talk at the Boston School of Finance and Commerce, an entry in their renowned Adam Smith Invisible Hand Lecture Series. My moment in the BSFC limelight had been billed as "Broderick Arbuthnot on the Enduring Legacy of Melina Kostopoulos," and I'd taken the opportunity to explicate the late Greek émigré's astute trifurcation of post-industrial humanity into three categories: parasites, practitioners, and prime movers. Although I concentrated on Kostopoulos's nonfiction work, especially *Capitalism Unbound* and *Marx without Tears*, I also noted the subtle ways in which this thinker's economic theories undergirded her novels, most conspicuously that astonishing 1168-page free-market swashbuckler, *Achilles Cringed.*

The Q&A session lasted nearly an hour, largely because nobody was anxious to venture into the storm-drenched streets of Back Bay. I'm pleased to report that my audience of impassioned young Kostopoulists accorded me a proper measure of deference, as befitted my status as the venerable paterfamilias and laurelled CEO of Synesthesia Capital. True, I had to cope with a couple of malcontents, ideologues who insisted that in celebrating Kostopoulos's philosophy I was "promoting a guru of greed" and "pimping for a whore of exploitation," but these detractors were more to be pitied than despised.

When Professor Ostrowski presented himself to me in all his aging but aristocratic glory—heavy gray overcoat, mellifluous voice, matinee-idol features (now supplemented by crow's feet and laugh lines but still striking)—I immediately discerned that he was no parasite, and obviously rather more than a practitioner. There he stood, as stolid and polished as the lectern around which my admirers had gathered, silencing the Kostopoulists with the power of his magnetic presence, and I soon realized I was entertaining that rarest of birds, a prime mover.

"Please call me Tomasz," said Ostrowski, shaking my right hand and pressing his business card into the left. A partially opened umbrella hung from his arm like an immense bat, the black fabric wicking droplets of rain. (Evidently he'd entered the BSFC auditorium during the final moments of the Q&A.) "By the time our collaboration is up and running, Dr. Arbuthnot, I hope I'll have earned the right to call you Brod."

"You may call me Brod right now," I assured him.

"My personal assistant will contact you before the week is out," said Ostrowski, depositing a data marble in my palm. "I'm offering you an unprecedented investment opportunity," he elaborated, then added, with a knowing wink, "No doubt you heard that exact same claim six times before breakfast."

"Seven, actually," I replied, smiling as I slipped the marble into my vest pocket.

"This is different, Brod," my prime mover insisted. "It's not simply a technological breakthrough. Call it a miracle." He turned and marched into the crowd, which parted under the pressure of his charisma, then called over his shoulder, "Ostrowski Enterprises will reward your faith beyond the dreams of avarice!"

***

Not until I was back home on the upper East Side, sharing take-out Szechuan with Valerie, my wife, did I remember about Ostrowski's data marble. I poured Valerie a second Chablis, replenished my own glass, and visited my cavernous closet, where I retrieved the little sphere from the charcoal suit I'd worn for my Boston talk. Sidling into my office, I popped the marble into the 3-D drive, then explained to Valerie that we were about to see a piece of puffery about an ostensibly revolutionary device whose inventor hoped to acquire my backing. But I was wrong. The video in question, *The Strange Case of Tomasz Ostrowski*, was an ancient PBS documentary chronicling the achievements of a brilliant mathematician who, in a single year, had solved two previously impenetrable Millennium Prize puzzles: the Hodge conjecture and the Reimann hypothesis. In both cases Ostrowski had refused to accept the million-dollar purse, explaining that "sharpshooters don't spend their time winning kewpie dolls in sideshows." Instead of basking in his accomplishment, Ostrowski disappeared from the public eye, devoting the next thirty years to creating a stone-by-stone replica of Italy's fabulous Castèllo Maciste, a project he pursued on Nobska Island off Cape Cod, using funds that came his way after it developed that his investigations of the Poincaré conjecture (proved by Grigori Perelman in 2003) had military applications. Despite Ostrowski's high-minded refusal to pocket the Millennium Prize money, he evidently had no qualms about selling his topology patents to the Defense Department for an astronomical sum.

During the decades that Castèllo Maciste was under construction, Ostrowski gave but one interview, to a hippie webzine called *Demimonde*, using this forum to announce that he was "working on the bedeviling technical conundrums posed by the three greatest science-fiction movies of the late nineteen-fifties, *The Fly*, *4D Man*, and *The Amazing Transparent Man*, each of which turns on an uncanny connection between flesh and physics." The documentary ended with a bright red question mark superimposed over a helicopter shot of Castèllo Maciste's granite doppelgänger, followed by the end credits.

"In other words, Ostrowski has accomplished the not uncommon transition from mathematical prodigy to delusional eccentric," said Valerie. "If I were you, I wouldn't invest a wooden nickel in his visions."

"Darling, you are, as always, the epitome of prudence and the soul of reason," I said. "And yet my instincts tell me he's the real thing, a genuine prime mover."

"*The Fly?* Give me a break, Brod."

"I've never heard of that movie," I confessed.

"It's about matter transmission."

"*4D Man?*"

"I caught it on the Tachyon Channel when I was a kid," said Valerie. "A scientist learns to defy matter, ends up walking through walls."

"There's a theme emerging here," I noted. "*The Amazing Transparent Man*—the title speaks for itself."

"You're supposed to be investing in technologies, not fantasies," Valerie noted.

"Matter transmission, matter transcendence, matter transparency: they all sound equally lucrative."

"Or at least equally alliterative," said Valerie. "Rather like prime movers, practitioners, and parasites," she added with a subtextual grin. She was not a Melina Kostopoulos fan. We all have our blind spots. "Take my advice and steer clear of Ostrowski. The man is several sandwiches short of a picnic. If and when you talk business with him, leave the Synesthesia piggy bank at home."

***

The following morning, just as my prime mover had promised, his personal assistant, a Ms. Leticia Attebury, telephoned me at the office. Ostrowski, she explained, had given her the week off so she could come to New York and chase down a couple of well-reviewed Tennessee Williams revivals, *The Rose Tattoo* and *The Glass Menagerie*. (Not much of a theatergoer myself, I routinely pass up opportunities to lose buckets of money backing Broadway plays.) We agreed to meet that afternoon for *Kaffee und Kuchen* at the Café Sabarsky on Fifth Avenue.

Thanks to the Cinema Caprice component of my cable package, I'd recently seen all three of Ostrowski's favorite late-fifties science-fiction movies, each of which posited a technology that indeed partook more of the miraculous than of the feasible. Thus it happened that, when Leticia Attebury walked into my life, clad in leather and swinging a Guggenheim Museum bag, she immediately put me in mind of the ravishing female engineer played by ex-Miss Universe Lee Meriwether in *4D Man*. Large eyes, high cheekbones, voluptuous proportions: all of these assets helped inspire my acquiescence to her employer's demands.

"First condition," said Leticia, according each syllable an enchanting Louisiana inflection. "You will tell nobody, neither friends, family members, nor business associates, of your impending audience with the Professor."

"Very well."

"Second condition. Nobody will accompany us to Castèllo Maciste, not even your wife, secrecy being imperative at this stage of your relationship with Ostrowski Enterprises."

"If you insist."

"Third condition. Plan to spend an entire weekend on Nobska Island, the better to appreciate the Professor's invention in all its facets."

"You'll be happy to hear I've done my Hollywood homework," I told the comely Leticia. "So which is it—

matter transmission, matter transcendence, or matter transparency? Personally, I hope your boss is following in the footsteps of the 4D Man. I've always wanted to walk through walls."

"I'm not free to identify the new device, and even if were to speak its name, I couldn't answer your questions —I haven't seen a demonstration yet."

"By the way, the Professor got one fact wrong. *The Amazing Transparent Man* is not a late-fifties movie. It was released in 1960."

"Keep that under your hat, sugar pie. It would spoil Tomasz's whole day. He isn't merely a genius—he's also a perfectionist. It makes us all a little crazy."

***

Three days later the Synesthesia Capital jet touched down in the precinct of Logan Airport reserved for private planes, and within the hour I was zooming south down Route 495 toward Cape Cod, Leticia at the wheel of her Fiat convertible, her bemused passenger using his Omphalos-101 to follow the progress of an impending Synesthesia deal: our intention to underwrite Corporality Incorporated, whose founders believe they are two years away from growing inexpensive human transplant organs in their Denver R&D facility.

As we approached the Bourne Bridge, Leticia took a sudden detour off Route 25 into the town of Stonewich. The further we advanced, the seedier the community became, until we reached a trailer park called, preposterously enough, Fairview Terrace, or so the sign atop the gateway proclaimed. Detached toilet bowls and rusting 55-gallon drums littered the landscape. The local religion seemed to be an especially primitive form of Catholic paganism, or so I surmised from the statuary dotting the grounds, including three plaster representations of the Virgin Mary and a carved limestone likeness of some dreary saint or other.

Leticia drove us to the hub of the park, a wide belt of crabgrass strewn with rusting lawn furniture on which lolled a dozen of Fairview's most prominent indigents. Grimy children roamed about this mockery of a village green, playing with a pack of barking, whimpering, doubtless unvaccinated dogs. We parked within spitting distance of a mobile home clad in ghastly pink aluminum. On all sides woebegone residents presented us with smiles compromised by erratic dental hygiene.

"Are we lost?" I asked.

"No, sweetie, but these people are," said Leticia, waving her arm in a gesture so sweeping it encompassed the entire enclave of New England hillbillies. "Half of them are unemployed, and the other half have dead-end, minimum-wage jobs. Were it not for the Professor's generosity, most Fairview tenants would be forced to choose between paying the rent on time and feeding their children nothing but macaroni. I'm happy to report that Tomasz's plans go far beyond charity. He hopes to locate his first factory—"

"Factory?"

"Once he gets the financing, Tomasz will put his miracle into mass production. He's already acquired the land—sixteen industrially zoned acres near Marshfield. The idea is to employ trailer park residents from all over the state, at wages high enough to convince even the most venal bank to give them mortgages."

"If our prime mover wants to become a local hero, that's fine with me," I said. "Synesthesia Capital is always happy to—"

"Turn parasites into taxpayers?"

"I wouldn't put it that way."

A middle-aged Fairview tenant, dressed in a beige cowboy shirt and dungarees, a black patch over his left eye, rose from his nylon-webbed chair, shuffled forward, and doffed his John Deere cap. "Hi there, Leticia. Who's your friend?"

"One of the Professor's business associates. Isaac Goshen, meet Broderick Arbuthnot."

Isaac presented me with an unwashed hand, and I saw

no choice but to shake it. "Any pal of Doc Ostrowski's is a pal of mine," said the counterfeit cowboy.

"Isaac's a concrete man," said Leticia. "Used to make good money repairing our nation's bridges, but then Congress decided that such spending was contrary to God's will."

Two more indigents approached the convertible, a plump middle-aged white woman and a grizzled old black guy, and the same ritual repeated itself: the introductions, the handshake, the artificial bonhomie. "Marge was once a reading specialist at Stonewich Elementary School," Leticia explained, "but then the taxpayers revolted, and her job disappeared. Delbert works part-time serving chicken burgers at Poultry Palace, no benefits, no possibility of a forty-hour week. Perhaps you'd like to stroll around Fairview Terrace a bit, get to know the Professor's future employees."

"I think not," I said.

"After all, they're *your* future employees, too, honey lamb."

"I haven't even seen Tomasz's business plan," I protested, my hands jerking to and fro as if I were using a cocktail shaker. "To say nothing of his miracle."

"Flesh and physics," said Leticia. "Nobody does it better."

***

After frittering away another twenty minutes chatting with her peasant friends, a hiatus during which I amused myself by scanning the Internet with my Omphalos-101, reading the latest round of Corporality Incorporated e-mails, Leticia finally restarted the car. We returned to Route 495, crossed the bridge to the Cape, and fought our way through the impacted traffic to Falmouth.

The fleet in the local marina included Ostrowski's private ferryboat: the *Pelican,* a coastal cruiser manned by an elderly husband-and-wife crew, Antonio and Anita Maniscalco. We left the harbor posthaste, sailing through a caul of mist and murk. Entering the frigid galley, I made myself some hot tea, but before I could take a sip Mrs. Maniscalco appeared and drew my attention to a dozen crayon drawings thumb-tacked to the walls, all rendered by a preadolescent artist whose preferred subject was sea monsters. The most vivid images included a giant squid attacking a frigate, a sperm whale capsizing a brigantine, and a crab the size of a backhoe holding a helpless swimmer in its claw.

"My grandson did those," Mrs. Maniscalco. "He's dyslexic. They're wonderful, don't you think?"

Wonderful was not the first word I would have used to describe young Bobby's oeuvre. *Imaginative*, perhaps. *Intense.*

"They're all for sale," Mrs. Maniscalco informed me.

"Fancy that."

"You can also buy them on Bobby's website. One dollar per drawing."

"Priced to sell," I muttered.

"Cephalopods dot com."

"I see."

"Which is your favorite?" asked Mrs. Maniscalco.

"I can't decide," I said, thinking that Ostrowski would have an easier time attracting investors if he didn't make them first run a gamut of trailer-park gypsies and entrepreneurial grandmothers.

***

At long last Nobska Island emerged from the haze, the sandy mass surmounted by a vast Gothic edifice whose magnificence had been ill-served by the half-dozen murky longshots featured in *The Strange Case of Tomasz Ostrowski*. In a tone that sounded alternately menacing and matter-of-fact, Leticia explained that throughout the weekend my personal electronic devices would have only limited utility. All the Professor's guests were "obliged to be incommunicado," for the island lay within "a bubble that screens out Wi-Fi and microwaves."

Two of Ostrowski's people were waiting for us on the dock, an elegant Brazilian butler named Almodovar and a zaftig Ukrainian maid called Natasha, grinning minions who promptly took charge of my luggage and guided us up a helical stone staircase to the central courtyard. Leticia bid us adieu beside a sundial guarded by marble cherubs, whereupon Almodovar and Natasha led me through a vestibule, down a corridor carpeted in red velvet, and into an elevator so spacious and agreeable I would happily have accepted it as my sleeping quarters—though of course my actual accommodations proved larger and more luxurious yet: a third-floor suite boasting a sauna, a wet-bar, a cabinet filled with high-end snacks, and paintings (not prints but pigment-on-canvas originals) of lobstermen and seascapes. Almodovar informed me that a full hour would elapse before he returned and escorted me to dinner, an interval that I profitably employed in consuming crackers-and-caviar, taking a shower, and changing into my evening clothes.

My first full meal at Castèllo Maciste was predictably resplendent, a candlelit affair keyed to lobster thermidor and Dom Pérignon, but the corresponding conversation was unexpectedly insipid. Dressed in a black silk caftan, Ostrowski offered only the most perfunctory responses to my queries about his youthful mathematical conquests, and Leticia was equally taciturn when I asked why a southern belle would decide to seek her fortune above the Mason-Dixon line. (She merely revealed that she'd attended Bryn Mawr, married a Philadelphia lawyer, divorced the man without remorse, and now looked forward to employing her organizational skills "for the greater good of Ostrowski Enterprises.") I wondered whether my prime mover and his personal assistant sought to stupefy me in the moment, so that the promised postprandial demonstration would seem awesome by comparison.

On the dot of 8:00 PM my host lifted a brass bell from beside his empty champagne glass and rang it thrice. A cadaverous man in the livery of an eighteenth-century footman strode into the dining hall—the majordomo of the castle, Ostrowski explained, Bartolomé—his outstretched arms cradling the most dazzling raiment I'd ever seen, an ensemble complete with hood, tunic, tights, boots, and gloves, its every thread seemingly spun by worms who dined exclusively on ambrosia and angel's milk. Accompanying Bartolomé was a tall, square-jawed, muscular young man, dressed only in a G-string and black socks, like an actor in a pornographic film.

"With apologies to H.G. Wells," said Ostrowski, "I submit that no drug engineered to make flesh and bone transparent could ever be of commercial value. The human visual system, you will recall, depends on retinal opacity. A pharmacologically created invisible man would be—"

"Blind?" I suggested.

"Stone blind, exactly," said Ostrowski. "Shortly after embarking on my search, I realized that the answer lay not in chemistry but in—curiously enough—legends and fairy tales: all those fantastical accounts of rings, hats, cloaks, and capes that render the wearer invisible. Behold the crowning achievement of my Poincaréan explorations, the world's first functional Tarnkappe, soon to make my nephew disappear from view."

As the young man clothed himself in his uncle's ingenuity, Ostrowski explained that the Tarnkappe's "epidermal layer" was festooned with millions of tiny "organic prisms." Spawn of recent breakthroughs in nano-topology and molecular optics, these "living, breathing jewels" were arrayed in such a matter as to collect the photons emanating from every opaque object in the immediate vicinity.

"Imagine a sphere with a ten-meter diameter, its axis running straight through my nephew to an imaginary north pole two meters above his hood and an imaginary south pole two meters below his boots," Ostrowski elaborated. "Once the prisms are set to spinning, they redistribute the photons along the entire outside surface of the Tarnkappe, thereby conferring upon the wearer the appearance—nonappearance, I should say—of transparency."

It all sounded plausible enough, but I wasn't yet ready to shatter the Synesthesia piggy bank. When it came to Ostrowski's invention, only seeing—or, to be precise, not seeing—would be believing.

With proficiency and panache, Gilles costumed himself until he glistened head-to-toe like a test pilot wearing a phosphorescent pressure suit. Ostrowski instructed him to touch the sensor above his left clavicle. The young man complied. Instantly the Tarnkappe's components melded into one another, gauntlets fusing to sleeves, hood to tunic, tunic to tights, tights to boots, so that Gilles's entire face and form seemed clothed in an incandescent leotard.

"Truth to tell, the inner layer was even more difficult to contrive than the prismatic coating," said Ostrowski. "The dermis had to be sufficiently porous for the wearer to suck up liquid nutrients, yet translucent enough to permit unimpeded vision. I further engineered the dermis to rapidly process every sort of human exudate. Saliva, mucus, semen, urine, fecal matter: all such substances are disintegrated and sluiced away within seconds of their appearance in the gap between flesh and fabric."

"And menstrual blood?" asked Leticia.

"Of course," said Ostrowski. "In other words, the consumer can live comfortably inside his Tarnkappe for weeks, even months, at a time. And now, Gilles, kindly spin the prisms."

The young man touched the sensor above his right collarbone, and a noise evocative of a hornets' nest filled the dining hall. As the drone built to a crescendo, Gilles suddenly vanished—poof!—and I found myself staring at the wallpaper and wainscoting behind him.

"Astounding!" cried Leticia. The drone dropped to a whisper, then to utter silence.

"More wine, uncle?" Gilles inquired from out of the aether.

The Professor nodded. Abruptly the champagne bottle levitated two feet off the credenza, floated toward Ostrowski's glass, and filled it to the brim.

"Amazing!" I gasped in spite of myself.

An instant later Leticia's butter knife defied gravity, ascending from her plate, soaring toward the bread basket, and implanting itself in a small baguette.

"Marvelous!" exclaimed Bartolomé.

Now a silver candle-snuffer leaped off the hutch, swooped across the dining table, and extinguished the flames in the central candelabra.

As the room darkened, Ostrowski said, "Come back to us, dear nephew," pitching his voice toward the young man's presumed location.

A disembodied match flared to life, then magically relit all the dormant candles. Seconds later a porcelain clock decorated with Dresden figurines flew off the mantle and glided through the air, borne by phantom hands.

"How time flies when you're having fun!" said the ghost.

"Come back *now!*" demanded Ostrowski.

The airborne clock returned to its original location, the hornets started buzzing again, and Gilles materialized before the mantle, bowing modestly as Leticia accorded him a round of playful applause.

"How is a Tarnkappe powered?" I asked the Professor. "Tiny dry cells?"

"The wearer's own electrochemical energy sustains the rotation of the prisms," Ostrowski replied. "In theory this technology could keep a person transparent until the moment of his death."

"How many have you produced so far?"

"You're looking at one of nine existing prototypes," said Ostrowski. "Gilles is wearing an ectomorph model, but I can just as easily outfit a mesomorph, an endomorph, and every intermediate sort of body."

"Tomasz, you have excellent marketing instincts," I said.

Gilles pressed his left clavicle, causing the Tarnkappe's components to separate. No sooner had he stripped back down to his porn-star attire than Almodovar entered the dining hall and announced that, per his master's instructions, coffee and pastries had just been served in the laboratory.

"If you prefer, I'll have the staff bring dessert up here," said Ostrowski, "but I'd like to show you the place where the prototypes were born."

Leticia retrieved her butter knife from the baguette, then turned to me and said, "This is a rare honor. Tomasz has never allowed me in his lair before."

**

Ostrowski led us out of the dining hall, down a spiral staircase, across a storage room, through a riveted bronze door, and into his private workshop. The subsequent hour found us sitting around an emergency generator savoring French roast coffee and a deliciously decadent assortment of éclairs, macaroons, petites madeleines, and Saint Honoré cakes, their sweet aroma counterpointing the ambient fragrance of ozone and battery acid.

"Naturally I have a thousand questions," I said, selecting a chocolate éclair.

"That's why you're here for the whole weekend," said Ostrowski.

Whether by design or serendipity, the immediate décor evoked my prime mover's cinematic inspirations. A towering Tesla coil reminiscent of the force-field amplifier in *4D Man* stood adjacent to the generator. Eight cuboid, free-standing booths not unlike the matter transmitters in *The Fly* rose along the nearest wall, each draped in a prototype Tarnkappe. A diode-encrusted cylinder suggestive of the phallic x-ray machine in *The Amazing Transparent Man* occupied the far corner.

"What do you see as the primary selling point of Tarnkappes?" I asked.

"If we ignore the criminal possibilities," Ostrowski replied, "voyeurism would probably head the list. On a higher moral plane, I can envision this product keeping marriages intact. It's much harder to cheat on your wife if she can follow you wherever you go."

"Unless the husband and his mistress are also wearing Tarnkappes," said Leticia, availing herself of a petite madeleine. "Tell me, Tomasz, is it possible for a couple to —"

"I don't see why not," said Ostrowski. "Their intercourse would lack complete tactile satisfaction—all that intervening fabric—but it could hardly be more discreet. And *en passant* the Tarnkappe provides reliable contraception."

"How convenient," said Leticia.

"The retail price for a single ensemble would be...what?" I inquired.

"We'll discuss that tomorrow," said Ostrowski.

"As much as an automobile?" I persisted.

"Probably as much as a house. Let's just enjoy our dessert, all right?"

"To build and staff a factory in Marshfield would require an investment of...?"

"Cocktail hour commences at four o'clock tomorrow afternoon," said Ostrowski, elevating his open palms like a policeman stopping traffic. "You'll find me on the south veranda. I'll bring my laptop. We'll talk about sex, religion, and spreadsheets."

***

Please try to understand. Accord me what sympathy you can. It was not my idea to investigate the concupiscent possibilities of Tarnkappes on that rainy Saturday morning. When Leticia knocked on my door shortly after 10:00 AM and, upon gaining admittance, slid a shimmering prism-suit from her portmanteau, I had no idea that she intended to seduce me.

"Does Tomasz know you have one of the prototypes?" I asked.

"I borrowed it with his blessing," Leticia explained. "He's anxious to learn how the device behaves when the wearer is in a state of sexual arousal."

"I don't understand."

She approached the bed and set the Tarnkappe on the top blanket—slowly, gently, as if the miraculous threads held a sleeper who must not to be awakened, lest a curse descend or a kingdom fall. Pivoting, she entered my personal space, then came nearer still. Like a safecracker plying his trade, she rotated the top button of my pajamas, north, north by northeast, northeast, east by northeast, east, and back again.

"Now do you understand, honey lamb?" she asked.

"Yes," I croaked. "I'm a married man," I added.

"This isn't adultery—it's product testing," said Leticia, pulling off her cashmere sweater. "Would you like to disappear first, sweetie, or shall I?"

"Product testing," I said, kissing Leticia on the lips. "The consumer—like the customer—is always right, and I stand eternally ready to serve him."

The Tarnkappe performed exceptionally well that morning, as did the humans who alternately wore it. Although our activity partook of fornication, I decided that, in light of what Ostrowski had called "all that intervening fabric," it fell short of unequivocal fucking. The spinning prisms were more stimulating that either of us expected, filling for Leticia a vibratory, near-cunnilingual function during my interval as an invisible man, and, when it was she who vanished, treating me to sensations commensurate with fellatio.

"So what did we just prove?" I asked. "That your boss has invented the world's most expensive sexual aid?"

"I like that, sugar pie," said Leticia, laughing. "When these suits start rolling off the assembly line, make sure Tomasz puts you in charge of the ad campaign."

***

I spent the balance of the afternoon learning about life inside a Tarnkappe. Prismatic transparency, I discovered, could be as disorienting as it was exhilarating. Because the fabric rendered my feet imperceptible and muted my tactile sense, the mere business of walking required considerable effort. With my hand invisible and my fingers drained of feeling, simply opening a door became a demanding task, accomplished largely through kinesthetic feedback.

This being the weekend, I reasoned that Natasha the maid had been allotted time for her personal amusements, and so I proceeded to the servants' quarters. Natasha's door was unlatched. I slipped in unobserved. She had recently stepped from the shower, a living, breathing iteration of Praxiteles's vision of Aphrodite. My eyes feasted on Natasha's form, my enraptured cock exploded, and I fled before my labored breathing betrayed my presence.

Following my puerile descent into voyeurism, for which I shall attempt no justification, I made my way to the kitchen, where I undertook the challenge of nourishing myself. While solid food was out of the question, the mesh over my mouth readily admitted fluids, and I proceeded to consume a lunch of carrot juice, yogurt, and India pale ale. My culinary experiment was not without mishap. In consequence of my limpid extremities and compromised sense of touch, my right hand bumped an orange-juice bottle, which toppled off the counter and smashed into a hundred pieces.

At four o'clock, having acquired reasonable proficiency in the art of imbibing while transparent, I proceeded to the south veranda for the scheduled cocktail hour. Swathed in a gold lamé caftan, his face shadowed by an immense straw hat, Ostrowski sat before a glass-topped, wrought-iron table overspread with the essentials of the moment—vodka, tequila, scotch, crème de menthe, Drambuie, Kahlúa—the six bottles encircling the Professor's laptop like obelisks hedging a sacrificial altar. Holding my breath, treading softly, I crept toward Ostrowski, reveling in my camouflaged condition.

"Boo!" I said.

"Boo yourself," Ostrowski replied, unperturbed. Evidently my arrival was noisier than I'd imagined.

"Who knows what evil lurks in the hearts of men?" I persisted, then added, cackling, "The Shadow knows!"

Now Almodovar arrived on the veranda, inquiring whether his master wanted "the usual." Receiving Ostrowski's nod, the butler set about preparing a cocktail of vodka and Kahlúa.

"Press your right clavicle, Brod," Ostrowski instructed me, accepting his black Russian from Almodovar. "I won't do business with a man I can't see."

I touched the relevant sensor, and the prisms spun to a halt. As my coruscating ensemble emerged from the void, I slipped into an empty chair and surveyed the placid harbor. The *Pelican* lay at anchor in the bay, the waters glittering in the setting sun like a vast tapestry woven of Tarnkappe fibers.

Ostrowski removed his straw hat and fanned himself with the brim. "Before you take off the hood, I'd like to observe your drinking technique," he told me. "What will you have? A black Russian? Rusty nail? Brave bull? Vodka stinger?"

"A brave bull."

Almodovar concocted the requested drink, then passed me the glass. I raised the crystal cone to my lips and sucked a mouthful of tequila-and-Kahlúa through the mesh.

"Well done." Ostrowski restored the straw hat to his cranium. "Do you mind leaving the hood in place for now? I want to watch for unseemly dribbling."

"As you wish."

"Leticia tells me you've been exploring the sensual dimensions of Tarnkappes."

"I've never strayed from Valerie before," I said, my voice diminutive, my manner abashed, then took a second sip. "Well, perhaps once or twice. In any case, Leticia insisted that we had your blessing."

"Everything that happens on this island has my blessing," said Ostrowski, "or it doesn't happen at all."

The brave bull was now loose within me, charging

through my blood, pleasurably pricking my brain with its horns. "Here's my verdict, Tomasz. I believe you're sitting on a gold mine, but it won't be easy extracting the ore. Building a profitable factory isn't like organizing a Sunday School picnic. Fortunately for Ostrowski Enterprises, I've had experience in these matters."

"Let me guess," said my prime mover, sipping his drink. "Eventually we'll be under siege from brigades of regulators."

I nodded and said, "It will turn out that Marshfield is the only breeding ground in North America for a rare species of ruby-throated hop-toad, so you'll have to either cancel the project or put the whole fucking plant up on stilts." I consumed another measure of my cocktail. "Not to worry. Synesthesia's lawyers are used to running interference with the EPA. They'll also provide whatever cover you need when the OSHA people start whining about workplace hazards."

"May I be excused, sir?" asked Almodovar. "Technically, it's—"

"Your day off, I know," said Ostrowski. "*Até mais tarde.*"

The butler bowed and slipped inconspicuously away.

"Believe it or not," Ostrowski told me, "I'm a partisan of hop-toads and all their amphibian kin, to say nothing of our planet's reptiles, birds, and mammals."

The veranda began to spin like an immense vinyl LP. Too much tequila, I decided. A surfeit of Kahlúa. "Unions," I said, slurring the word. "Emission standards. Health coverage. There are ways to work around all those things."

An itching arose in my crown, so I resolved to uncover my head and appease the unruly patch of skin. But when I poked my left collarbone, the Tarnkappe failed to resolve itself into hood, tunic, tights, boots, and gloves.

"Something's wrong," I said.

Ostrowski answered my distress by pulling a large jade scarab beetle from his coat pocket and plunking it onto the table. A blue button lay embedded in the left wing, a red button in the right. A yellow dial sat atop the insect's head like a miniature fez.

"Nothing's wrong," said Ostrowski. "I simply pressed the blue button, which overrides the sensor above your left clavicle. Unless I press it again, you'll never be free of the Tarnkappe."

"Then press it again."

"All in good time."

"What are you trying to prove?" I asked, glowering at the Professor. "Do I have to cut my way out with scissors?"

"Easier to puncture a brick with a banana."

"Shall I try tinsnips, then? Pruning shears? A hacksaw?"

"The fabric is impervious to steel."

"Push the blue button!"

"I'd prefer not do."

The brave bull found its way to my stomach. I feared I was about to slather the veranda with vomitus. "Prefer not to?" Again I prodded the deconstruction sensor—to no avail. *"Prefer not to?!"*

"Alas, I've not been entirely honest with you, Brod. I didn't bring you to Nobska Island because I need Synesthesia funding for my factory. Ostrowski Enterprises is already fully capitalized: the military-industrial complex giveth—and giveth and giveth and giveth, and only rarely taketh away. I brought you here to measure your rectitude."

"Push the button, damn it."

"I'm afraid you got a pretty low score. Care for another brave bull?"

"Push the fucking button!" I screamed. "Get me out of this fucking monkey suit!"

"I'll wager you're curious about the scarab's other functions," said Ostrowski. "The red button overrides the sensor in your right clavicle, which means I can make you transparent for as long as I want. A day. A month. A year. Forever. *Voilà!*"

Ostrowski pressed the red button, setting the prisms in motion. As the hornets' drone filled the air, I descended once again into invisibility.

"Bring me back!" With my erect thumb I repeatedly jabbed the sensor above my right collarbone. "Bring me back *now!*"

"As for the yellow dial, it guarantees that you can never make yourself perceptible merely by putting on pajamas—or wrapping yourself in bandages, or packing yourself in mud, or throwing a shawl over your shoulders. One twist, and the epidermis goes into incendiary mode, bad news for all adjacent substances: plant fibers, synthetic textiles, animal hides, clay. Care for a demonstration?"

"No!" I cried.

Ostrowski rotated the yellow dial, and the prisms issued a sound suggesting a raw steak encountering a red-hot barbecue grill.

"Lunatic!" I wailed.

As the sizzling faded to a soft whistle, then to quietude, Ostrowski lifted a pristine cloth napkin from his lap and hurled it in my direction. It found the region wherein my left shoulder seemingly lay—in its new mode, the Tarnkappe had reduced my tactile competence almost to zero—and burst into flames. The sea breeze caught the fiery bits of cloth and wafted them across the veranda.

"Tomasz, this isn't funny!"

Alternately smirking and sneering, Ostrowski removed his enormous hat and, after several failed attempts, fitted it over my head. Like a grass hut struck by lightning, the straw dome turned into a ball of fire.

"Fucking psychopath!" I screamed.

"I've deceived you in a second way as well," Ostrowski confessed. "Your brave bull contained not only tequila and Kahlúa but also a soporific."

As the red embers settled onto the veranda, dark vapors enshrouded my reeling mind.

"The drug's called chloral hydrate," said Ostrowski, "though I much prefer its colloquial name, Mickey Finn, after the notorious Chicago saloon keeper."

Mickey Finn. Meekee Feen. Feeney Meek. Keemee Neeef. And then everything went black.

***

When at last I awoke, my head spinning, intestines torqued, flesh and bones stretched across an inflatable Coleman mattress, I gradually apprehended that, while the Tarnkappe still enveloped me, its incendiary mode had been deactivated and its fabric restored to visibility. Once again my prism-pent arms, legs, hands, feet, and trunk were available to my sense of sight. My ankles, I saw, were fastened together with nylon rope. My wrists were likewise bound.

As the fog lifted from my skull, my ears began throbbing with the hum and clatter of an internal combustion engine. A shaft of morning light pierced a porthole and set my epidermis to glittering. The walls displayed a dozen crayon drawings of sea monsters, each rendered in Bobby Maniscalco's inimitable style. Evidently I'd been taken to the *Pelican* and deposited in a below-decks cuddy.

"Good morning, sugar pie," said Leticia in her most beguiling Dixie drawl. Swathed in a wool blanket, she sat on the opposite berth, clutching a pair of tinsnips, the jade scarab dangling from her neck like a pendant. "We just docked in the Falmouth marina."

"Leticia—thank God!"

"I appreciate the sentiment, honey lamb, but I don't believe in God."

I brought my bound wrists to my left clavicle and pressed the sensor. The Tarnkappe remained intact. "Why the bindings?" I asked.

"Once upon a time you and I were lovers," Leticia replied cryptically, "but we can never be friends."

"Cut these damn ropes."

Firming her grip on the tinsnips, Leticia rose and approached me, but instead of severing my bonds, she pulled a taut lobe of Tarnkappe fabric away from my forearm and attempted, with seemingly genuine resolve, to penetrate the material with a clipper blade.

Leticia whispered, "And now you see that, when Ostrowski told you the fabric was impervious to steel, he spoke the truth."

"But these *ropes* aren't impervious to steel!"

Saying nothing, Leticia made an about-face. She summoned Antonio Maniscalco, then enlisted his assistance in dragging my trussed and flustered self up the companionway to the pilot house, and from there to the foredeck, where a Persian rug lay waiting to receive me. Ignoring my sputtering objections, my captors spooled me up like Cleopatra. Although the rug obscured my vision and the Tarnkappe blunted my tactile sense, I easily discerned my subsequent forced itinerary: down the gangplank, across the marina, and into the back seat of an automobile—Leticia's Fiat convertible, I reasoned.

"By the way, your wife believes you're dead," Leticia told me as the car rumbled out of the marina.

"Dead?"

"It seems that, during the crossing from Falmouth to Nobska Island, you fell off the *Pelican* and drowned. They're still dredging the bay for your waterlogged corpse."

"This is outrageous!"

"True enough, sweetie, but so was firing Marge Bowman from her reading specialist job."

Now Antonio, who evidently occupied the passenger seat, piped up. "Until she got canned, Marge met with my dyslexic grandson every Tuesday and Thursday. He was making real progress."

"I remember about your grandson. Make me visible again, and I'll go right to his website and pay him five dollars for every drawing. Ten dollars. A hundred dollars. Call me the world's foremost Bobby Maniscalco collector."

"You know something, Dr. Arbuthnot?" said Antonio. "I find you an extremely boring person."

After an indeterminate interval, during which I continued making bootless promises to Antonio—I would buy him a sports car, pay off his mortgage, send Bobby to college—the Fiat stopped. My captors pulled me out of the back seat and, keeping me imprisoned in the rug, carried me on a journey of perhaps twenty minutes duration. The parade halted abruptly. Leticia and Antonio unraveled the rug, spilling me onto the wet ground. I rolled over the bank of a drainage ditch and crashed into a rivulet of muddy water.

Dazed, I jabbed my left collarbone, hoping to shed the Tarnkappe. Nothing happened. "Fuck!"

Peering over the edge of the ditch, Leticia extended her right arm. The jade scarab lay in her grasp. "I hate to do this, sweetie, but I have my orders from Tomasz."

She pressed the red button, causing my Tarnkappe and its resident flesh to vanish. Next she twisted the yellow dial, shifting the suit into incendiary mode and rendering me incapable of clothing myself. Straightaway the hot prisms interacted with the rivulet, vaporizing the water with a sibilant sound that filled the ditch like the hissing of an immense viper.

"The Professor suggests you go to Stonewich, two miles south as the crow flies," said Antonio. "The trailer park tenants will feed and shelter you. It's your only hope."

"You're both going to jail, and so is your fucking boss!" I screamed.

"That could very well be the case, honey lamb," said Leticia. "But first *you're* going to Fairview Terrace, probably for the rest of your life. Try and make the best of it."

***

The alienation of Broderick Arbuthnot was now complete. My body had been amputated from itself—I stood on phantom legs, clenched phantom fists, bobbed a phantom head. Step by uncertain step, inch by fitful inch, I ascended the wall of my grave, my incendiary epidermis sizzling as it met the mud. At last I gained the surrounding terrain, then struck out for the trailer park, shuffling across the swampland like an ambulatory coma victim. I felt that at any minute I might faint from hunger or stumble from miscalculation, my phantom foot having gotten snagged by a root or trapped in a rabbit hole.

Two hours later I entered Fairview Terrace, lurching toward the central tract of crabgrass, that ersatz village green Leticia had insisted on visiting during our motor trip to Falmouth. The lawn furniture held the usual indigents. In time I reached the corroded framework of a chaise lounge, the nylon webbing long since rotted away. I heaved a sigh, sprawled across the aluminum rods, and proceeded to catch my breath.

"I'm thirsty," I rasped. "Water, please—and something to eat."

"Did you hear that, Delbert?" said chubby Marge Bowman, speaking with mock bewilderment to a silver-haired old black man. I recalled that Delbert worked at Grab-a-Crab or Cosa Nostra Pizza or one of those ghastly franchises. "Did you hear a voice?"

"You heard *my* voice," I wailed.

"You're right, Marge, there's definitely an extraneous set of tonsils around here," said Delbert. "Do you suppose this place is haunted? I thought ghosts came out only at night."

"It's me, Brod Arbuthnot," I moaned.

Delbert rose and, approaching my chaise lounge, stared at the zone where my eyes presumably resided. "That's funny, Dr. Arbuthnot, I'm simply unable to *see* you. Are you sure you're really *there?*"

"Stop playing games, Delbert!"

The black man turned to Marge and said, "Arbuthnot would have us believe he's here, but I'm not observing much evidence for that hypothesis."

Marge abandoned her chair and, joining her friend, squinted strenuously in my direction. "Maybe he's one of those invisible men we've been hearing so much about."

"No, that can't be," said Delbert. "Only *poor* people are invisible. I heard that Arbuthnot's richer than Scrooge McDuck."

A hefty Hispanic woman with a limp appeared on the

scene, hobbling up to my chaise lounge. "Did I hear you say 'one of those invisible men,' Marge? This must be the person Leticia told us to expect. Is that you, Dr. Arbuthnot?"

"Of course it's me! Tell Marge and Delbert it's me!"

"They know it's you," said the Hispanic woman. "They're just amusing themselves at your expense."

"Laughs aren't easy to come by around here," said Marge.

"Do any of you have one of those scarab gadgets?" I asked.

"'Fraid not," the Hispanic woman informed me. "I'm Paloma, by the way. When I can get the work, I clean toilets and make beds for the Nirvana Hotel chain. Don't you move a goddamn inch, Dr. Arbuthnot. I'm gonna alert Celeste and Gabriel. They're the hospitality committee."

Paloma tottered away, disappearing into a hideous turquoise trailer surrounded by American flags stuck into the ground like pickets. She returned accompanied by a sturdy black woman wearing a floral print dress and lugging a large copper kettle by its handle, an endeavor in which she was assisted by a bearish white man, bald as an eight ball, a wooden spoon tucked under his arm like a drum major's baton. The hospitality committee set the kettle before my chaise lounge. Paloma took the spoon from the white man and dipped it into the kettle.

"We thought beef bouillon ought to work," said Paloma, jabbing the spoon in the general direction of my face.

"An old family recipe," said the black woman. "Call me Celeste. I also made you pea soup and plenty of borscht."

The bouillon strategy indeed proved successful. Although the incendiary prisms did their worst, vaporizing the broth as it dribbled down my chest, I managed to suck considerable nourishment through the mesh. As Paloma continued to slake my thirst and assuage my hunger, the bald guy, Gabriel, insisted on telling me about his marginal existence as a checkout clerk at the local Giveaway City, run by a corporation that declined to accord him either medical insurance or full-time hours. Celeste made me listen to her lament as well, all about how, owing to her ex-husband's refusal to pay child support, she now spent six days a week oscillating between two adjacent households in Quincy, cooking meals, doing laundry, and minding toddlers.

"The phrase you're groping for, I believe, is 'Thank you,'" Marge told me.

"Perhaps even, 'Thank you very much,'" said Delbert.

"I'm truly appreciative," I said.

Within twenty minutes the kettle was emptied—what Ostrowski's invention hadn't boiled away now sustained my grateful flesh—and I was free to concentrate on the problem at hand: liberating myself from the damnable Tarnkappe. Somehow I must return to Castèllo Maciste and persuade the Professor to wield the jade scarab on my behalf. When I suggested to Marge, Delbert, Paloma, Gabriel, and Celeste that they might aid me in this project, the five of them snickered in unison.

"I'll make you all the bouillon you want," said Celeste, "but you're crazy if you think we're gonna help you shoot Doc Ostrowski."

"I don't want to shoot him," he said. "But I must inform him how unreasonable he's being. He had no right to entomb me like this."

"I see your point of view," said Gabriel.

"The fucker told my wife I'm dead," I said.

"My, my," said Paloma.

"Think of that," said Marge.

"You can stay with Gabriel and me in our trailer as long as you like," said Delbert. "Our hovel is your hovel. But leave the Doc alone."

***

But for a rusted Chevy Blazer owned by Isaac Goshen —Isaac the one-eyed concrete man, forever strutting about in his cowboy garb—I might still be living in the trailer park. As it happened, though, the third morning of my Fairview residency found me stumbling past Isaac's vehicle when a side-view mirror, the one adjacent to the steering wheel, revealed something unexpected. The strange reflection was I, Broderick Arbuthnot, swathed head-to-toe in a luminous prism-suit.

I laughed out loud. Could it be that the brilliant Tomasz Ostrowski had neglected to test the effect of a simple mirror on an activated Tarnkappe? Evidently. Was it possible that the mundane phenomenon of reflection canceled the illusion generated by the spinning prisms? So it seemed.

As the sun climbed toward its apex, a scheme for salvation took shape in my brain. The Blazer's side-view mirror was too small for my purposes, which meant I must break into a Stonewich men's store or dress shop under cover of night, find a clothier's mirror, and appropriate a full-length panel. By holding the stolen looking glass at arm's length—the frame must be metal, of course, not wood, plastic, or any material easily burned or melted —I should be able to observe precisely how my legs and feet moved in response to each instruction I gave my motor cortex, rather the way a video-game player adjusts his joystick according to the feedback he receives from his screen avatar.

It was a splendid plan, worthy of the CEO of Synesthesia Capital. Moreover, it worked: making my way to the Stonewich business district, finding a clothing store, jimmying open a back-alley window, stealing a full-length mirror—everything fell into place. At first my journey through the nocturnal streets, looking glass in hand, proved grotesquely comic, the sort of scene that might grace a Three Stooges movie directed by Salvador Dalí. A midtown Manhattan huckster outfitted with a plywood sandwich board, BEST NYC SOUVENIRS SOLD HERE, TOUR BUS STRAIGHT AHEAD, EAT AT THE HARD ROCK CAFE, could not have felt more burdened. But eventually, like a rehabilitated vampire, I learned to love my mirror, and I pursued my mission with a confident stride.

As you might imagine, it took me all night to walk from the Bourne Bridge to the Falmouth marina. Furtively I hauled myself and my mirror aboard the *Pelican*, soon ascertaining to my immense relief that Antonio and Anita were evidently sleeping elsewhere. I loosed the lines, started the engine, and sailed free of the harbor.

As dawn broke over Cape Cod, I piloted the *Pelican* to Nobska Island, running her aground on the beach. Before disembarking, I once again jabbed my left clavicle. The prism-suit and I remained invisible. My distress was acute but bearable, for I had my therapeutic mirror now, and my Fairview Terrace sanctuary, and my determination to make Ostrowski know that, in exchanging my flesh for glass, he'd made the worst mistake of his life.

***

Although my bones ached with exhaustion and my tissues cried out for nourishment, I knew I must not squander precious time on a nap or a meal. With catlike stealth I entered the vestibule of Castèllo Maciste, crept down the red-carpeted corridor, and, taking care to avoid clanking the mirror against the railing, descended the spiral staircase.

Reaching the basement, I sidled into the storage room and undertook a search for flammable liquids, a quest that culminated in nine one-gallon cans of gasoline, doubtless stockpiled to fuel the emergency generator. I grabbed a can by the handle, holding it at arm's length lest my incendiary prisms cause the contents to explode, and, dragging the mirror behind me, passed through the bronze door and into the laboratory. Upon determining that the Professor was nowhere to be seen, I secluded the gasoline behind a water heater, then set the contraband looking glass upright in the far corner. There remained the problem of concealing my secret from Ostrowski. Soon the solution caught my eye, a green canvas tarpaulin draped across a device suggesting an office stapler inflated to the size of a snowmobile. I picked up the tarpaulin using a length of copper tubing, lest my incendiary prisms set the material on fire, and dropped it neatly over the mirror.

The stage was set. All lay in readiness. Satisfied, I approached the rank of free-standing booths (those installations that, on my previous visit, had evoked for me the matter transmitters in *The Fly*), then sat down on a drafting stool and waited for Ostrowski to appear.

My nemesis entered within the hour, dressed in a white lab coat and black leather apron. He sauntered across the room and, taking hold of a microfiber cloth, began buffing the dust from his high-frequency transformer circuit, the ascending loops rising toward the ceiling in a configuration suggesting an immense cobra. But the Tesla coil wasn't the only serpent in Ostrowski's garden. I was there, too.

"Good morning, Tomasz," I said, then abandoned the drafting stool and, advancing clumsily, without benefit of the mirror, positioned myself imperceptibly before Ostrowski.

"Brod?" he said. "Is that you? Where are you?"

"I am everywhere," I replied. "Like microbes and dust and God."

Apparently there was no jade scarab within reach, or Ostrowski would surely have conjured me into visibility.

"My terms are simple," I continued. "Free me from this damned regalia, and I'll do you no harm."

"Harm is the last thing of which you transparents are capable."

"That remains to be seen."

The Professor began speaking at twice normal speed, as if his larynx were wired to a hyperkinetic rheostat. "Lots of things remain to be seen, Arbuthnot. A proof of the Swinnerton-Dyer conjecture remains to be seen. A solid theoretical framework for the Navier–Stokes equations remains to be seen. But know this. Before the end of the decade, our Marshfield factory will be fully functional, turning out five hundred Tarnkappes a day, each priced at two million dollars." He chattered more rapidly still. "Shortly thereafter, a prism-suit will become the primary index of a person's worth, until the human race has neatly sorted itself into two classes, the transparents and the opaques." He stroked the Tesla coil as he might a lover's thigh. "And then one day—shazam!—Tomasz Ostrowski takes up his jade scarab and condemns the transparents to perpetual invisibility. Are you following me, Arbuthnot? In the blink of an eye, I shall reverse the poles of the prevailing order, so that our planet's once proud pluto-crats, now pathetic specters, must beg their victims for bread and water!"

"All I want is to go home to my wife," I said. "Kindly fetch the scarab before this confrontation takes an ugly turn."

"When I first devised my scheme," said Ostrowski, ignoring my plea, "I realized I was morally obligated to question its underlying premises, and so I lured you to Castèllo Maciste by way of the trailer park. It was just as I suspected. The first time you found yourself among those tenants, you made no attempt to comprehend them. Only after you *yourself* became invisible did you deign to perceive the unseen casualties of capitalism or the maxim-um-profit motive or galloping Kostopoulism or whatever you want to call it."

"That hardly gives you the right to bury people alive," I protested. "Maybe I'm not a typical case. Maybe if you took other financiers to the trailer park, they would behave more to your liking."

The Professor kissed his Tesla coil. "Don't worry, Arbuthnot. For the next six months I'll keep trying to disprove my theory, administering the Fairview test to tycoon after tycoon, though I'd be surprised if I don't get the same result each time."

Did I imagine that Ostrowski's demented vision might actually come to pass? A bifurcated society, wealthy transparents on one side, impoverished opaques on the other, the tables suddenly turning at the press of a button and the twist of a dial? Not really, no. It was all too unwieldy, too grand, too Napoleonic. But I *did* believe that before long some equally horrendous design would emerge from this *faux* prime mover's diseased mind, and many an innocent financier would perish in consequence. For the sake of my free-market brethren, I must thwart this megalomaniac posthaste.

"The scarab, Professor!"

"The future is forever lost to you, Arbuthnot! It's lost to you and your wife and your whole fucking ruling class!"

Like a steroidal werewolf, I transmuted instantaneously. The civilized Broderick Arbuthnot became a savage Mickey Finn. In a blind fury I lurched toward the tarpaulin, the canvas fabric turning to embers as I yanked it away, revealing the vital mirror. Cued by my reflection, I threw myself at Ostrowski. I embraced him. The incendiary prisms did their worst, melting his leather apron—the stench seemed to sear my nostrils—then setting fire to his white coat. His cries bespoke first astonishment, then outrage, then physical torment. Staggering about the laboratory, the burning man wrenched the torus off his Tesla coil and hurled it at the mirror, shattering the glass.

But Ostrowski's gesture came too late, for I had already seized and uncapped the gasoline can. Methodically I splashed the pungent fuel across the Professor's limbs and chest, feeding the extant flames, turning him into a humanoid torch. I shall never forget his screams. Those sounds will haunt me till the end of my days.

∗∗∗

Thus did I become a ghost. By these actions did I condemn myself to a permanent spectral state. Day in, day out, my limpid self wanders the halls of Castèllo Maciste, searching for a jade scarab.

The other residents regard me with profound ambivalence. Occasionally Leticia, Almodovar, Natasha, and Bartolomé feel favorably disposed toward the man who'd assassinated their insane employer. When in a benevolent mood, my keepers give me water and soup, and they even supply me with legal pads and stainless steel pens, so that I might continue composing this memoir. But usually Leticia and the others treat me as an enemy. They hide all the mirrors, laugh when I ask for the scarab, chain me up when the *Pelican* comes to Nobska Island, and refuse to contact Valerie on my behalf.

Unlike Melina Kostopoulos, I have great respect for pre-industrial communities. Such societies in my view boasted several distinct virtues, most notably the coherence of their reigning fables. Don't kill a goose that lays golden eggs. Embrace the generosity of dwarves. Make no promise you aren't prepared to keep.

Were I to recast my memoir as a contemporary fairy tale, however, I have no idea what moral I would expect the reader to take away. If my story contains an edifying message, then it is you, not I, who must discover what that lesson might be.

Here's a suggestion. Don't begin your quest by attempting to build your own Tarnkappe. Don't try to solve a Millennium Prize puzzle. Don't purchase shares in Corporality Incorporated. Start, rather, by visiting Bobby Maniscalco's website and acquiring some of his drawings. The lad will be thrilled.

I especially recommend his vision of the enormous cephalopod dismantling the frigate. Remarkably, our young artist got all the morphology correct: eight short arms, two long ones, the whole slimy nightmare brimming with suckers and teeth. Were I a free man, I would buy Bobby's masterpiece myself, hang it on my wall, and contemplate it every day. In its own outré way, I feel, deep-sea gigantism is the hope of the future. Tentacles will save us yet. You can never go wrong with a squid.

James Morrow has been writing fiction ever since, at age seven, he dictated "The Story of the Dog Family" to his mother, who dutifully typed it up and bound the pages with yarn. Upon reaching adulthood, Morrow wrote such satiric novels as *Towing Jehovah* (World Fantasy Award), *Blameless in Abaddon* (a *New York Times* Notable Book of the Year), *The Last Witchfinder* (called "an inventive feat" by critic Janet Maslin), and *The Philosopher's Apprentice* ("an ingenious riff on *Frankenstein*" according to NPR). His short fiction has won the Nebula Award (twice), the Rickie Award, and the Theodore Sturgeon Memorial Award.

Concerning "The Amazing Transparent Man" he writes: "I remember encountering, at age eleven, a novel called *Invisible Man* in my local library and being disappointed to discover it wasn't science fiction. And now, fifty-five years later, Judith K. Dial and Thomas A. Easton have given me the opportunity to juxtapose—and perhaps reconcile—H. G. Wells's materialist narrative with Ralph Ellison's indelible metaphor."

THE EDITORS

Judith K. Dial was born in Hollywood, CA, a circumstance she's never quite overcome. For many years she was a bookseller and book store owner, specializing in science fiction and accumulating far too many books. She is a former dude ranch waitress, electronic assemblist and technical writer. She lives in New England.

Tom Easton was the book columnist for *Analog* for 30 years. He holds a doctorate in theoretical biology from the University of Chicago and teaches at Thomas College in Waterville, Maine.

His latest nonfiction books are *Taking Sides: Clashing Views in Energy and Society, 2nd ed.* (McGraw-Hill, 2012), *Taking Sides: Clashing Views in Science, Technology, and Society* (McGraw-Hill, 11th ed., 2014), *Taking Sides: Clashing Views on Environmental Issues* (McGraw-Hill, 14th ed. Rev., 2013), and *Classic Editions Sources: Environmental Studies* (McGraw-Hill, 4th., 2012). His latest novels are *Firefight* (Betancourt, 2003) and *The Great Flying Saucer Conspiracy* (Wildside, 2002) (both available as e-books from Naked Reader Press).